THE PRICE OF DESIRE

PE KAVANAGH

BOLD
SOUL
BOOKS

PRAISE FOR The Price of Desire
(previously released as Fish Tails & Lady Legs)

"Pascale has a way of embodying the essence of human emotion through written word. While reading along one cannot help but find one's own story being told. An easy to read book for pleasure yet personal growth is inevitable."

Sarah Jenkins, UK

"Pascale Kavanagh's character, Nik, has just the right mix of sass and vulnerability. At times, I felt the character was speaking both my own desire and doubts. As she conquered the doubts and moved into her sensuality, it made all things for me seem possible. Brava!"

Priscilla Orr, Pushcart Prize-nominated author of Losing the Horizon

"Pascale Kavanagh creates a fiery love story where the reality of ordinary life is juxtaposed with a mystical, glorious sensuality that takes your breath away."

Carole Oligario, Hollywood writer and director

Fish Tails & Lady Legs is a fun read that will entertain and inspire. The reader gets two stories for the price of one. Lalune's story is that of a mermaid whose true passion is to sing, obviously stifled by the fact that she lives underwater. Whether you believe in the existence of mermaids is inconsequential - her struggles and journey are relatable to those of us 'land-dwellers'.

The second story of Monique, who left her true calling as a chef for a more 'traditional' life, chronicles the effects of going against her passion and her journey back to life. Pascale's writing is eloquent and entertaining - equally perfect for a cozy Winter evening or an afternoon in the Summer sun.

M. Linehan

A superbly written and perceptive novel, by turns graceful and tren-chant. Kavanagh is particularly good at rendering the inner life of a woman in love, her dreams and insecurities. Every man in a relation-ship with a woman should read this book.

Gregory Dime

For my own little mermaid, whose song changed everything.

1

UNDERWATER

She let out a deep sigh, the bubble containing her would-be sound floating all the way up to the surface, untouched. There it lingered for just a moment before popping softly, heard by no one. There were numerous sounds deep in the ocean, but none of that variety. A sigh was not a productive issuance from a mermaid and so dissolved into nothing.

It was another day in the cold, dark ocean for Lalune. Another day yearning for anything outside her watery home.

"Lalune! Where are you?" She heard her sisters calling for her. Or more accurately, she felt the vibration of the sound. She supposed it was time enough to get started with the day. Floating around wasn't going to grow her legs any faster.

Lalune was partly glad to have her reveries interrupted. Pondering the hopelessness of her life did not make for a wonderful start of the day. There was plenty to do to keep busy in the vast ocean, and many creatures to keep her occupied and even entertained. Maybe a bit of distraction would be helpful.

"Lalune, why are you always hiding out in Nori Cove? Do you have treasure back there? I can't imagine what could be so interesting?!"

"I like to have a little private time, for my thoughts. Is that so bad? I'm not hiding anything, I promise." Did anyone believe her? Did she believe herself?

"That sounds terribly boring, sister. And it makes you morose. Who's ever heard of a sad mermaid?? It's just not natural. We are the most beautiful and interesting creatures on the planet. What is there to be sad about?"

"I'm not sad, necessarily. I just like to think about things. And I think all of the world's creatures are beautiful and interesting. Even... the land-walkers." She knew this statement would not be taken well, but said it anyway.

"Ughhh. They are just awful! Clumsy, rude, unkind. Haven't you seen how they act? Thank goodness they could never be in our world. And I would never want to go out there. Especially since everything is perfect down here."

Lalune nodded, pretending she agreed. In her heart, that was the furthest from the truth. Most mermaids had nothing but disdain for the land-walkers, but Lalune felt differently. In her eyes, they were splendid.

Not that she knew this from any personal experience. The stories she heard from her friends and family were amplified to grand proportions by her own imagination. An entire fantasy lived in her head, about their charmed lives, and the wide variety of experiences they must be having. The one that was most intriguing, of course, was their ability to make music. She could hear it sometimes, all the way from the distant shore, vibrating through the water. It was mesmerizing.

Many of the creatures in her world could make music – she especially loved the whales' song – but it was not the same. A sense of joy, not just utility, permeated the land-walker's music. They made music for the sheer pleasure of it, not just for basic communication. Lalune knew this had to be true based on how the sounds she heard made her feel.

Despite all the others thinking it was reckless and ridiculous, because only land-walkers sing and sea creatures hum, Lalune loved to sing. The pleasure of hearing her sound, carried on the soft breeze above her home, made her feel alive. Yet her song was stifled and muted in the sea, where she was supposed to keep herself hidden.

She knew that on land it could be heard in its fullness, from the few times she had snuck over to the island and let herself sing. She knew, without knowing why or how, that it would be on land that her voice, and her life, would find its purpose. Each day, it became more and more difficult to stay silent in the depths.

Lalune had known since she was a child that she had been built for something different than the life she was living, if only she could figure out how to get it. What she wanted most in the world, enough to give up everything she currently knew, was to be a land-walker. To have two beautiful legs that would carry her around on the land, and to hear her song, her true voice, carried through the air. This would be her salvation.

Still, the ocean contained everything she knew. Why couldn't she be satisfied with that life? Why did she come to believe that her only hope was to leave everything behind? No one else seemed to suffer this same malady, this discontent. Her friends and family were perfectly happy with their glorious kingdom.

A large tail flapping in front of her once again startled her out of her daydreams. Her sisters had swum away and she was supposed to be following them.

Off she went to live another day in the life of a magical mermaid. There were adornments to create, games to play, and beautiful scenes to explore. She and her sisters were close (other than the big secret Lalune carried) and had a vast repertoire of diversions to keep them occupied. Occasionally they would sneak up towards the surface and watch the land-walkers fumble around in the water. It caused no shortage of giggles, except from Lalune, who observed with awe.

She could see herself, wiggling those legs and needing that funny facemask to breathe. All their awkwardness was endearing and she could only imagine how poorly she would do in their environment. It would be impossible, actually.

She wanted to know the feeling of sand between her toes, sun on her skin and the beauty of her song in the faces of those who heard it. Could she find her boldness, her voice, and take her place in the other world?

The legends said it was possible to transform, to grow legs where her tail used to be, but what if it wasn't true? What if Lalune was destined to live out her days swallowing this secret, ashamed and unheard?

It was too easy to hide in the darkness, and nearly impossible to live with her desire. Without being able to sing freely, all the magic in the ocean was useless to her. Her beauty, her talent, even the love in her heart, were all wasted.

There was no one to talk to about this, and certainly no guides she could ask for help. The land-walkers knew of song, but not of mermaids, and the mermaids knew nothing of a two-legged life. It was a leap of faith, to believe all the pieces would come together, but what choice did she have?

Lalune's search for someone to guide her, someone who knew the way, had to be done in secrecy. No one could discover her desire to leave their underwater kingdom. There were severe consequences for mermaids who tried to cross over and did not succeed. Making it all the way through to the other side would be her only option.

What scared her most was knowing she could never come back. The comfort and familiarity of her dark depths, as unsatisfactory as they were, would be lost to her forever. She would live or die as a land-walker.

2

MONIQUE

"Mama!"

Was it wrong to wish that your children were mute?

"Maamaa!!"

Okay, maybe it would've been easier if I were deaf.

"MAAAAAAAAMMMMAAAAAAAA!!!"

Somebody better be about to lose a limb over there, I fumed, as I stomped over to the bedroom.

"Yes! What requires so much yelling?" I was also yelling. They looked at me with wide eyes, startled by my testy response. Guilt poured over me.

"Mama, Lola was doing a perfect handstand! She did it, she really did it! Oh my gosh, it was so amazing. She just balanced there like her hands were her feet. It was so cool..."

My baby Claire jumped up and down, just like her aunt Lizzy always did.

Lola couldn't have been standing any taller or smiling any broader. She'd been working so hard to do this, and now couldn't even speak, while happily accepting the accolades from her usually critical little sister.

"Let me see," I said with a broad smile.

The girls set themselves up near the wall and Claire positioned herself as the spotter. I noticed how much she had grown; she was nearly as tall as her older sister. I had stopped being confused by the balance of power between my girls. Lola was older but her sister was the boss.

Claire had exhibited brilliance and domination from the outset. I prayed she would find the right outlet for those strong characteristics. Lola on the other hand, was a natural athlete, but spent more time in her inner world than with others. I wondered what medium she would eventually use to express the thoughts she naturally withheld.

I looked at both girls, one standing so powerfully upside down, not even using the wall for balance, and the other being an encouraging and supportive coach. There was almost too much pride to fit in my adult body. They embodied everything I lacked. Lola had an uncanny sense of her body, so graceful and strong, and so unlike the gangly, clumsy one I carried around, while Claire was a born leader, which I certainly was not.

Lola landed fluidly and asked, "How did it look, Mama?"

"It was perfect, baby. You totally nailed it. Like a flagpole. I really liked how you held your arms really straight and pointed your feet. Wow! I am completely impressed.

"And you, Claire... what a great coach you are! I didn't know you could do that. You guys are incredible."

I wrapped my arms around my girls. My strong, beautiful, talented girls. I was happy. And lucky. To be their mother and to have this life and to witness their greatness. I buried them with deep squeezes and slurpy kisses. "Who's hungry?"

We all scrambled to the kitchen so that I could finish making their dinner. This was our brand new life, which still felt awkward, even after more than a year. Just like relearning how to ride a bike, the process was causing some soreness in tender places.

My knives were getting dull, leaving me frustrated with the extra effort I had to put in to get through the carrots. I had gotten lazy, after having been so fanatical for all those years. Everything was harder, now that I was out of practice. But the girls loved it anyway. They didn't complain that my vegetables weren't perfectly diced, or that my sauces were lumpy instead of silken.

That meal was all delicious flavors and sweet little-girl giggles. With every smile and compliment from them, I remembered how unaccommodating I had been to their calls just a short while before. And all they wanted was to celebrate with me. My frequent companions - shame and inadequacy - settled in to either side of my squeaky chair at the kitchen table.

I couldn't claim that motherhood was new to me - Lola was eleven and Claire was about to turn seven - but the learning curve just hadn't let up. Sometimes I reverted to being the selfish little girl who had always been in the middle of all my siblings' needs, and just wanted her own time and privacy. I didn't want to share and I didn't want to be responsible. Sometimes, all I wanted was to be invisible.

That little girl had grown up and become somebody else's mother. Despite how much I adored my own girls, I couldn't seem to get past my own self-centeredness. What had made me so selfish and needy? Why couldn't I just be the person I wanted to be?

I was resisting allowing the answer to complete itself in my head, when my phone rang with the pop song Lola had installed as my ringtone. It was Nora, my older sister.

"What's up?" I asked, startled out of a potential spiral.

"Can you come over tomorrow night?"

"I guess… is something going on?"

"Nope." Her answer was sharper than I expected. "We just want to see you. I know it's been a shit-storm over there. Just come over, okay?"

I wasn't really in the mood to hang out with my sisters. They'd want to talk about all the drama and it was just too exhausting. I would've much rather avoided and denied, frankly. But there was no getting out of it. When Nora wanted something, she got it.

"Fine." I knew I sounded ungracious. "Thanks Nora. See you tomorrow."

Family. Mine was better than most, I had to admit, but we were an odd bunch with such diverse interests, strengths, and personalities. Of my siblings, Nora, the oldest, had been given an extra portion of brains, Danny got the best personality and Lizzy, the baby, got exuberance. My gift? A strange affinity to blades and flames, and the ability to create something from nearly nothing.

That skill had served me well in the kitchen, but kept me constantly in the world of my imaginings. It made me a daydreamer, like our mother and my oldest daughter. It also allowed my hypersensitivity to blossom into fantastical stories that helped me easily escape the world, for better or worse. Family, however, was something I had yet to successfully escape.

Bedtime was easier than usual. The meal seemed to have shifted us past my earlier grumpiness and everyone was in a good mood. I didn't allow the worry about going to my sister's consume me, although I could feel it trying to make its way to the front of my thoughts.

The girls and I fell into bed playful and snuggly, a tangle of little bodies and big bodies, all vying for the best patch of bed and the most comfortable corner of pillow. We didn't do it as often anymore, but when we piled into my enormous bed, I had a glimpse into the feelings I used to have... that everything, in fact, was perfectly fine. The next thing I realized, we'd all fallen asleep. As it had been for so many nights, sleep did not last.

I squinted at the clock across the room. Shit, my eyesight seemed to get worse by the day. Did it say 2 or 3? Did it matter? I was awake.

A few attempts at re-settling didn't prove useful, so I undertook the task of untangling myself from my babies and heading downstairs to my little office. There was nothing so urgent that it needed my attention in the middle of the night, but still I felt it was important to use the rare stretch of peace and quiet fully. Might as well get some work done.

I couldn't shake the bad feeling about the next day. Sure, I'd been avoiding my family since all hell broke loose in my life. Everyone else seemed to be doing so well in their lives, and it had been one disaster after another for me. After such an illustrious start, too. Oh well, I knew it was just temporary. At least I hoped so.

I just didn't want to get lectured. Or questioned. I knew they disapproved of my career change, leaving my soul's calling. They wanted me to live the grand life I used to, the rising star chef whose life was all passion and glory. I didn't know how to be that woman anymore and I just didn't have the strength. My girls had to come first. My sisters didn't understand.

It was no secret that I had walked away from the only area in my life in which I had consistently felt successful. I had been flying, then cut my own wings off to be with the other land-dwellers. There, on the hard ground, I was hardly good for anything other than cooking, which I wasn't doing any more.

My relationships were pathetic, I was never satisfied with how much time or attention I gave my girls, and the work of suppressing my primary creative outlet had left me tired and grumpy. But I couldn't see any other choice. At least for the moment. I was a single mom – I needed a paycheck and a career that did not have me out all night, every night.

The job at the magazine had been a godsend. It not only payed the bills, but also let me do something that was useful to the world. I could live in the inventions of my imagination, a place I landed in quite often, and was happy enough to be writing. Sure, it wasn't the same passion I felt for the kitchen, but it was good enough. It was the right choice for my family.

The bright lights of my screensaver reminded me that the Valentine's Day article about romantic meals in the city needed finishing. Having already done the research on restaurants offering the most unique experiences, all that remained was to include recipes for people to cook at home. Romantic meals were a part of my distant past, at that point, and I could just as easily have been researching Mars.

I rarely let myself feel the depth of my loneliness, but it was always with me. It had been a string of failed attempts at love since my failed marriage. I had to be thankful that Jeff and I were now on good terms, but the road getting there nearly destroyed me.

All the stories – my divorce, the end of my career as a rising star in the restaurant world, the recent deaths of my brother and parents – streamed before my eyes like a personalized movie from which I couldn't pull myself away.

So often life, in all its dimensions, had been too much for me to handle, and it had been feeling like that quite often during those days. When I turned away from reality and slipped into the stories in my head, or on the page, life became Goldilocks' version of *just right*. In my fantasies I was brave, kind and utterly capable. I stopped betrayal in its tracks, and dished out a healthy dose of whatever was needed for any situation. My daydreams replaced my relationships and my time in the kitchen. No need for lovers when the ones in my mind were always perfect.

A blade of light pierced through the darkness of the night. I was surprised to see that I was still sitting in front of my computer, believing instead that I had traveled back in time to relive the tumultuous events that still shook everything around me. It was a good story, I thought to myself. I wondered if I would ever write it down. First, I had to complete those darned recipes, before the sun rose and a new day began.

3

A FAMILY AFFAIR

I t had been seriously high tension at the magazine during the previous week, and I was pleased to have an excuse to leave early. Unlike my sisters, the staff seemed afraid to talk to me, the recent events as ugly as things got in gourmet cuisine publishing. Not that I was looking forward to going to Nora's either. At least I had the 45-minute drive to clear my head.

I had recently published an article about one-upmanship among younger chefs, and how that was negatively impacting the level of art in our culinary community. It included a mention of one of the rising stars in our city. My point had been the bigger issue of over-the-top cuisine, but it was true that I had not spoken very kindly of that chef, and he didn't like it.

The scorned chef publicly called me the has-been that never was, flaming me in every media outlet he could. It created quite the storm, not only at my magazine, but also throughout the restaurant world. He had used his huge audience and willing media attention to express his rage at what he took as my defamation of his skills.

The magazine continued to be conflicted about whether to respond or not, and so we all stewed in the hot water, waiting for someone to do something. Most people thought that someone was me.

The truth was that I knew chefs; I used to be one. I knew the industry rewarded hot-headedness. This young man had felt his fifteen minutes of fame being threatened by some nobody and lashed out. It really wasn't as dramatic as everyone was making it out to be, but no one wanted to be left out of the conversation, so a slew of media had been devoted to this ridiculous battle.

He and I had become the polarizing points for anyone who had an opinion about food. There were those who saw his behavior as histrionic and were extremely insulted on my behalf. Then there were those who took my commentary personally, as if I had called their children dumb and ugly. I'd been doing what I did best – staying silent.

I only hoped my sisters hadn't caught wind of this scandal. It would be yet another point on which to berate me.

I arrived at Nora's house, the implicit shared ground for all family matters, to find my two sisters sitting in the living room looking very serious. The only one missing was Sam, Nora's long-time partner. Something big was about to go down – I could feel it in the room. Lizzy, my expressive baby sister, was trying to hold the solemnity, but I knew she would be the first to crack.

The questions began almost immediately. Why wasn't I showing any emotion or taking action to resolve all the messes in my life? How was I tolerating all these personal attacks? Why wasn't I defending myself? How could I let him call me a no-talent nobody?

I found it all too ridiculous and childish to respond to, so I let them rant while I stayed silent. It did not stop them.

"What happened to you?" Lizzy asked through the tears that began falling almost immediately. "You used to be the most passionate person I'd ever met. You loved food like most people love sex."

"Maybe just how you love sex, Lizzy," I reminded my historically horny sister.

"Whatever. Now you don't even care that your entire reputation as a chef was just defamed and the work you're doing now is being totally ridiculed. Did you die in that divorce? What happened, Nik? What happened?"

I didn't understand. I had made a series of decisions, quite good I thought, to save my family. To move into a life that was much more reasonable and realistic. What was Lizzy saying? That my passion had died?

"I love what I do," I said in a soft voice, not quite sure how much I believed it. "This guy is a wack-job, probably on his way to rehab as we speak. Why should I get all riled up about what he's saying?" I was genuinely curious.

"Because it's true," Nora said in an even softer voice. This made Lizzy start crying harder.

I looked around in confusion. Was this really happening? How could they think the awful things that man had said were true? My feelings were hurt more by that quiet statement then by all the yelling and screaming by the angry chef.

Nora began again. "We love you so much, Nik. You were the one who lived her dream. Defied convention and did something you were really, really good at, not just what you were expected to." My older sister spoke from experience.

"Ever since the divorce, and your working at that magazine, it's as if you put your soul in cold storage. You just work and take care of the girls and have no life. Do you even do anything you love anymore?"

"I LOVE MY GIRLS!" It was much louder than I intended. Everyone froze. "Why are you doing this to me? Isn't it bad enough that I had to be publicly humiliated? Now my family has to tell me what a loser I am too? Are you guys for real?"

"We just want the old Monique back," Lizzy said. "My big sister who was my hero and my inspiration and everything I wanted to be when I grew up. Now you're gone. You're nearly invisible."

A tremor pulsed through my body, followed by a stream of tears.

"Even the girls notice, you know," Nora said. "They say you're not as much fun. Lola says it's because you have a serious job now and you have to be a serious person. But that's not who you are. You are a wild, crazy, creative woman. Who was born free and unique, like a fairy or a mermaid."

That was the last straw. "How dare you! To bring up my kids? You have no idea what I've been through and what I had to do just to survive. My family is doing GREAT now. Better than we ever have. We are happy and stable and we get to see each other and I'm not working crazy hours..."

I stopped to regroup and rethink my approach.

"Why am I even explaining myself to you? You spent your whole lives just doing what you were told, not a creative or free bone in your entire bodies, and you sit there and insult me? You wouldn't last a day in my shoes. Not even five minutes. So maybe you should start looking at your own pathetic excuses for lives before you start insulting mine."

I bolted off the couch. "I don't need to listen to this. I will never forgive you. Never."

Lizzy was sobbing so hard I worried she might gag or throw up. Nora softened her gaze. What did she want from me? To admit they were right? Never.

Lizzy began pleading. "No, Nik. No. You can't leave. You're the best mother I know. The best one I've ever known and the best sister too. You can't leave and you can't hate us. I need you Nik! I need you now. I can't do it without you."

"Not now, Lizzy," Nora said with a slow deep voice.

"What are you two talking about?" I asked, frozen in my path toward the door.

"I'M PREGNANT, Nik. Really pregnant. I can't do it without you."

"No fucking way," I said, while finding somewhere to set myself down again.

We sat silently. Well nearly silently, as Lizzy was still sobbing and Nora was whispering to her, "It's alright sweet girl, it's okay. We're going to be there for you, okay? You're not alone. You're not alone."

I couldn't believe it. My baby sister, pregnant. No boyfriend that

I'd heard of. And her crazy career in advertising. What the hell was she going to do?

"How far along?" was all I could ask.

"Almost eight weeks."

"Holy shit." She didn't show at all. But maybe that explained why she'd been looking so busty lately.

"That's not why we're here," said Nora, the pain-in-the-ass voice of reason. Always so rational. I hated that about her.

"So why *are* we here?" Bitterness seethed through my words.

Nora cleared her voice. "We're here because our sister needs help. And that's you we're talking about Monique. We can see the girl we have all known and loved just dying in there. You look nearly the same on the outside, but we know you're not the same on the inside. Why won't you let us in? It's okay if you have to live a lie, Nik, but you don't have to live it with us."

No one spoke for so long that my words startled everyone. "I'm not dying, I'm living. And I like my job, I really do. The girls and I are doing great. We are happy and healthy and living our lives. You have no right to say otherwise.

"Maybe when they're a bit older, I can go back to the kitchen. For now, it's just not appropriate. I don't see how you can't understand that! Who wants a mother that comes home at 2am every night? It's completely ridiculous to even contemplate. There's a season for everything and right now it's about my family. There will be a season for me. Again."

"When?" Lizzy managed to say between her subdued sobs.

"I can't answer that! When it feels right." I needed to move attention off of me. "Who's the father Lizzy?"

"It's Mike. You don't know him. It was quick, and he pretty much told me he didn't want anything to do with me."

"She hasn't told him," added Nora.

"What? You have to tell him!"

"Why? So he can reject me even worse? No thanks. I can do it on my own. At least I think I can. I don't know..."

We all exhaled together.

"I wish Danny was here," she said. Our brother. Our beloved baby brother, who died right before Mom and Dad. No brother had ever been so loved and so wonderful. I thought about him every day and missed him even more often.

He had been our mediator for most of our lives. The voice of practicality and magic, all at the same time. He had a way of saying the most ridiculous things in a way that made you absolutely believe him. During the numerous girl-wars that had erupted in our house, he would take us all out in the woods and pretend to do an incantation to cure us all of the devil energy he claimed had taken us over. We would invariably end up in a huge giggle pile on the forest floor and spend the night picking leaves and twigs out of our hair.

The emptiness since he died had not shrunk a single inch. He had been our boy, in a house overly full of women.

He seemed to always have the answers to anything. He would have known what to tell Lizzy about the baby, and he would have known how to soothe my hurt feelings.

Danny understood me. My sweet baby brother, who felt about the ocean the way I felt about the kitchen, was the first to really *get* me. He had explained to the others what I could not verbalize, until I had gotten successful enough that he no longer had to.

I wondered what he would have thought of my new life, since I'd let go of *the dream*. He would have understood that I made the choice for my family. That it was the right and reasonable thing to do.

Nora broke me out of my reverie. "You know what Danny would say? He would say, 'You need to just get the devil out of you. Go outside and sing until your throats are all sore. Then come in, each do at least one shot of whiskey and then lay in bed together.'"

Norah had known him the longest and it showed in her ability to channel him as needed. That was exactly what he would have said.

"You're right," I said.

They both looked at me, as if I'd just snapped out of a trance. They waited on my next words, but I had none.

"Okay, then... whiskey anyone? Except you, Lizzy. Sorry," offered Nora.

"Fine," she responded.

"No whiskey needed," I added. "But I do want to understand why you called me here tonight. Do you really think my life is so screwed up? Are my daughters damaged from all the hell we went through?"

"No, no, no..." Lizzy began to cry again. "We LOVE you Nik. So much. We just wanted you to hear that you're not alone. You think you have to do everything on your own, and you don't. We're here and you never ask for help. We can help with the girls, or money or whatever you need. We just want you to be happy again."

"What makes you think I'm not happy?"

"Because you're not. It's as simple as... like when you tried being a blonde for a little while. It didn't look bad, but we knew it wasn't actually who you are," Nora said.

"And you need to get laid more," said Lizzy.

"Look where that got you, missy." Nora's stiffness softened and Lizzy's tear-stained face couldn't hold back a chuckle. It felt like we'd torn down the walls and opened the doors.

"Are the girls with Jeff tonight?" asked Nora.

"Yup."

"Great. You are going to stay here tonight. We all are. Just like we used to do, all curled up in Mom and Dad's giant bed. Except it's my giant bed, but whatever. We have to stick together. We're it ladies, the last of the Malones. And Lizzy is going to be a mom, and Nik is going to go back to cooking, and we all need lots of help and we're all we have. It's time to go."

With that, Nora walked toward the bedroom. Like good little soldiers, we followed.

"I'll get the water," I said, and filled three huge glasses for our bedtime thirst. We had all inherited this love of water from our mom, needing to drink constantly, day and night. I emptied half my glass before even reaching the bedroom, desperately hoping for relief from the pain that just wouldn't stop.

4

A SCARY STEP

We laughed and cried and slept very little. We crafted the speech Lizzy would give to her boss about being pregnant, composed the letter to the father, and hatched a plan for my illustrious return back to the kitchen. I'd start small, maybe just a part-time job to get my skills back, and slowly make my way up the ladder again. My girls would spend more time with their beloved aunties, which might actually be good for all of them.

Being a chef was a lot like being a celebrity – you were only as good as your last movie or meal - and I hadn't cooked in a long time. Other than the recent hooplah, I was dead to the cooking world. I would have to prove my chops once again.

I was so tickled with excitement that even after my sisters had fallen asleep, I stayed awake. So many different ideas flowed through my mind. I could find a place that just did breakfast and lunch. A small place with exemplary food without all the pressure. Or I could become a private chef, even though that was less interesting. My ultimate dream was to run the kitchen at a B&B, maybe even in wine country, a few hours away from our home in San Francisco.

Jeff and I had spent many hours plotting out our retirement in Sonoma - he would be the concierge doctor in a quaint little town, running our world-famous inn, and I would turn out the most fabulous food the world had ever seen, in very small scale.

That dream had always brought a smile to my face, no matter how distant it seemed. I could have almost tasted it.

But there were so many problems. First, I had no money to start a B&B and now that Jeff was starting a family with his nurse-girlfriend, he would have no interest in funding my little venture. And I was fairly certain that he no longer had any interest in moving out of the city. Since we shared custody of the girls, neither of us could go very far without the other's consent. How could this ever work?

Despite the impossibility of it all, I eventually fell asleep. We woke up in age order with Nora a few steps ahead of me into the kitchen to make the coffee, and Lizzy sleeping till noon. I had a copy deadline that day, but had already completed the piece and could give myself a leisurely morning. It was nice to be with my sisters again. It had been such a long time since we'd had agenda-less time together.

A pang from last night hit me. I hadn't responded to what they said to me, just picked up and went along with the plan. Was it real? Did they really want to help me get back into cooking? It seemed like such a long shot, especially with their already full lives.

As Lizzy rolled out of bed, we could hear her stumble into the bathroom and throw up. Disgust filled Nora's expression. Excitement filled mine. I was going to be an auntie! After my oldest sister had declared she was living child-free, I'd given up hope. But now... there was a chance.

"Should we go help her?" I asked.

"That's revolting. She'll come out when she's ready."

"Aaaaahhh... the voice of compassion."

Lizzy came out and Nora handed her a tea that I hadn't even seen her make.

"Thanks. Sorry about that," she said, knowing Nora's aversion to bodily functions. "It was worse for me, in case you were wondering."

I gave her a hug. "You know that means the baby is good and

strong, right? It's what you want. And it will pass, maybe even in the next week or so. My morning sickness went away right on my 12th week, each time. It was a miracle!"

"Let's hope..."

"Shall we go out for breakfast?" Nora asked.

"Just toast for me, thanks," said Lizzy, still slightly green.

"Why don't I make something?" They both stared at me, open-jawed, not attempting to hide their disbelief.

I blazed my evil eye at the both of them. "If you don't watch out, I just might poison you both, assuming that Nora actually has any food in her house."

"Feast your eyes on this, sis." A flourishing sweep of the refrigerator door revealed a bounty of goodies.

Lizzy and I were both incredulous. "Where did all that come from?" I asked.

"Sam hired someone to fill my fridge. It's nice. I like it."

My oldest sister had one of the oddest lives I knew, having followed in the footsteps of our father and become a scientist. A very successful one.

With what appeared to be a conspicuous lack of effort, she had gotten tenure in one of the most prestigious universities in the country and was working her way up the ladder there, too. Nothing short of a Nobel would stop my sister.

Her partner, whom she swore she would never marry, was in the philosophy department of the same university, and possessed the complete counterpoint to her obsessive logic. We all loved Sam, sometimes more than we loved Nora. We couldn't believe that she had found this amazing man, who loved her more than life itself, and agreed to all her crazy demands.

They were to keep separate houses, she demanded. And vacation separately at least once a year. No kids. That was an absolute. He was mesmerized by her, much like our father had been mesmerized by our mother.

And now he was making sure she was fed. Unlike Lizzy or me, Nora had a tendency to get too skinny. She forgot to eat (imagine that!), sometimes for days at a time, hunkered down in the lab, afire with her research into the genetics of endangered species.

Like the rest of us, she also held this soft, secret sadness, but hers was harder to diagnose. On the surface, she'd created the life of her dreams, including the perfect man and career. She was in excellent health, meal skipping aside, and didn't want for anything financially. The sadness was nearly imperceptible, and reminded me of our mother.

"You did mean breakfast today, right?" said a sarcastic Nora.

I realized I'd been standing in front of the open refrigerator for minutes.

"Extra poison in yours, darling," I said with a wink.

And then I began. Cooking to me felt like music did to the rest of the family. I didn't have their musical skill (although I tried) but I could make a symphony on a plate or palate.

Nora's kitchen was stocked with the best of everything, as expected, and I was excited to create. Fancy food wasn't my thing, but I was thrilled by absolutely delicious, simple food that made you feel like someone loved you, not just that someone was trying to impress you.

I made eggs, French toast, fruit salad and smoothies as well as stir-fried greens, curry rice and ginger soup. I figured that Nora and Sam could enjoy any of the leftovers.

Even Lizzy ate, in small tentative bites. I was filled with love for my sisters.

That feeling of feeding my family, of coming together to share what nourishes us, of rediscovering our humanity and our neediness and our hunger, was like a deep breath. I wondered when I'd be fully ready to respond to my sisters' plea to really live my authentic life. It would likely be some time.

For now I had a plan to create.

First I had to call Emile, my friend and mentor, who also happened to be the most well-connected person in the culinary world. He'd know where to start. Maybe even be happy that I wanted to go back. He'd always been my biggest fan, if not my best lover.

I felt a tickle of excitement and a tremor of trepidation. *What's next for me?*

The reality of the day arrived suddenly. Phones started ringing, schedules became important and obligations came to call. The end of breakfast and the beginning of the rest of the day came so swiftly that it was almost as if the morning never happened. Now it was time to get on with our full lives.

On my drive back to the city, I felt the urge to deal with the situation around my inflammatory article and the angry chef. Should I wait until I've re-established myself as a chef? Or would that take too long? The world (or the small part of the world that cared about such things) was waiting to hear from me and I'd been mostly unwilling to engage. But perhaps it was time to be heard.

I arrived home a few hours before the girls, but spent most of the time staring at my computer screen. What to say to someone who'd thrown down the gauntlet that you weren't ready to pick up? What to say to defend your honor against petulance, immaturity and unreasonable competition? I wasn't interested in going after this guy. I knew he just felt attacked and was defending himself, no matter how excessive the response.

I simply wanted to state my case, unapologetically, and let the matter die its inevitable death. But where to start? Slowly the words came to me, about the integrity of food and the subjectivity of taste and the power of free speech. Then I began to feel how much I loved food and cooking and the business of eating and the words began to pour from me.

I'd been obsessed with food most of my life. In a good way. I loved everything about it - the alchemy of bringing simple ingredients together to create something much greater than its parts, the understanding of how food formed culture and determined health. My sister Nora used to say that I would have made a great chemist, considering how similar the two activities are, but I had no interest in science. I wanted to make something that was beautiful and delicious. Her discoveries as a biologist might have been changing the world, but I wanted to feed people. To nourish them.

I could feel it in my body when I thought about my old life, as a chef. And not just any chef, but one whose rise to fame had been charmed. My family of artists and scientists hardly understood me, the one whose favorite room in the house was the kitchen, where magic was made. But it made perfect sense to me, because art, science and magic all lived in that room, where the simplest materials could become something that made people happy.

My sisters were wrong. My work as a writer wasn't merely obligation and the need to make a living. I really did find joy and value in it, and stood by my choice. At the time, trying to survive the implosion of my family, being a chef felt impractical. Certainly not what a single mom should be doing to support her family. I was going to survive the awful divorce and create stability for myself and my family. Soft dreams gave way to hard realities and I found a way to make it work. I walked away from the stove and into the office.

The position at the magazine was a miracle find, after all. But it wasn't my heart's desire. That I had to agree. Did I feel it was sucking my soul dry? No, not at all. But was I just fooling myself? Had I moved so far from my authentic expression that I couldn't even tell anymore?

The shrill ring of my alarm surprised me. It was time for school pick-ups. I looked forward to giving my girls a loving squeeze. They were the light of my life, and even if I never did anything of value in my life I knew I achieved something by bringing these remarkable people into the world.

The rest of the day unfolded into ordinariness. There were activities, dinner, homework, and then baths and bedtime.

I spent extra time snuggling my girls and we said our grate-fulls. I let them know, as I did every night, that I was deeply grateful for them in my life. They talked about not having too much homework, doing well on surprise quizzes, and having parents who loved them.

I couldn't hold it in and told them about my plan to go back to cooking. Lola had known me back in those early days, but Claire didn't really understand. We both explained to her that Mama used to be a famous cook (okay, we embellished a bit). She seemed to find it unbelievable.

I sat back and watched as Lola described how she saw me, before the big change.

"Mama was really popular. She worked in big and famous restaurants too, and sometimes famous people would come and eat there. She was a really good chef."

I couldn't help but smile at my little girl, who never once mentioned my previous profession or indicated that she thought I did anything of interest or importance. Maybe this change wouldn't be so hard after all.

5

RULE OF THREES

I barely recovered from 'The Intervention' and the ego battle at the magazine before the next storm hit. Or storm cluster, to be more precise.

When I saw the middle school's number flashing on my phone, I was sure it wasn't not good. And I was right.

My talented Claire had always had a song on her lips, and often forgot that she was singing or humming. The whole family, and all her friends, understood, and loved this quirky quality. Apparently one of the boys at school hadn't found it quite as charming, and smacked her across the face – hard.

By the time I got to her school, the pink marks had faded, covered now with the tracks of her tears. The school official was devastated about the alleged violence, but considering he couldn't get a straight story out of the hysterical participants and bystanders, decided to make it a no-fault issue.

I was furious, but thankfully thought better than exacting my own revenge on that little boy.

"Are you okay, sweetie?" I asked as she sat quietly in the car.

"Yeah, Mama. I'm fine. It doesn't really sting anymore."

"Do you think your singing was bothering him for some reason?"

I wasn't sure where I was going with these questions, but my curiosity was killing me. "What exactly happened?"

"I don't know, Mama. He just got so mad when he asked me to be quiet and I wouldn't. I didn't even realize I was humming, but I guess he could hear it."

"That must have been awful baby. I wish I could take it all away for you." I did.

"I think he just forgot I was a girl. I mean, that's how all the boys act toward each other. They're always hitting and wrestling, like bears or something. I think he just forgot for a second... that I wasn't a bear."

My wise girl.

"I really appreciate how you're being so cool and fair about all this. I'm very proud of you."

"I know, Mama."

We decided to pick up Lola and get some ice cream. It was definitely a good day for ice cream.

The visual of boys as bears was going to stay with me for some time. It reinforced everything I felt about men and betrayal: Expressing the song in your heart got you a smack across the face.

It was less than a week later when I saw Jeff's number on my phone in the middle of the day. It was unlike my ex-husband to call during his workday. I assumed he butt-dialed me.

"Hi there. What's up?" I asked, expecting silence on the other end.

"Hi, Nik."

Something was wrong. His voice was off.

"It's my dad, Nik. He's gone." The breath left my body in a whoosh, punctuated by Jeff's sobs. His father was one of my favorite people on the planet. He'd been there for me even through the worst of our divorce.

"No... that can't be right. No, Jeff."

"It's true. Mom said he was feeling tired, and laid down for a nap, which he would never do. Then his heart stopped. Everyone thinks it was painless. I don't know..."

"Oh my God, Jeff. I can't believe it. Can I do anything for you? Do you need me to take care of anything?" How quickly we fell into our old connection.

"Patti's getting our stuff together now." Funny, I had forgotten all about her. "We're flying out in a few hours. I just thought you'd want to know."

"Of course. Thanks for calling. Do you want me to tell the girls, or do you want to?"

"Why don't you do it, Nik? I just don't think I could keep it together for them."

"Anything you need, Jeff. Will you let me know when the service is? Maybe we can come out."

"It's so far, Nik." They lived across the country. "You don't have to. But I'll let you know."

"Okay. Safe flight."

"Thanks. Talk soon."

The feeling of the chair around me made me realize that I'd sat down. My body had lost the ability to hold itself up, and the tears began to flow. The stream of grief began with Jeff's father, but moved quickly to my own parents, and to Danny. So many people gone, it was too much to process.

My heart broke for Jeff. I knew exactly what it was like to lose a parent unexpectedly. But he'd always been stronger than me.

I could remember so clearly the first time I saw Jeff. It was my first week cooking at a prestigious restaurant, and getting *paid*, after having apprenticed for the hottest chef in the city. Of the four apprentices they selected from my cooking school, they chose me to continue on. It was nothing short of a miracle.

Jeff's arm was wrapped securely around a woman whose proportions made me wonder how she didn't topple over. I had this natural mistrust of 'breast men', easily explained by my own lacking in that department - it was all legs and bottom for me – but he caught and kept my attention anyway.

I couldn't decide if he was handsome, or just so blatantly confident that I couldn't help myself from staring as he walked toward me. They sat in front of the open kitchen, in the most prized seats in the restaurant, only given to very special customers, so I knew he was either important or rich. Probably both.

He oozed cool flawlessness. I was a nervous wreck, convinced that any wrong move, no matter how slight, would get me kicked out on my butt. I have never experienced anywhere more competitive than a fine dining kitchen, and all eyes were on the new girl.

His eyes were certainly on me as well, to the dismay of his pouting date. He asked about all the dishes I was working on, and then wanted to know about how I started cooking. Speaking was limited, as everything was so busy, but he stayed attentive.

As soon as his date headed toward the bathroom, he slipped me his card, making some excuse about the possibility of my needing a good surgeon should one of those knives slip. I wasn't sure how cardiac surgeon would re-attach one of my severed digits, but thankfully it never came to that.

Of course, so consumed with my new job, working 12-15 hour days, I never called him. And there was the complication that he had been with a woman when we met. Then he started coming to the restaurant regularly, by himself, and sitting at the counter. The fourth time I saw him, he asked me out.

As soon as he arrived at my apartment to pick me up that night, I knew I would have to up my game. This guy was super smooth, and I was an awkward mess. The only love in my life to that point had been my career, and I had never before met anyone who understood what it meant to be passionately in love with your job.

He felt the same way about medicine as I did about food, and could talk about surgery like a child talking about candy. It was his life's dream to be a doctor, and I could only guess how talented he was. He treated me like a grown-up. Not like a new chef, or an inexperienced girl, but like a grown woman whose opinions mattered and whose dreams were as important as his own.

Our courtship was slowed down by our busy schedules, but the commitment was clear, nearly from the beginning. Despite the romance of the early days, Jeff never actually proposed. We just sat down one day and started planning our wedding. As obvious and expected as our summer vacations in France.

Our lives settled into an ease, lubricated by frequent separations and our own passionate immersions into our careers. When we were actually together, it was nice enough. Jeff was interested in and supportive of my life, our families got along quite well, and we never lacked for anything. Perhaps I didn't notice how little intimacy there was, as I was so absorbed and fulfilled by my work. My dream was expanding, and the world was accommodating. I was being touted as one of the next generation of great chefs. There was talk about creating a signature restaurant. Just for me.

Things began to change between us after Lola was born. I never realized how much I could love another human being until my daughter came into my life. It made the feelings for my husband even more painful in comparison.

Being her mother should have been the easiest job in the world. Lola was a gift of a child, so easy-going and beautiful. She had this other-worldliness about her, like my brother Danny did. Lola had been his favorite song.

I was equally mesmerized and terrified by this tiny creature who was now mine to protect, torn between wanting to be with her every moment, and wanting to be living my dream life as a chef. Neither part of my life felt right anymore – my time at the restaurant was tainted with an urgency to be with my baby, and my time with Lola would leave me with rising anxiety about my ability to be a mother, my leaving behind the only thing in my life I had ever been really good at, and the impossibility of how I could possibly do everything that was being asked of me.

The internal battle raged every time I had to leave her, but every night (or morning as it happened on occasion) I would come home to my baby and know that it was all as it was supposed to be. At least for a few hours.

In a strange role reversal, she became my source of solace and comfort. She had this intuitive sense that told her exactly what to do and say. Sometimes I would feel embarrassed to be the weak and needy one, but had to accept that that's how it was for us.

I wanted it all to work, although the unlikelihood stared me right in the face. The crazy hours Jeff and I were tied to were not conducive to the round-the-clock care a baby needed, and tensions built quickly about our respective responsibilities. Jeff was taking on more and more at the hospital, and even traveling to train other doctors and speak at conferences. He was proud of how well he was providing for our family, even if not in person. Although my culinary star kept getting brighter, it didn't mean any fewer hours for me either.

"It's time for you to leave your frivolous career behind and stay home to take care of our child, Monique," he eventually said.

That's when I stopped speaking, so overtaken by betrayal. Jeff grew more and more insistent, my suffering apparently not a consideration. How could I leave the only thing in my life, other than my daughter, that filled my heart with joy? Yes, it was an enormous amount of work, and yes it brought in nearly no money and was very stressful and time-consuming. But it was my life. It was how I defined myself - I was a chef, before anything else. How dare he demand I leave my career?

He grew louder and I grew silent. He grew larger, and I shrank into my two unsatisfying worlds of mother and chef.

Silence became my husband's lover. A lifetime of meticulously chosen words, and a short period of incoherent raging, left me mute. No need to wonder what happened after one screamed so violently that the voice failed. Silence, of course.

Whose hand is over my mouth, I wondered, powerless to move my mouth with an inexplicable case of lockjaw. Being incapable of complaining also meant no oral sex. He would suffer for what he had done.

By not speaking, I could bear the dishonesty. By feigning agreement, I would keep the peace. By locking my jaw, I could stop being force fed his chilling torment.

Silence cooked for him, silence slept with him and silence hung on his arm, right alongside the Rolex, neither making even a tick.

Maybe I had used up my quota of words. A bit soon, I thought, but not impossible. Or maybe, by using words like weapons, which I had done with so many others, I had broken some covenant and been banned to the land of the speechless.

Be seen and not heard, resurrected from childhood. Silent AND deadly.

How much venom could be produced with a wordless gaze, a tight-lipped grimace, a rigid backed response? A nearly fatal dose, I came to understand, without the need to bare the fangs locked behind the prison of my mouth.

Everyone could see the cause of this strange symptom, the locking of my jaw. But I dared not even think the thought – my life was sealing my lips shut.

What would I have to admit, about my own part in the tragic farce, to say – "He did this, and I let him?"

Silence was the price for security, the counterfeit for connection, as valuable as any of the constant lies. Whether spoken or not, dishonesty was our secret code.

I would win this one. If shutting up and shutting off were the rules of engagement, I would be the silent victor.

"You won't talk to me," he would say. *No shit*, I thought, and that was that. I won the round, again.

But he changed the rules, so quickly I could not veer from the strategy to manipulate him into acquiescence. I rounded the bend to find that he had left me, emotionally.

Unable to bear the hypocrisy, or the silence of lies, he stopped playing mid-game, took his heart and left. The only pleas were silent as I realized it was my own hand over my mouth.

When lies are all you tell, what is the value of your word? When the truth is too hard to bear what is the value of your life?

Does silence burn in the consumption of rage or stand at the doorway to ecstasy? Who holds the barometer, the perfectly precise gauge of 'rightness' by which to assess the opening and closing of one's mouth... the opening and closing of one's heart?

Fill the hole with whatever is around to keep it busy, or seal it so tightly for no trespassing, I told myself. Breathe, moan, whisper, cry, scream, laugh. But speak not or forever hold your peace.

In a rare moment of courage, when the rift had grown enormous, I began to plot my escape from the marriage. Jeff had already commenced his next relationship, with no concern whether I knew or not. Not sure how I would manage financially or as a single mom, but I could not take the hostile environment in my own house and the slow crushing of my dream.

The whole process with the lawyer was much easier than I thought. As I was about to secretly file papers, Jeff and I had an unexpected reconnection, courtesy of a wine-tasting at my favorite vineyard and an especially soft energy from my husband. Our sex life had dwindled to almost nothing since Lola's birth, partly because of the changes in my body and the exhaustion, but mostly because of our toxic relationship. I considered myself nearly asexual during those years. No desire, no thoughts, no interest.

Our lovemaking had been beautiful that night, reminiscent of the early days of our courtship. We were in no rush, as Lola was at a friend's house, and neither of us had to work in the morning.

We took our time and rediscovered each other. Things between us got a bit better after that. I noticed that he was more helpful around the house, less denigrating about my work, and even kinder to our daughter. My fantasies turned to the rebirth of our marriage, the return of the life I thought I wanted.

It all shifted again when I realized I was pregnant. No way could I handle another kid, now that Lola was in preschool. I'd been looking forward to greater independence and more time for myself, if even just to sleep. No possibility for that to happen with another baby on the way.

I panicked and withdrew again. Jeff reverted to his previous coldness and disdain. We fell into our old patterns like a hole in the road. I waited a very long time to tell him I was pregnant, even to the point that strangers began to notice. I was too far along to do anything about it. I just kept willing it to go away and at the same time, knowing somehow that this baby would save me. It would prevent me from continuing down this path of a loveless marriage and self-hatred.

When I told him I was pregnant, he barely changed expression, as if I had just announced we were having lasagna for dinner. He nodded and said, "Great. Maybe we'll have a boy this time," then went back to what he was reading.

I thought the crack in my heart would be irreparable. I didn't mind anger or other strong emotions, but apathy was my kryptonite. I felt my face burn and my heart shatter. Part of me wanted him to be furious. To rail and cry about the absurdity of bringing another human being into the farce of our marriage. Part of me wanted my transformation into a mother again to create a shift for him, back to the man who wanted me so deeply, and cared.

There was no way I could be in this marriage one minute longer. But there was no leaving now. What would I do? Move into a shelter? I could not support myself with my work, at least not the way we had been living, and I could not put in any more hours with a small child to take care of. I didn't want to assume that Jeff would take care of us, financially, given his feelings about the situation. I had heard too many horror stories about divorces going terribly wrong.

Claire was born in the middle of the night, after everyone was already exhausted from a challenging day of labor. She came out of me like a lion, full of roar and fury, the scream impossible not to hear.

It was much harder than with Lola, and made worse by the fact that everyone had said that the second would be so much easier. I resented Jeff's presence during the birth, but he seemed insistent on staying. My body was trying to birth a baby and my heart was trying to flee from everything I'd created. The man I no longer loved or wanted to be with. The prospect that I would have to leave my world of cooking. And yet another life in my hands, when I was making such a mess of the one I already had.

Holding Claire in my arms, I found a source of strength that transcended my exhausted body and beleaguered mind. That night, after cradling my new baby girl, my second daughter, the mother bear arose. I knew I would not raise my girls in a house of mediocrity, lovelessness, or powerlessness.

"I'm not doing this anymore. I'm leaving. With the girls."

Jeff held his newborn daughter and cried, knowing the inevitable had just happened. We spent the next several days in a peaceful silence, enjoying the short time as a family that would soon dissolve. I appreciated the quiet and the lack of conflict or interrogation. Little did I know that Jeff had been plotting a full-scale attack. He would do anything to prevent me from leaving, either kindly or not.

He offered me anything I wanted. Separate rooms, money, time at a prestigious cooking school in Europe. All I wanted to do was leave, but he would not have it. The break-up of his family was not on the very specific agenda for his life.

The divorce raged on for five years, while Jeff tried to find any means to pull me back in. He knew better than to play the child card - he loved his daughters and knew that he could never take them away from their mother. For this, I was eternally grateful, even though I didn't know it at the time. This would become the thread that eventually rebuilt our relationship as co-parents and friends.

My emotional departure was mirrored by his physical one, as he moved on to his next relationship. That act, painful as it was for me, was the first sign that the divorce would actually happen, which had been unclear before then.

When I was finally free, I had to completely undo and redo my life, alone with the girls. Restaurant hours would no longer work with my abbreviated family and I had very little money to hire a round-the-clock nanny. My dearest friend Emile, the man who knew everyone in the culinary world, found me a job at a national food magazine, as a writer. He knew I had been writing informally for some time, and enjoyed it.

The move to journalism would solve all the problems - a steady paycheck, stability and best of all, hours that work with raising two young children. Without even thinking about it, I said yes. Exuberantly. It was the answer to my dreams.

I went off to my new corporate job happily. It was the solution I had been searching for, without knowing it existed. It kept me in that world I so cherished, utilized my writing skills, put food on the table and me at home with my kids. I could not believe my luck.

The divorce became final, by default, as it happened in our state, on an anticlimactic day. I told my sisters and poured myself a beer. It had been an extremely long and bitter road. I had lost nearly everything - my kindness, compassion, perseverance and self-awareness - but I still had my beautiful girls. And the strength to wake up another day and do it again. In the scheme of things, it could have been worse. Not much, but some.

This is where we'd ended up. Making our way back to a place of respect, and even love. Without him, I never would've had these human beings in my life – my beloved girls. My heart ached for the loss of his father. And mine.

The girls and I hunkered down in our own processes of hurting and healing. We talked about all the grandparents they'd lost, and how it made them feel. I didn't even pretend to be the strong one, my own grief relentlessly rising to the surface like a thousand tiny bubbles.

6

VEGAS, BABY

Even with Emile's help, it was a tough road back to the kitchen. I swallowed my pride a hundred times, as chefs I could out-cook with both hands behind my back decided I wasn't good enough. Or too old. Or too constrained. I was worse than old news – I was no news at all.

I got my first *yes* in the most unlikely place - at a hot new restaurant that had just lost two kitchen staff that week. Their desperation was my salvation, and the chef agreed to take me on as an apprentice. There was no money, of course, but the experience would get me back in top shape in lightning speed.

I worked at the magazine during the day and spent a few evenings every week at the restaurant. None of the kids working beside me had ever heard of me, but my skills came back quickly. I resisted saying, "Do you know who I am?!" about a thousand times during my comeback.

In the moments when I tied my apron, and unrolled my knife bag, I felt alive again. All the chaos – prep chefs busily working in the back, produce delivery people in and out, even the business guys yelling about the books in the office – faded into a distant hum as I found my own rhythm. All I heard was the sound of my knives against the sharpening steel, the whoosh of the gas ovens catching, and the sizzle of my creations. I began to know joy again, in a way that I had forgotten for so long.

A new me was emerging. I couldn't help but sense that there were more surprises to come.

No one, however, was particularly surprised when Nora got nominated for a national science award, but the fact that she offered to take us all to Las Vegas for the ceremony made us jump up and down like game show contestants. Lizzy was finally moving past her morning sickness and wanted to go, maybe as her last hurrah before she got too big. We promised to fund as much spa time as she needs. Nora forbade Sam from coming and dubbed this 'girls' weekend'. I was sure he was disappointed but there was no changing Nora's mind once she decided something.

Nora had gotten us adjoining rooms at the hottest hotel, and planned the entire itinerary around enjoying the best restaurants and clubs. The schedule was packed, with very little time for actual sleeping. I knew I would need multiple outfits per day.

I was excited. Maybe more than I should have been. I didn't care that the chef at the restaurant was annoyed about my needing time off. I didn't care that Jeff was questioning why I needed to go to Las Vegas. I didn't care that I had nothing cool to wear.

I hadn't been out in a big way for far too long. I spent so much time going through my closet trying to find something acceptable (in Vegas terms) for the long weekend that Lola declared we had to go shopping. I wanted to be a little bit racy, but not ridiculous, for a woman of my age.

As I scrutinized myself in the dressing room mirrors, I acknowledged that I was doing okay. I'd let my hair grow a bit longer, so that it was easier to tie back for the kitchen, and my face didn't look quite as drawn as it had recently. There was a rosiness underneath my skin that looked good, I had to admit.

My body had settled into a 40-something combination of strength and curves, which filled my clothes in an attractive way. Even if everything else was a wreck, I realized I still had those legs. The ones that made buying pants off the rack nearly impossible, but were undoubtedly my strong suit.

Lola noticed me looking pleased with myself.

"You are really beautiful, Mama. I like when you're this happy. And this is definitely a step up from your jeans and sweatshirts."

"You're right, sweetie. Thank you for helping me." I never thought anyone noticed my wardrobe, but my daughter apparently did.

"You should get dressed up more often. All these fancy clothes look so good on you!"

"Well, maybe one day I'll have a fancy life to warrant all these fancy clothes."

"I bet you will Mama. I bet you will. Now try on the stack over there. We've got lots more to do."

The shopping trip was fruitful - I put together several great outfits, even bought a celebratory pair of shoes. It wasn't clear how I would actually walk around in them, but for those few moments that I was able to stay upright, I was going to look fabulous!

The day finally came, my luggage filled with little black dresses, sequined stilettos and cherry red lipstick. Yes, I was going to party, as well as make some high profile connections. Vegas had become a culinary Mecca up there with New York and Paris, and with Emile's interventions, I was set up for VIP treatment wherever I wanted to go. Nora was suitably impressed. There might not have been sleep in our schedule, but at least we were going to eat very well.

I realized how long it'd been since I last travelled as I moved in slow-motion through the airport. Everything was new and interesting. Even the crowds, unhappy people, and rude workers didn't rile me. I was wearing my *I am going to Vegas* grin, nearly as big as my head. I made sure I began on the right foot by getting decked out for the flight, and I was pleased I did. It didn't matter that it was only a few hours – still an opportunity for me to show up as the fabulous babe I was going to unveil in the lighted city. This was the beginning of my grand coming-out party.

I stopped at an airport shop to buy a bottle of water. I must have begun daydreaming on line and was awoken from my Vegas fantasies by a deep, slightly accented voice saying, "Excuse me, ma'am. Excuse me, are you ready?"

I looked ahead at the huge gap in the line ahead and the clearly impatient sales girl at the register. The gentle beckoning certainly had not come from her. I turned around to see a man smiling at me.

"I'm so sorry," I said breathlessly. Wow, he was very good looking. Too good looking. The kind of man with whom I tended to act like a complete idiot.

"Gosh, I must have been daydreaming..."

"NEXT!" came the insistent urge from the cashier. I paid for my water and magazine, then walked out, afraid to look back at the man. Not that I needed to because his face was indelibly etched into my mind.

I arrived back at the gate just as boarding began, my generous sister kind enough to have upgraded me to first class. The experience was growing more and more perfect, and I settled into my big comfy seat and accepted a glass of champagne from the attendant.

I realized, a bit too late, that I hadn't set myself up well for the flight. I needed to get my magazine out of my bag, put away my phone and buckle my seat belt. But all my hands were full. I sat, awkwardly, trying to figure out what to put down and how to juggle everything.

"Would you like some help?" someone asked. Not just someone, but that same voice from the store. Could it be?

I turned around to see one seat behind me, on the other side of the aisle, the gorgeous man with the beautiful smile. How did he know what I was doing? Was my clumsiness transmitting seats away?

I decide to bypass my potential embarrassment, as this was an omen of great things, and I wasn't going to let *Monique the Dork* rule the day. *Monique the Goddess/Diva/Sex Kitten* was coming out to play. And play with this man I would.

"Why yes, I would," I said in as coy a voice as I could muster. *Did that really come out of my mouth?* Holy shit, I was embarrassed for myself already. But no, must keep going. No retreat.

"What can I do for you?" he asked, right back in that fucking sexy voice of his, so deep and tinted with just a hint of an accent. Italian? Or Spanish? *Holy crap this man could probably talk me into an orgasm. Right here on this plane.*

"Well, would you mind pulling my tray out for me? I seem to have a shortage of hands." I looked up just in time to see the flight attendants eyeing me quizzically. I flashed right back - *Back off bitches. He's mine.*

"Absolutely," he volunteered. He rose from his seat and was by my side in one easy step. He removed my elbow from the armrest and pulled out the small extension of the middle tray, which I'd already filled with my phone and headphones.

I could smell him as he leaned in to me, and thought, this man cannot be for real. I was getting more and more turned on. I wondered if the lady sitting next to me would switch seats.

"Anything else I can do for you?" he asked with the most enticing smile I had ever seen. *The champagne must be going to my head...*

"Well, yes, since you asked. A refill would be wonderful." I handed him my nearly empty champagne glass.

He took my glass, walked to the galley, and asked the shocked attendants for more champagne. They admonished him to return to his seat, as we were about to take off. He smiled at them and they filled the glass without any more commentary. He was a charmer and knew it. I wondered if this guy was ever denied what he wanted. Part of me wanted to be the one who rejected him, but who was I kidding. This man could've invited me into the airplane bathroom and I would probably have gone.

"Champagne for the beautiful lady." He stood in front of me, handing me my newly filled glass. Did he really just call me a beautiful lady? I tried not to look so obvious while searching to see who else he could have been referring to. *What an ass I am.*

He laughed softly.

"Why, thank you. I will definitely recommend you for a generous raise." And I winked. Seriously, I winked. I must have been channeling some celebrity vixen; something was fueling my newfound brazenness. We hadn't even taken off yet, and it was already the most fun plane ride I had ever taken.

He returned to his seat and I looked down, pretending to flip through my magazine. OH MY GOD. I knew I was breathing hard and tried to calm myself down. *Take it easy, babe. I'm sure this guy is used to women falling all over him. Play it cool!*

I pretended to skim my magazine through the remainder of take-off. Every now and then I felt like he was looking at me, but I dared not turn back and check. Too obvious, too desperate, even though I was both of those things. *Just keep reading,* I told myself.

I remembered my headphones and decide to put some music on. Yes, that would be just distracting enough to keep me from obsessing.

His hand was on my arm. HIS HAND WAS ON MY ARM! I turned hesitatingly, removing my headphones as if in slow motion.

"Hi," I squeaked.

"Hi." Then nothing. He smiled at me.

"My name is Marco. I, um, I'm going to a friend's wedding in Vegas. Not that you asked." He laughed at himself and shook his head slightly. Maybe he was nervous too. Wow. This was good stuff.

"My name is Monique, though nearly everyone calls me Nik. My sister was nominated for a science research award and I'm going to the ceremony. My younger sister too. The three of us are having a bit of a girl's weekend I guess." I laughed shyly, wondering if he had any idea what girls do with a weekend in Vegas.

"Staying anywhere good?" he asked.

"We're at the Wynn, where the conference is."

"Great!" he said a bit too quickly. "That's actually where the wedding is. Have you been there? It's a beautiful hotel."

"I haven't been, no. But I hear good things. Then again, is there anything in Vegas that isn't amazing?"

"Good point," he agreed. "I am sure you and your sisters will add beauty and grace to anything there."

"Or maybe there will be three very drunk women, completely unused to all that glitz, making fools of themselves." *Did I really just say that?? Ughhhh. Get yourself together, girl.*

"You are very funny, Monique. And I really can't imagine that happening. So, what are the husbands doing with themselves?"

Wow. He was digging for info. My gosh, this was too much fun.

"Missing us," I said with a playful grin. His face fell, slightly. "Just kidding. No husbands between us."

"Lucky Vegas," he said, flashing that smile again. This was too much. I was having such a great time with this guy that I forgot to notice that he was totally out of my league. No, I wasn't going to let that stop me. I was going to rise to the occasion.

As I turned to respond to him, the flight attendant stepped directly in my view. "Have you decided on your meal?" Snippy. Very snippy.

I ordered and let her finish her survey before turning back to Marco.

"Do you live in San Francisco, Marco?" I tried to sound as nonchalant as possible.

"Yes, I do. I have offices in New York and Argentina as well so I spend some time there."

"That's a wonderful combination of places to be. What do you do?" Cool and calm, not looking like I care too much.

"I'm an architect. Mostly private homes but a few public buildings. In the US and South America."

"That's very impressive. I've always been fascinated by architecture. It's such a cool mixture of art and science, don't you think? Creative and functional at the same time. Built anything I would have seen?"

"Well, maybe. We could turn around in Vegas and go to South America so I could show you myself."

Okay, that was some serious flirting. And I could keep up. I might have been rusty, but I wasn't dead.

"Sounds great. Shall we tell my sisters and your friends, or just run away secretly?"

"I'm all for full disclosure. And I can just have my assistant take care of it all so we don't have to deal with any emotional backlash. You know how people tend to take awards and weddings so seriously."

We were both laughing pretty hard by then. I kept reminding myself to stay present to how fun this was, in that moment, without projecting how badly it would inevitably end and how much suffering was in store. *This does not have to be another example of failure, Monique. You've had plenty of those.* Maybe this is the perfect setup for a juicy Vegas affair, or even just a lovely interaction with another human being that is bringing me pleasure. *This is enough,* I kept telling myself.

"I am a chef." It came out of my mouth before I knew what I was saying. Oh boy. Now, I'd really set us up for a fantasy.

His eyes widened. "Amazing," he said. "Now that's what I call art and science... and magic. I would give any of my buildings to be able to cook something that makes people experience how I feel after a good meal."

"You don't cook?"

"Yes, actually I do. But not very well. My family is Argentinean and Italian - food is everything. It's in our blood, but unfortunately mine is buried a little bit deeper. I do okay, I guess, but nothing like what you must do. I can only imagine what you must create in the kitchen," he said, making me immediately think of sex. What was this guy doing to my mind?

Everything he said was seductive. Flamingly seductive. I flashed into a scene of us in my kitchen with lots of food and very little clothing. Yum.

"Maybe when we are in Argentina, you will cook something for me." That jolted me out of my reverie, forcing me to remember his joke just minutes before.

"Fair enough I suppose, in exchange for you taking me on a tour of South America to view your buildings."

This was getting so rich and delicious I could hardly stand it.

We spent the rest of the flight talking about our lives, joking about our fantasy trip and comparing Vegas itineraries. We disembarked together and headed to baggage claim together (even though neither of us checked luggage) and walked outside together.

"Are your sisters picking you up?" he asked.

I laughed. Too loudly perhaps.

"We're not that kind of family. It's all about independence with us. And besides, they are much too busy getting the party started. It's fine. It's such a short taxi ride."

He cleared his throat, clearly wanting to say something. "I would love if you came with me. I mean... I have a car. I mean I'm getting picked up... a car service... and we're going to the same place. And you could come."

7

SLEEK BLACK LIMO

He stopped talking and lowered his head. He'd had a hard time with that. The thought of him feeling a bit nervous with me was too ridiculous to believe. I was just this boring mom pretending to be glamorous, living a fake life to go with my fake weekend. He was this gorgeous, most likely brilliant architect with a global business. Did I mention gorgeous? Oh and smart. And really well spoken, with great manners and sweet breath... Oh, I had to stop.

"Yes, that would be great. If you don't mind." Sexy smile.

"I would love it. But I think I said that already," he chuckled.

I followed him as he strode toward door number six. I noticed, as it was my favorite number. Good sign. A quick glimpse in the reflective glass soothed my worries just a bit. I actually looked pretty damn good. At least for me. Things were holding up and those extra sessions at the gym (to work off all my sexual tension) were paying off. Maybe I wasn't so far out of his league.

Just outside was a sleek black limo with his name in the window. As he approached confidently, the driver asked, "Mr. Gonzales?"

"Yes, thank you."

He opened the door for me, and stood as I entered. I noticed him looking at my legs. Good. Very good. We had all inherited those great legs from Mom, whose legs were out of some fashion magazine. Absolutely perfect. Even when I couldn't stand the rest of me, I knew my legs could stand up to scrutiny. No problem to linger there a little bit.

We sat very close to each other in the limo. Closer than strangers normally would.

"You are leaving on Monday right?" He had asked me that already. What was up, I wondered?

"Yes. After we recover from our raucous celebration of Nora's big win. She's convinced that she has no chance but my sister is the golden girl. She works her ass off and wins. A lot. Lizzy and I are both expecting to see her up on stage with a no-tears acceptance speech. She's not one for soft emotions."

"And you? Will you be crying?"

"Most certainly. I'll probably be crying during the boring speeches. I may even start if we see an especially touching billboard on the way there. Yup. That's me."

"Lovely," he said looking at me so deeply I thought he might have been reading my mind. It felt as if hours had passed. Or at least minutes. I wasn't sure.

"I have to ask you something, Monique."

"Yes?" Curious. So curious.

"Would you have time to go somewhere with me?"

"You mean other than Argentina?"

"Yes. Somewhere local. For now at least." Gosh that smile was going to be the end of me.

"There is a restaurant I have been wanting to try. It is supposed to be spectacular. I would like to take you there, if you have time."

Oh my God, he just asked me out. On a date. Perhaps I misheard. No, it was definitely a date. Shit. What was I going to do? Would the girls understand? I knew they were hoping to spend all our time together. But how could I say no to this man? Oh boy...

"That sounds really nice. As long as you understand I love to eat. People have been frightened when taking me out to dinner."

"I can't wait to experience that. I am definitely up for the challenge." The grin again. "Does tomorrow work for you?"

"Actually, could I just check with my sisters? Nora is a real stickler and likes to have everything planned out. I just need to see if Friday or Saturday is better."

As if we were using our sibling ESP, my phone beeped with a message. Nora, I was sure.

Where are you, Nik? Do I really need to be the only one drinking in this family??

"Excuse me," I said to him. "I need to get back to the boss."

On my way. In a shiny black limo. You are welcome to pull yourself off the barstool and greet me at the entrance, like a sister with manners would do.

Limo?? Who are you? And what have you done with my simpleton sister??

I showed him the text exchange, which sent him into gales of laughter.

"I see all of you are very funny. I can tell you love each other a lot."

"Yes. Despite outer appearances, we do. And this is the real me... the simpleton sister. Now you know."

"I can't imagine what your family must be like to think you are a simpleton. You are not in the Gabor family, are you?"

We both laughed.

"While you have your phone out, why don't I give you my number so you can let me know about tomorrow? I don't want to intrude on your time with your sisters, really. But I would love to spend some time with you. It has been a wonderful afternoon, talking to you."

I handed him my phone like a star-struck teenager. I even giggled, embarrassingly enough.

He took it confidently and began to type in lots of characters. Many more than I would have expected. I held myself back from peeking over his shoulder but the anticipation was killing me. What the heck was he writing? Did he have one of these extra-long Latin names? Was he writing me a love note? Hee, hee hee. The girlish giggles came out again.

He handed me the phone.

"Okay, I put my full name, so you can find me at the hotel. Also my cell and email. And a little note so you remember who I am."

"Do you think I would forget you?" I was really surprised. Had this guy not looked in the mirror lately?

"I would never presume that I made nearly as much of an impression on you as you made on me."

Humble to top it all. I was toast!

We were mostly silent for the last few minutes of the trip. I liked sitting next to him, hearing and feeling his breath. Every now and then we looked over at each other and smiled. No words needed. Also surprisingly, not awkward.

We arrived and someone from the hotel opened my door. Marco came around from his side and took my hand to help me out of the car. I could almost swear that he pushed the valet out of the way. His hand felt soooooooo nice. Big and warm and not too soft. The hands of a man who used them. Unspeakably sexy.

We stood face to face for the briefest moment and the idea of kissing him crossed my mind. Not something that *regular* me would do in a million years. But the goddess diva? Definitely. The moment passed before I could move on my impulse. Perhaps I'd be given another opportunity. Hopefully.

We followed the bellboys, with our luggage, into the hotel and the bustle of Las Vegas. This town was a secret passion of mine. Not something I admitted to too many people - it didn't really match my down-to-earth image - but the part of me that loved glitz and glam and stardom felt at home here. I couldn't help but grin.

I headed toward the unfortunately long check-in line when Marco wrapped his arm around my waist and whispered, "Come with me."

We moved past the crowds to a desk, off to one side. I thought the sign said VIP or concierge or something like that. I was too busy taking in the sights and sounds of Vegas. Gosh, I was happy to be there. And not only because that amazing man had his arm around me.

He provided his information, to which the stunning woman behind the counter cooed, "Welcome to the Wynn, Mr. Gonzales. So wonderful to have you back." He told her that I'd also be checking in and he'd appreciate her help. She obliged.

My sister had reserved us fabulous rooms, certainly, but I wasn't not sure I would have gotten this level of service. I was very grateful.

He listened closely as she told me my room number. I noticed.

We stepped away from the desk and paused for a moment, neither of us sure of what to do next. Did we go up to our rooms together? Would he even use the same pedestrian elevator the rest of us use? Did I shake hands, hug, or kiss as the Europeans and South Americans did? So confusing.

The problem was solved by the piercing shriek of my baby sister, her tiny yet curvy frame bobbing across the lobby toward me. Right behind, not stooping to excitement, was my equally-pleased older sister. They looked fabulous, in full Vegas style.

"You're finally here! Oh my God, we were waiting for you for so long." Lizzy kept talking, even as she wrapped her body around mine. "Sooooo glad you're here. Oh my God, Nik, this place is amazing! I might want to live here. It is the BEST EVER," said the soon-to-be mom.

Even Nora gave me a sweet hug. "So glad you're here, Nik," she whispered in my ear. I knew she meant it.

They barely noticed the man waiting patiently next to me. "Hey guys, this is Marco. We flew in together."

"Whaaaaaat?!" screeched Lizzy. "You know this guy? Oh my God!" It was hard to believe that this girl had not been drinking.

"We met in the..."

"Hello. I'm Nora. I'm the reason we're here. And you are?" My sister, always the professional, always the boss.

He took Nora's hand, then pulled her in and kissed both her cheeks. She was kissed into silence. A very rare occurrence.

"I am Marco Gonzales. Your beautiful sister graced me with her presence on what would otherwise have been an uneventful plane ride. I am so pleased to meet you. She described you quite well."

Nora couldn't speak and neither of us knew what to do. It was unheard of. Lizzy took the moment of silence to make her introduction, which she did by jumping up for her own hug and kiss. Except that Lizzy was so small and Marco was so tall that she jumped up on him like a small child on her father. He caught her, thankfully and gracefully put her down.

We all erupted in laughter that lasted minutes. Lizzy, not one to hold onto embarrassment, happily accepted his two-cheeked kiss.

"Wow, you are so handsome!" she exclaimed. I would have turned red if my olive skin didn't hide it so well. "Did you really just meet Nik on the plane? And was it your limo she came in? That is so awesome! I love meeting awesome people on the plane. Did she tell you I'm pregnant? Yup, it's true. At first I was like, oh shit! But now I'm super excited and I feel really good now that all the throwing up is done and my fabulous sisters have offered to help me and Nik is the best mom I have ever met and she's going to teach me how to be the best mom ever and-."

"Lizzy, shall we save some of our life history for later? Marco probably has somewhere he needs to be," the voice of reason chimed in.

"Well, yes and no. I am meeting my friends fairly soon, but it's

Vegas, which means that time is flexible. And this is MUCH more interesting." Marco graced them all with the killer smile.

"I am very excited for you, Lizabetta."

Now did he really have to say it in the most sexy and glamorous way?

"Parenthood is the journey of heroes and holds riches beyond anything you could imagine."

"You have kids?" she asked.

"Yes, two boys although they are nearly men now. Both in college."

I did not know this. I felt awkward about it.

"Cool," she said. "Too bad they're not a teensy bit older, because they are probably HOT!"

"Lizzy!" I had to intervene this time, but Marco just laughed.

"Yes, I think they are very handsome. And they seem to like slightly older women, so maybe..." He winked.

When Lizzy laughed it was like drinking champagne. So light and effervescent. It's wonderful to see her this happy.

"So, when will we see you again?"

"Lizzy!" I thought I might just die of embarrassment. Right there in the hotel lobby.

"Funny you should ask. I have invited your sister to dinner with me, and she is wondering when it would be convenient for you to be without her. For a night."

Did he say *A* night, or *THE* night?

"Oh, whenever is fine. We're just hanging out. Other than Nora's thing on Sunday, but that won't take very long."

All Nora or I could do was sigh.

"Good to hear."

Exasperated, Nora said, "Shall we?" as she led us toward the elevators.

Awkwardness filled the space as we waited for one of the doors to open. Lizzy looked like she was trying hard to contain her excitement and I couldn't tell what Nora was feeling. I felt strange, a little ashamed of my family but heck, this was the reality of my life.

We got into a packed elevator and Marco made his way next to me. Our bodies were very close and mine was warming up. I definitely wanted this man, if nothing more for than a seriously good romp. Maybe lots more.

He bent down as if to kiss my neck and whispered in my ear, "I apologize for intruding on your schedule. I did not mean to bring it up with your sisters. I know you would have talked to them. I hope you don't think I was too forward."

I couldn't believe what I was hearing and had to take a breath before responding. And boy, did I like having his face so close to mine.

I turned toward his ear and replied, "It's okay. No problem, really. It looks like we are good for tomorrow night."

"That's wonderful."

And then he kissed me. Slowly, lingering, one kiss on each cheek. As he passed my lips I imagined what that would feel like. My arousal raised the temperature in the elevator by several more degrees.

I beamed back at him as I made my way through the doors onto our floor.

"Call me later, okay?"

"Absolutely," I responded.

The three of us stepped off the elevator and held our composure until the doors closed. The laughing began and we hardly made it to the room before we completely let loose.

8

GET THE PARTY STARTED

"Nik, that man is unbelievable. Oh my God, you have to do him. You have to. He probably has an amazing body too." Lizzy was the most sexual of the three of us and pregnancy hadn't appeared to slow her down.

"He is very charming, Nik. Well done. I approve," the boss added. Marco seemed to have infiltrated Nora's typical skepticism.

"Well now, I feel so much better because I was like, eh, about the whole thing." The screaming began again.

"This is going to be the weekend to end all weekends, girls!"

"Yes, Lizzy, I think you're right," I added. "And you, the reason why we're here. Anything to say?"

"I'm glad you guys came. It's been too long since we did this."

"Don't get soft on us, girl!" said Lizzy.

They gave me a tour of our adjoining rooms, with mine in the middle. With all the interior doors open, we had a huge great space, but decided that my room would be party central. I was happy to oblige.

"Can a girl get something to eat around here? I have to take care of some serious pent-up sexual energy!"

"Yes, yes, let's eat! You know I'm always up for that. Where should we go?" asked Lizzy.

"Nik, we've got this great fruit and cheese spread here. Would that work? Then we can get ready and go out for the night a little later?" My sister, the planner, always had the most logical solutions.

"What are you guys going to wear? I'm going to get ready for our big night. Music! We need music!" Lizzy had already begun dancing around, even before the music started.

Lizzy and Nora provided the soundtrack for our preparations, complete with singing, drumming on the furniture and a few rounds of the hustle. I hadn't felt that happy and alive and... like a woman... in so long.

I prepared outfit number one for the weekend. Understatedly sexy. Well, maybe not so understated.

Inspired by the dance party, we got dressed and strutted out of the rooms as if Vegas was our own personal runway. There were yards of legs on display, each of us knowing which asset to feature. Lizzy had chosen a flouncy skirt and, in acknowledgment of her pregnancy-inspired bust-line, a low cut top. The baby bump was hardly visible.

Nora wore a leather pencil skirt to accentuate her slimness and nonstop legs. I wore shorts. Silver glitter shorts that Lola (my resident fashion diva) forced me to buy but that I never expected to in public. Where else but Vegas?

It reminded me of Mom and her short skirts. Even as she got older (not that she actually aged), she knew exactly what she was going to feature on her body and wasn't shy about it.

Crossing the casino, I watched heads turn and eyes follow. It felt spectacular. To be desired again was like the first breath after being underwater. This is what it feels like to be alive, I realized.

Was that my name I heard? No, couldn't be. Then again. We all stopped and Lizzy saw him first. "Marco! It's Marco!" she said.

I turned around to see an outline of a man straight from his own runway. Royal blue cashmere sweater and dark jeans. I thought Lizzy was right, this man had an amazing body, much more apparent now that he wasn't in the suit he had on earlier. I really had to play it cool, even though I wanted to swoon.

He walked directly to me and I went straight in. First to one cheek, and then slowly to the other. I gave his arm a squeeze and confirmed everything I believed to be underneath that silky soft sweater. We were frozen in space, just the two of us, my happily hopping sister aside.

"Well, hello," I said.

"Ladies." Long pause. "You have made it impossible for any of these other poor women who have worked so hard, to get any male attention." He turned to Lizzy first, who was dying for her double cheek kisses. "You have forever redefined what an expectant mother looks like. I hope you never worry about being sexy, my dear."

She beamed at him, as if he had read her mind about a big part of her anxiety about pregnancy.

Nora was next.

"And you. The serious Nora with the mile-long legs. I can see why you need all that seriousness to contain those legs. They are lethal."

Once again, Nora was silenced. This was good.

I realized he'd been holding my hand the whole time. He turned to me and kissed my hand, ever so softly. He didn't speak and I thought maybe he had nothing to say. I was starting to feel a bit embarrassed and unsure about my garish outfit choice.

"Come meet my friends. I'm not sure I can let you out of my sight tonight. You outshine the whole Vegas strip." His gaze never wavered from my eyes.

I would have followed him anywhere he led me at that point. Without saying anything more, we headed toward a lounge across the casino. I didn't know how he'd spotted me from there, with all these people around. Vegas was never short of eye candy and I was so glad he found me.

"Monique is hungry! She needs to eat!" Lizzy added. Oh yeah, I'd completely forgotten. The snacks were delicious, but my body was asking for real food. Among other things.

"Well, may I feed you then?"

Everything in my body said yes. Feed me, consume me, anything you want.

We walked through a busy collection of bodies, hand in hand. I was unsure where he was leading us, and was surprised when he walked into a room that you couldn't tell existed from the front of the lounge. It grew surprisingly quiet.

This was clearly some VIP area, with a much more subdued feel than the rest of the place. It was beautiful, sexy, elegant. Just like him.

With our hands still clasped, he led me and my sisters up to a group of men, who stopped as if on cue. They couldn't tell which of us to look at first. They were impressed. I was pleased.

It could've been a Latin supermodel convention, each man better looking than the next. Please join us, said the young one in black. Lizzy's eyes got very wide. He was definitely her type.

"Amigos, this is Monique." A nod of recognition moved through the group. Had he told them about me? "And her sisters, Lizabetta and Nora." They each in turn got up to kiss us and introduce themselves. This ritual was really growing on me.

I looked back to see if Nora was okay with this change of plans. She had a restaurant in mind that she wanted to try and did not like to deviate from the plan.

When our eyes met, she smiled and I knew it was fine.

"They serve food here right? Nik is hungry!"

I loved how Lizzy was always looking out for us in just the sweetest way. She was going to make a great mom.

The men made room for us to join in and the party began. I didn't know who was ordering the food and drinks but everything just kept coming. Marco never let our bodies get more than a foot away from each other. His hand remained around my waist, on my back or holding mine. I felt like a queen. A very sexy queen.

Hours passed and no one made a move to leave. The conversations flowed with Nora showing off her Spanish and talking about her time in South America. They regaled her with stories of each of their homelands and made her promise to visit. Lizzy and her young man created their own dance floor and practiced the salsa or the rumba. I couldn't tell.

Marco and I floated in our private bubble, speaking with our faces inches away, about life and food and buildings and beauty. I started to feel like I could love this man. What wasn't there to love?

Somehow we agreed to move the party to the dance club. The groom's brother has gotten VIP passes and there was apparently Latin music in one of the rooms.

Moving back out into the fray was a shock but Marco glued his body to mine. The crush of bodies trying to get into the club almost separated us, but the men created a protective wall. I was being completely protected and taken care of. This fantasy of a night just kept getting better.

The pulse of the music hit my body well before we entered the club and I wanted to move. My sisters were the singers of the family, but I was the dancer. I felt music in my hips and my back and my legs and could express it well. I was already moving when Marco pulled me to the dance floor. "Let's see what you can do, my chef."

My chef. He said my chef. I didn't think anyone had ever called me *their* chef. The implications were too much to contemplate. Now, I just needed to move. He was surprised that I could follow him. We went from a close embrace Latin-style to freeform dance and back again. My body was free, taken by the music.

At several points he reached down to whisper something in my ear. Every time his face came close to mine, I gave a start. There was undeniable electricity there.

Occasionally, I remembered my sisters, and had a look around the club. We'd deviated pretty seriously from the plan, and I wanted to make sure they were okay. As far as I could tell, they were both having fun.

"I have to ask you something," he said fairly seriously. Nervousness flooded my body. Will this be the proposition? Or the dump? *Stop projecting, Monique, just enjoy the moment.* He lead me into a quieter part of the club, where we could hear each other a bit better.

"I don't know quite how to say this."

Uh-oh is all I hear in my head.

"I know you are here for your sisters. But I don't really know why you are here. I mean, I don't know if you wanted to meet some... people and have fun. I mean of course you wanted to have fun. That was stupid to say."

He was the one who was nervous. What was going on for him?

"What I'm trying to say is that, I don't know if you want this. All this time with me. I feel like maybe I am keeping you from something."

Had he been he worried about my looking around the room for my sisters? Had he felt my nervousness and thought it was lack of interest? I needed to be powerful. "What do you want to know, Marco?" All of a sudden, I became the cool one. Calm, collected, expressive. The power of it all was nearly ecstatic.

"Yes, the question," he said nodding. "I want to know if you want to be with me. I mean, if it's okay that I am keeping you here. I just... We are having so much fun, and I would like to spend this time with you, but not force you, if you don't want."

"Does it look like I don't want?" Power was a dangerous thing and now I was playing with him. This was my MO, to take advantage of men when they were being vulnerable with me. To attack when they were defenseless. I was disgusted that this was coming out now, with this man.

Before I could retract the question, he answered. "I think you are enjoying yourself," he said strongly. "And so are your sisters. But Vegas is a funny place. Sometimes... it can be easy to misread things and I don't want to do that. I want to be clear."

"Yes, me too. I am here to enjoy myself, in whatever form that takes. And if I wasn't, I wouldn't still be here."

"That is very clear."

A moment of awkward silence was broken when I touched his arm. I wanted to tell him that I was completely in awe of his directness and his consideration. That the whole power trip was a pretense. That I felt thrilled and terrified in his presence. I couldn't quite muster the courage for any of that.

"I'm going to the bathroom. Be right back."

"Okay."

I took extra time in the bathroom to review what had just happened. He was right. It was easy to misread and misunderstand. I had done it quite enough in my life. Part of me was terrified about how I already felt about him, after just a few hours together. And the other part heard what I said - *I am here to enjoy myself. In whatever form that takes.* And desperately wanted to believe it.

Marco was talking to a friend when I came out. Spanish flew between their lips and I struggled to understand what was being said. Damn! I wish I had paid more attention in Spanish class!

"Hola Bella," he said as he took my hand and kissed it.

"Everything alright?" I asked, expecting to hear otherwise.

"Of course. Except that we are here and the music is out there. Shall we?"

"Absolutely."

Any tentativeness he had about our being together was lost, which he showed me on the dance floor. He held my body so close to his that sometimes I couldn't breathe. I thought I could feel him hard, through his pants, but convinced myself it couldn't possibly be, even though we were dancing as if we were making love. Our bodies were filled with fire and spark; I'm certain he felt the music through my own pulse. His hands explored me and I liked it. Nearly as much as my hands on his body.

The way we moved together definitely bode well for anything that might happen further along. This man could really move, and more importantly he could move with me. He was a very strong leader, and I let myself surrender to him. It was delicious.

And sexy and magical and so erotic. Even if nothing happened between us, I would look back at this night and know I had a hot moment with a hot guy. And had a great time.

I wanted him to kiss me so badly. My mouth ached for his. But he didn't. What did this man want and would I be able to give it to him?

9

PENTHOUSE VIEW

I immersed myself in those moments with him so many times that I completely lost track of time. It was only when Lizzy found me to say she needed to eat that I realized it was morning. No windows in Vegas meant morning and night were indistinguishable.

Lizzy's handsome friend offered to take her to breakfast but I wasn't sure she wanted to be alone with him. Normally she would have been the first person to leave with a guy, but pregnancy had made her a bit more skittish. And sensitive maybe. And sensible, certainly.

Thankfully, Marco made the decision.

"I'm hungry too. Your wild sister kept me dancing all night with no sustenance. Can we accompany you to breakfast?"

"Yes! That's great!" said my always enthusiastic Lizzy.

Before the four of us headed out, I remembered Nora.

"Where's Nora?"

"She's still out there," said Lizzy. "Said she didn't want to eat. She's in the middle of a group of men, doing her snake dance."

That's what we called Nora's dancing. She was so tall and skinny and didn't really have rhythm but did this slithery sinewy movement that seemed to mesmerize everyone around her. She loved being the center of attention and I knew she was having fun.

We decided on the German pancake house, which tickled Lizzy to no end, but it was a cab ride away, which meant having to go outside into the light of day. I was terrified about what I must have looked like after so many hours of dancing. Hard. Maybe this wasn't a good idea. But it was too late and I was being led along.

I didn't realize how hungry I was until I saw the food around us. This was a superbly good choice and we all ate until we were almost sick. The enormous pancakes were probably meant for Bavarian lumberjacks, but we devoured them. Marco watched me eat as if he was studying a piece of art, grinning at my exuberant enjoyment.

"I need to eat many meals with you Monique. It makes everything more delicious."

My fork stopped midway to my mouth as I contemplated where I wanted his mouth to be.

We all hit a wall. At least I did. It was time to call it a night. Or a morning, as the case might have been.

We made the trek back to the hotel, and at one point I fell asleep on Marco's shoulder. I awoke as he kissed my forehead.

"Time to go, Bella." I liked that he called me that, cheesy as it was. We held hands all the way down the hallway to my room, hardly speaking. Would he make a move? Would I invite him in? It was all so unclear, the long night and the events of the day creating quite a blur in my mind.

Maybe tonight wasn't the night. I was so sweaty. But so was he. Would showering together be out of the question? What I really wanted was to just sleep with him, really just sleep. But no, it was too soon for that, I rationalized.

All four of us stopped at Lizzy's door. It was awkward. Marco probably knew his friend would make a move and wanted to give him some privacy. What could we do? My room was only next door, not enough space for us to be inconspicuous. Wow, this was weird, a flashback to my teen years.

"Come with me," he said.

I was exhausted, but I followed him anyway, back into the elevator, to the very top of the hotel. To his penthouse. Holy shit. He was taking me up to his room. Was I ready? Willing? I tried to summon my good decision-making skills right there, but couldn't. I followed my body, which wanted his body, right into his room.

The view took my breath away. The entire Las Vegas strip laid out in front of me through floor-to-ceiling windows. It was spectacular. I put my hands on the cool glass, mesmerized, and stared out. He disappeared into the kitchen and returned with two glasses of water.

What a thoughtful guy. He just didn't quit.

"I didn't mean to rush you in here," he said sheepishly. "I just didn't know what to do because Esteban and Liz..."

"Yes, I understand. It's beautiful up here. I can't imagine how you got this room."

"Aaaahhh. It's Esteban. He is a high roller here. Brings lots of clients who pay big money. And we are having the wedding here, so they gave us this whole floor. It is beautiful, though, isn't it?"

"Yes," I spoke over a yawn.

"You are very tired." He turned to look in my eyes.

"Yes." Again just yes.

"Please let me know when you want me to walk you back to your room. I imagine they have made some decision by now." We both snickered, then I remembered…

"Doesn't he mind that she's pregnant?" I didn't know where that came from.

Marco laughed. "Well, it's actually quite funny. Esteban is younger than me. Youngest in the group and the first one to want children. More than any man I have ever known, this man wants children. Lots of them. I think he saw her, and she is very beautiful, of course, and when he saw that she was pregnant... well, I think he fell in love instantly.

A bit like when I saw you daydreaming at the airport. A woman who could dream things that make her face light up like that must have magic in her soul."

I wanted to be more wide awake to process what I'd just heard. Did he really just say...

"Are you thinking of those things now?" he inquired.

"No. There are other things now. Maybe even better things."

He liked that answer and took my face in his hands.

"This face... this magnificent face. How has any man managed to let you go?"

"Well, some quite easily," I joked. The moment was getting more serious than I was capable of handling.

"Foolish." He moved toward me, still holding my face. My breath quickened. He was so close to me. Just one more inch and our lips would touch, but he stayed there. Just outside me. I thought I would dissolve or catch on fire or both at the same time. This was too much. Was he playing with me?

So slowly that I barely knew he'd moved I felt his warm mouth on mine. He held me there as his kiss grew firmer. His lips parted mine and next we were devouring each other. My God, I wanted to consume him, take him into every part of me.

He pressed into me and then backed away, in a rhythm I could instantly understand. Just like our dance, he was constantly reading my body, my breath, my mouth. My fatigue began to slip away as he took me further and further into him.

"Marco..." I breathed into his mouth.

"I have been waiting all day for that," he said. "It was well worth it."

My eyes stay closed to take in what he was saying but I found his mouth again. And now my hands began to explore his body. All the curves and angles of his bones and muscles felt like something surreal.

As he moved to my neck, I fell under the tidal wave of my desire. This man ignited me. He listened and paid attention and figured out exactly what to do. I moaned aloud, despite myself. He responded with his own groan.

His hands grasped my bottom, pulling me toward him and removing any doubt about what I was feeling. He was fully aroused and wanted me to know. He found the skin beneath my blouse and the sensation of flesh on flesh shocked me. He stopped, unsure of whether I was signaling him to stop. I assured him with my mouth that all was fine. Better than fine.

"Stay with me," he whispered. I wasn't sure I heard him and moved just far enough away to look directly into his face.

"Stay with me," he repeated, stronger. Our faces moved apart, but he never stopped holding me tightly against him. "I don't expect anything from you, I just want you to stay with me tonight."

"Today." I was disgusted with my unnecessary need to clarify and correct. My inexperience and clumsiness were starting to show.

"Yes. Today. Right now."

He waited for my answer and I tried to find one. I desperately wanted to stay with him. I wanted to rip his clothes off and fuck him like there was no tomorrow. I wanted to scream and writhe in ecstasy.

"Not tonight," I said instead, unsure of why those words came out of my mouth.

He looked disappointed, but not surprised.

"I promise you, I don't expect anything. I'm just not ready to let you go yet."

I considered his promise, and realized I believe him. Perhaps I could stay there, and not have sex with him. It would've been delightful to be held by this man while I fell asleep.

"I...I..." Nothing. I couldn't find an answer.

"You are worried about something. Can I ease your worries somehow?"

"I don't know. I would love to stay with you, but..."

"You are not comfortable. Yet. I understand. You don't know me." He nodded, convincing himself more than anything else, I believe.

"Maybe I should go." I didn't want to go. *Please convince me to stay!*

"As you wish, Bella. Let's go down."

We walked hand-in-hand all the way to my door, in silence. What was there to say? Had I just totally blown this opportunity? Would I get another one?

"I really look forward to seeing you tonight. Just us, right?"

"Right. Good night, Marco. Thank you for a wonderful evening. I had a great time."

He moved toward me, perhaps with the intention of a gentle kiss goodnight, but the energy caught me and I responded passionately. I pulled him in this time, with insistence. I wanted him to understand that my decision did not reflect my current state of desire. Or my feelings for him (God help me!).

With my back pressed against the door and our bodies grinding, my body was changing my mind. All I had to do was open the door and we would fall into my bed and there would be no more false no's, no more insecurity, no more ridiculous restraint.

But he pulled away first, this time. Had he felt my resolve fading?

"Good night, Bella. I can't wait to see you again."

Though my mouth must have been open, I couldn't say anything as he walked away.

I entered my room in a daze. Had all of this really happened?

Knock, knock. *Is he at the door?*

I got excited. No, it was the internal door. Lizzy.

"Are you up? Let me in!"

I opened the door to my baby sister, not hopping so much but grinning from ear to ear.

"I can't believe you didn't stay with him. What happened? Okay you have to tell me everything. I have to say the two of you are the hottest couple I have ever seen. More sex appeal and chemistry than Brad and Angelina. Seriously. It was so hot to watch you – he's a seriously good dancer too. So why didn't you stay? Did something weird happen?"

I knew that Lizzy would just continue talking unless I stopped her.

"Nothing happened. I just really like this guy. I mean *really* and I sort of... panicked. Maybe he's not a one-night kind of guy. Maybe I should wait and make it... important. Maybe I'm just full of shit and scared. It's been a while for me, you know."

"Of course I know! Which is why you should have totally jumped his bones!"

"Who says that? What are we, twelve?"

Lizzy slid into my bed.

"Well, make yourself comfortable."

"Oh, come on. You know you want to snuggle. The baby wants her favorite auntie to stay with her."

How could I resist?

"I want to hear about your young man. There were some serious sparks, baby girl."

My baby sister and I, and her baby, all snuggled under the covers late in the morning after a wild night in Vegas and slept. Like babies.

10

WANTING AND HAVING

The next thing I heard was a knock followed by the unmistakable voice of big sis.

"Rise and shine you lazy-bones."

I swore Nora was not human. Part alien, part sea creature, part robot. Seriously. She strode into the room as if she had just spent the last few hours in a salon. Lizzy buried herself further under the blankets, with a slight groan.

Without opening my eyes I asked, "Why do you even knock, if you're just going to come in anyway?" I couldn't hide the bitterness in my voice. What was so important that we needed to be awoken?

"Listen, we need to nail down the agenda for today. There are a lot of moving parts. I've got some important meetings this afternoon, Lizzy, you've got all the spa appointments and Nik, well, I'm not sure if the plan to do some chef schmoozing has been superseded by getting laid. You'll have to sort that one out yourself."

"Screw you," I barely had the energy to say.

"In any case, I'll be expecting to see you all at 6pm tonight, which is really not that many hours from now. And I expect you to be looking fabulous, relatively of course. These are important people to meet and I am serious about being impressive. Got it?"

"Nik can't make it," groaned the voice under the covers. I gave my thoughtful baby sis an extra squeeze for remembering my date, which I had nearly forgotten. "She's got dinner with the Latin hottie. Remember? We all agreed. Or was I the only sober one?"

Nora sighed in exasperation. "Okay, I really am interested in what's happening with you two. I all looks excessively interesting. I just want to make sure you guys know what I expect."

"Stop acting like our mother, Nora. She wasn't even like this. We're here for fun, remember?" Lizzy was getting angry.

This was going to escalate.

"Don't worry Nora. We will be there," I reassured her. "I will be there to meet and greet, then I'm off with Marco. We are here for you. We know this is a big deal. Okay?"

"Fine." She really wanted to pout and continue making her point but didn't have a basis for complaint. Sometimes it was quite helpful that she had that scientific mind. Logic ruled.

Lizzy peeked her head out to make sure everyone was okay.

"Okay, sleepyheads. Can't wait to hear about your Latin lovers. Have a great day and I'll see you later. Love you."

"Love you too Nona," we said at the same time, using our child-hood pet name for her. "Knock 'em dead Dr. Bad-ass!"

I realized going back to sleep wasn't going to be an option for me, no matter how bleary I felt.

"I want to get some sun. How about you, baby girl?"

"Sleep. Just me and this bed. Maybe some room service and massage. Mmmmmmmm..."

"Sounds lovely. I'm going to check out the pool and I'll see you back in time to get ready. Love you sweet girl." I gave her a big hug, kiss, and belly rub.

The first look in the mirror was a bit of a shocker. It was going to take some major work to get things back to a presentable state. At my age, a long night out made itself very apparent: dark circles, splotches, immovable makeup remnants. The work began.

A bit of breakfast, or lunch, would do me good. I hadn't drunk that much, thankfully, but not enough rest left me ravenous. Even after that pancake fest we'd just enjoyed a few hours before.

I was in the bathroom when I heard more knocks. Did Nora really need to check on us again? Goodness gracious! But then another round of knocks. This wasn't Nora. Housekeeping maybe? I forgot to hang the Do Not Disturb sign. I could hear Lizzy muttering under the blankets.

I opened the door just a crack, prepared to ask them to come back later, when I saw the beautifully set table.

"Room service," said the cheery older man. Confusion kept me silent for a beat. "We didn't order room service," I said, quizzically.

"Yes, ma'am. It was ordered for you. A nice gift." His smile broadened.

Nora, I believed, ensuring our rising promptly and being in decent shape for her event later. Nice, if it wasn't so damn controlling.

"From Nora," I asked, knowing the answer. He shook his head. Perhaps he didn't understand what I was saying.

"No ma'am. This is from..." he paused to pick up a sheet of paper to make sure he was getting it right. "It's from Mr. Gonzales in the penthouse. Will you accept?"

Surprise silenced me for a moment, but I moved my body away from the door enough for him to enter. I pointed to the bed and made a sound of shushing.

He nodded and smiled, then quietly set up the beautiful brunch Marco had sent for me, complete with a magnificent bouquet. I flushed at the memory of our last few moments together. It could so easily have ended with us together, fully together, and didn't. Still he sent me this amazing gift. What I had missed? What was the trick? How was it that this situation kept proving itself too good to be true?

Everything was scrumptious, clearly hand selected. He'd really thought of my tastes. Part of me wanted to run upstairs and thank him. With my body. Then I remembered I couldn't even get up there anyway, as it required a special key.

Okay, don't get ahead of yourself. The day was young, and I needed something in my system. I finished eating, while Lizzy slept, convincing myself a bit of distraction from this man would do me good. I worried about how obsessive I was feeling and decided to be content in this quiet moment. Or pretend to be content.

Vegas-ready swimsuit on, I made my way down to the pool, which in true Vegas style, looked more like an outdoor nightclub than swimming spot. The music was pumping, the drinks were flowing and all the beautiful Vegas-ites were continuing the party. By sheer luck, I happened to see a group leaving and scored one of their lounge chairs. Perfect. Absolutely perfect.

It didn't take long before I started to feel conspicuously alone. I fiddled with my phone, hoping it would be a good distraction. *Maybe I should send him a quick thank-you note. For brunch.* That would have been the polite thing to do, certainly, ulterior motives aside.

I looked up his number and saw, for the first time, the note he had written me the first day we met - yesterday:

Looking forward to our trip to Argentina.

Wow, this guy really had a hold on me. The energy in my body spiked as I thought about him. The memory of his hands on my face, and his lips finding mine, kept replaying itself in my head. It was making everything just a little bit warmer than even this hot desert day.

I typed: *Brunch was a wonderful surprise. Much like you have been.* (Wow. A bit provocative, if I did say so myself.) *Deepest thanks for your thoughtfulness. When Lizzy wakes up I'm sure she will also thank you.* Smiley face. Send.

My body began shaking. Actually shaking. What did I expect, that my text would magically summon him and he would appear before me, ready to pick up where we'd left off?

Alright, I said thank you. I reached out. Did my part. Now I would just sit back and enjoy this beautiful day. I was about to take a magazine from my bag when my phone buzzed.

Oh boy. It was probably him. Nervous as anything I turned the phone over to see what he said. I appreciated his prompt response in any case.

Where are you?

Funny. Direct. Okay, I'd play along.

At the pool. Watching the beautiful people do their thing.
You must mean BEING the beautiful people. Excellent.

Not quite sure how to respond to that. Thank you? Maybe some modest phrase? I stared at the message as if it was in another language. Was I supposed to ask him his whereabouts in return? Wasn't that a bit too intrusive? But he did it, so maybe that was okay. I sat there pondering the rules of communication and appropriate behavior for minutes. I began responses then erased them, finding them too provocative or serious or ridiculous. It amazed me how much time I could spend analyzing just a few words...

"Excuse me, ma'am? Here is your champagne." A Vegas-style, scantily clad server appeared before me. She was a knockout. Wow.

"No, I'm sorry I didn't order this." She held two glasses anyway and I was clearly by myself.

"Hmmmm..." she wondered. "Um, Ms. Malone, right?"

Now she had my attention.

"How did you know my name?"

"That gentleman, by the bar, sent them over for you." And there, of course, was Marco, grinning from ear to ear. He enjoyed these surprises too much - finding me across a crowded casino, sending me brunch and now my favorite beverage. A girl could get used to this.

His linen shirt fell open as he walked toward me, and I saw just enough to keep me from actually breathing. I'd seen him in a suit, jeans, and now swimwear, and he just kept getting better looking.

"You are everywhere, my friend," I laughed and shook my head at him.

"If only that were true." Were we both thinking about our separate sleeping arrangements last night?

He bent down to kiss me, and I expected to offer my cheeks but he caught my mouth. We were both surprised, but lingered there. Everything from last night came bubbling to the surface again. Daylight and a change of scenery hadn't dimmed this fire.

"How are you today?" he asked.

"Doing pretty well, considering..."

"I would say you are doing quite well, just from external evidence. May I join you?"

"Of course, but I consider both of those glasses for me, so you'll have to get your own."

"As you wish," he said, with that smile that made me want to rip my clothes off.

"I'm going to start to think you've secretly embedded a locator chip in my arm, or something. Your ability to find me in the most unlikely places is quite impressive."

"We are like magnets, Bella. Can't you feel it? It is inevitable that I find you."

All I could do was take a slow sip from my glass, and avoid his gaze. This was too much.

He helped me with a change of topic. "Are you swimming, or just laying here being gorgeous?"

"Actually, I was planning on reading a bit. Maybe having a bit of a catnap. It is Vegas after all. All about pleasure."

This made him laugh. "Yes, pleasure. What a thing to pursue."

"I'm not sure what to say to that Marco. Are we making a point?" Defensiveness about last night's events, or non-events, seeped into my tone.

"No point, Bella." He returned my look with a huge grin, not saying anything more. I was sure he was thinking what a nut-job I must be.

"I'm not sure if you're attached to this particular spot, but we have a private cabana just behind the bar, if you are interested."

"I would love to," I said graciously.

He picked up the glasses, offered me his arm, then wrapped the other one around my waist and held me for a moment before moving. When he kissed me again, ever so lightly, a shiver ran down my spine that nearly set me down on my ass. But there he was, holding me up in his strong arms.

11

FAMILY HISTORY

He led me to a much more private area, with its own pool. A wonderful piece of sun and shade and civil behavior. A few of the guys from last night spread out on their own loungers.

We sat on the largest one, the size of a bed, and made ourselves comfortable. It was downright sexy.

"Are you swimming, Marco?"

"Yes, I did already. The water is very nice."

"So, you were already here when I texted you?"

"Right here, thinking about you."

"But you don't look wet." Okay that sounded very strange. Couldn't take it back now.

As he took his shirt off, I couldn't believe it was even better than the initial view I had gotten. He was sculpted and bronzed and flaw-less. I desperately wanted something to be wrong with this man. Otherwise, I had no chance.

He rubbed his hands along his arms and chest, and I immediately flashed to something pornographic.

"I suppose you're right. I have dried off. Which means it's time for another dip."

He pulled me up again, right after I chugged down the rest of my glass of champagne. I was about to be in front of this god of a man in my swimsuit. Heaven help me.

I peeled my dress off slowly, trying to be as seductive as possible, while feeling as awkward as I could imagine. A schoolgirl trying to be a seductress. The story of my life.

As soon as my dress was off, I pulled him toward the pool, trying to conceal myself underwater as quickly as possible. He was right. It was wonderfully refreshing. And quiet enough that it felt tranquil.

I began to float on my back and his hands moved underneath me, holding me up and gliding me across the water. It was delightful to feel him touching me, without the hot urgency of desire. It was still there, certainly, but muted by the cool lapping of water on my flesh.

Occasionally he bent me around his body, holding me close to him, like a baby. I stroked his body gently, enjoying the opportunity to experience him this way. I was tall enough rarely to feel small with a man, but in his arms I was completely contained.

"I am very grateful for this pool right now," he said after we'd been floating around for a few minutes.

I gave him a quizzical look.

"I get to enjoy you, with my eyes and my hands, while we're both wearing very little."

He was grinning but all I wanted was to sink to the bottom of the pool. He noticed.

"You are so… what is the word? Inscrutable. Sometimes you are so confident and commanding, and sometimes I feel you are like a little girl - shy and nervous."

"I'm not sure inscrutable is the right word." There I went again with my pathological need to correct. What could I say to vault over that gaff? "Isn't that like all women?"

"No, Bella. You are not like any woman I have ever known. I am so intrigued by you."

He paused and I watched him form a thought.

"You are very charming. And mysterious. And of course, strikingly beautiful. It makes me want to study you, like a piece of art."

"I'm not sure I want to be studied like that. Seems very impersonal."

"Maybe like a meal, then. Which I would consume. With pleasure."

It took everything I had to maintain my composure, which I wasn't sure I did successfully.

"You are very smooth, Marco. You say these things... they are unbelievable."

"Aaah, do you not believe me?"

He brushed his lips against my shoulder. I shivered in the warm water.

The smallest move of his hand, and my top would be off. I could have slid my hands down his shorts, and he could have taken me, right there, in view of all of Las Vegas. I wanted to scream: Take me! Love me! Right now! I believe you with all my heart!

I couldn't look at him. "I don't know what to believe."

"So it is my job to make you believe."

I desperately wanted to move to a neutral topic. "Tell me something about your life, Marco."

He smiled with a look that told me he knew I was uncomfortable with the intensity of the conversation. He abided.

"What would you like to know, Bella?"

"Anything you want to tell me."

"We'll start at the beginning. I was born in Buenos Aires, the oldest of three children. My father is Argentinian and my mother was Italian. They met when they were young, both students."

"How did they meet?"

"My father had gone to Italy to study architecture. Actually, I think he was studying women, but that's another story. My mother was working in a gallery, studying painting, when they met. He says he went in to ask for directions, and he left with the love of his life. It's all very romantic, you know."

His eyes sparkled with mischief and I just wanted to keep looking at him.

"The story is that he whisked her away to Argentina, despite her parents' refusal. My grandparents always denied all of that. They claim that they gave their blessing."

"Were they happy?"

"Yes, they were very happy. My father got more and more successful and my mother got to live a life as an artist and a mother, which is what she always wanted."

"I mean together. Were they happy together?"

"Yes. But it was a different time. Every man in Argentina had mistresses. And he was no exception."

"How did you feel about that?"

He was clearly uncomfortable. Maybe I was asking him to reveal too much.

"I know it's not right. But I don't think we can judge other people's relationships. They were better together than most couples I've seen in my life."

I wanted to stop myself, but I couldn't. "How do you feel about fidelity?"

"I think it's hard. And not necessarily natural. It's tempting to get what you want whenever you want it. But I think that is the price you pay for... love. That sometimes you sacrifice what you want in order to get what you need."

I was stunned by that answer, unsure whether I agreed or not.

"How do *you* feel about fidelity?" he asked me.

I wanted to get this right. "It's hard enough for me to share myself with one person. More than one at a time is out of the question."

He laughed and I realized what I said was funny. It was not intended that way. I slid myself out of his arms and submerged myself in the water. I needed a break.

He was floating when I rose out from underwater. I just wanted to watch him, stretched out in all his glory, but he stood up as soon as he saw me.

"Would you like to go sit down for a while?" he asked.

"Yes, that sounds like a great idea."

He held my hand the short walk over to the lounge area. I loved how physically attentive he was to me. I tried to think about the quality that most impressed me and it lay in the mixture of tenderness and courage. He'd been fearless in showing me his interest, without being aggressive. Whatever he was doing, it was working.

I lay down first on the lounger, leaving him plenty of room to spread out, but he brought his body right up to mine. The view of the cloudless sky was wonderful, but I turned on my side to get a better view of the man next to me.

"Tell me about your siblings," I asked.

"My sister lives near my father, still, outside of Buenos Aires. She is the baby, but I feel like she has been taking care of us her whole life. She is a natural mother – which is good, as she has five kids. We are very close.

My brother lives in Milan, near where my mother lived. He is a designer. For fashion. Quite good actually. But a bit like a child. Always so competitive, with me and the world. Never got married or settled down. Just enjoying himself with all the models."

"Sounds like that trait runs in your family." I realized how rude that must have sounded and I regretted it immediately.

He didn't respond.

"I'm sorry for saying that. I guess I'm a bit sensitive about men cheating. I didn't mean to offend you."

"Did your husband cheat on you?"

"Yes. Many men have. My history is fairly… sordid."

"I'm sorry to hear that. It surprises me. You are so amazing, Monique. What could these men have wanted that you did not give them?"

"Aaaaah… that would be quite a long list, I believe. I've made many mistakes, Marco. And behaved quite badly on many occasions. I tend to withdraw, or shut down, if I feel threatened. This is not conducive to a loving, trusting relationship, apparently."

It was unclear where this level of honesty was coming from. It was not my typical way.

"Do you feel uncomfortable talking about this?"

"Yes, a little bit. Maybe a lot."

He put his hand on my cheek and held it there for a moment before bringing his face to mine. Feeling his warm mouth gave me the goosebumps.

"You seem so open to me, Monique. I can't imagine you being withdrawn. Maybe you chose the wrong men."

"Perhaps. But I was the common denominator. Somehow I got in my head that men are not to be trusted. Which is strange because the two most important men in my life – my father and brother – were the most trustworthy people I've ever known."

"Were your parents happy?"

"They had a fairy tale romance. I've never seen anything like it. They met on the beach in the islands and fell in love at first sight. They even died together."

"I'm so sorry, Bella. How terrible for the rest of you."

"Yes, I can't say I'm fully recovered from that. My brother died shortly before them, so I feel this huge gaping hole where my family used to be. At least I have my sisters. They are my lifesavers."

He didn't stop looking at me, but I had to avert my eyes. Tears began to build at the bottom of my throat.

Something a bit less sharp was needed to cut the emotion.

"Even Jeff, my evil ex-husband, was supportive about my family." I was only mostly kidding.

"I guess you don't have the best relationship."

"Actually, we do now. But it was very bad. For very long."

"How long have you been divorced?"

"About three years now, but we had started living separate lives years before that. It was very messy and slightly complicated."

"Will you tell me about it?"

"Are you sure you're ready?"

"I'm absolutely ready, Monique."

That statement sent chills down my spine.

"But first," he continued, "can you lay right here, on my arm?"

Marco stretched his right arm toward me, and tapped the area of his chest just below his shoulder. I was happy to slide my head into that most wonderful resting spot.

"Are you sure you won't get too hot?"

"Monique, Bella, it's hot whenever you're around. That's how that works."

I flushed, knowing how hot I felt with him. I took a deep breath of his scent and my body tingled.

"We were kind of a strange couple, well suited in so many ways, but never this grand love affair. It just made logical sense for us to be together. I was hypnotized by how powerful and sure of himself he was and I think he saw me as a unique possession to go with his other possessions. He had plotted out our whole lives, he liked things to be well thought out and predictable. But I wanted an adventure.

We did okay. For a while. We were both so absorbed in our careers and happy enough, and then when Lola was born, the whole precarious house of cards came tumbling down."

He listened intently. Part of me wished he wouldn't. I wasn't particularly proud of this period of my life.

"Jeff started resenting my career and insisted that I quit and stay at home. It was really hard for me to do that. I just became more and more indignant until it didn't work anymore to even be in the same room. It was ugly for a long time but eventually we found our way back to being good co-parents and even friends. He's happily involved now, about to start a brand new family and it's all very exciting for him."

"Did he cheat on you?"

"Jeff is not one to be neglected very long and when the trouble started he began a relationship with a nurse at his hospital. What a cliché, right? The reality is that they're a perfect couple. She's very young, and completely interested in subsuming her life for his needs. I have to admit she's a lovely girl and much better suited to him than I ever was. She's great with the girls and I'm happy with their relationship."

I paused to collect myself. "What about your marriage, Marco? What happened?"

"Like you, we did okay too. We were very convivial. Like brother and sister. My father began doing business with her father when we were kids and the families became friends. We grew up together, and I was so obsessed with following in my father's footsteps that I just made the decision I would marry this Italian girl, just as my father had. I didn't think it through, obviously, and well… we know how it ended.

The irony is that we would have probably had a lifelong friendship, if it hadn't been ruined by forcing it to be romantic."

"What exactly ended the marriage?"

I hoped I wasn't being too intrusive, but the curiosity was killing me.

"My career started taking off right after the boys were born so I left the firm I was working for and decided to start my own. I built this very successful company from nothing but the price was time away from my family. It was really painful for me and Anna was very unhappy to be alone most of the time with our two boys while I was traveling the world.

She thought it was very glamorous but the reality is that it was brutally hard work. Because all the intimacy was gone, she was convinced I was having an affair, or many affairs, I don't know. She couldn't get it out of her mind. I couldn't handle how she questioned everything I did. Every interaction we had felt like an interrogation. I couldn't do anything right, in her eyes."

"Were you?"

"Was I?" He didn't understand.

"Were you having an affair?"

"No, Monique. No, I wasn't and it wasn't because I didn't have the opportunity or even the desire. It was because I didn't want to be that person. It would have been the easiest thing in the world for me to have someone in my bed, every night if I wanted. But I didn't. I wouldn't. Anyway, she wouldn't believe me and she… she… had an affair. She says it was to spite me. I don't know. It involved someone very close to me and that was the end. I couldn't…"

I couldn't believe what I had just heard.

"Did she stay with this guy?"

"Oh, no. He wasn't interested in that. He just wanted to have her and spite me."

"Wow. This doesn't sound like a very good friend, Marco."

"No, it wasn't a friend. It was actually my brother."

My face froze in shock and disbelief.

"Holy shit, Marco! That is... too much to believe. Do you still speak?"

"Of course. We are family. And frankly, that's who he is, Monique. He... I don't want to defend him but now I know better. That's all."

Nothing I could have said would have been worthy or appropriate, so I stayed silent.

He startled me with the first words after our quiet moment.

"That feels good."

I'd been gently stroking his chest and stomach.

"Your skin, Marco. It's the color of the most perfectly buttery caramel."

"I wish I was nearly as delicious as you make me sound."

I bet you are.

"You take very good care of your body. It's very impressive. You must spend hours at the gym."

"Not really hours, but I do go. I like the feeling of finding my limits. And pushing them. What I really love is soccer. I try to play a few times a week with a league I'm in. They're all much younger than I am so I get quite a good workout."

He paused as if looking for the right words.

"Do you like my body?"

I dropped my jaw, awed at his courage to say what I would have found impossible.

"Marco, your body is... flawless. You are a very handsome man."

He tilted my face up to look in my eyes. I realized for the first time, in the bright sunlight, that our eyes were the same color. An unusual hazel hue that I rarely saw. Mine was from one brown-eyed and one blue-eyed parent. Maybe his were too.

"I'm very happy you think that, Bella. You know I think you are remarkable – physically and otherwise."

"Thank you." Keeping it simple forced me to swallow all the denials I would have expressed.

I slid my face back down and kissed his chest several times before settling back into a contented quiet.

The tone of our relationship shifted, becoming much softer and more intimate. We connected like adults who'd acknowledged their attraction for each other. He held me, either on the lounger or in the water, where I let myself sink into his supportive arms and set all my insecurities free. I hadn't been with a man like this in so long, but Marco was making it feel easier than any man in my life ever had. The idea that this was too good to be true never strayed more than a moment away from my thoughts, however.

The afternoon passed too quickly, and soon it was time for me to get ready for Nora's meeting. We'd been laying on the lounger, in and out of luxurious naps. It was excruciating to pull myself out of his arms.

"I have to go now, Marco. Nora has a reception tonight, and I promised I would make an appearance."

He held me against him. "I understand, Bella, although I would happily spend the rest of the day here with you."

I forced myself to separate our bodies. "It was so nice to spend the day with you, like this, so relaxed."

"And it's only a few hours until we see each other again, right?"

Was he questioning whether I still wanted to see him later? His modesty kept surprising me.

"Of course. I'm really looking forward to it."

"Me too."

I noticed him gathering his belongings. "You don't have to leave on my account. Stay, and enjoy the rest of the afternoon."

"I will walk you to your room, if you don't mind."

The chivalry was really working for me. We strolled back inside, never losing touch with each other. He paused uncomfortably when we got to my door. He couldn't possibly be nervous about kissing me goodbye, could he?

"I want to ask you something."

"You are a man of many questions, Marco."

His laugh lightened the tension. "I want to invite you to the wedding. As my guest. Actually your sisters too. What do you think?"

I must have had the most dumbfounded expression on my face, as if I had suddenly gone deaf and mute, which caused him to repeat the whole thing.

Still, I had to ask, "You want me to be your date for the wedding? Don't you already have a date?" What a stupid question.

"Well, I was going to go with my sister, but she had to cancel at the last minute, because two of the kids are sick. Does that mean you will come?"

"I'm just so surprised, Marco. Can you really do that?"

"Of course I can. Besides, this is Vegas. Half the casino floor will probably be crashing anyway."

I paused, lost for words. "I would love to go, but I have to check with the girls, of course. And Nora's award ceremony on Sunday..."

"The wedding does not start until that night, after Nora's event."

"You've thought of everything, haven't you?"

"I doubt it. But I want you to come with me. If you want to."

"I don't see why not. I'll let you know for sure tonight, after I talk to the girls. And none of us have anything to wear!" The extent of my idiocy couldn't be overstated.

"You're kidding, right? I would be very happy if you wore those shorts from last night. Although I might not be such a gentleman next time around."

I caught my breath, and he noticed. If this man knew how much I wanted him, he would run screaming from this hotel.

"Thank you, Marco. For the invitation. It really is too kind. Like everything you've done..."

"Maybe I am pursuing pleasure as well," he said, provocatively.

"I'll see you in a few hours," I said as I opened the door to my room. I turned around and kissed him lightly on the lips.

———

Nora's event passed in a daze. I tried to be present, but I kept thinking about my afternoon with Marco. What would our dinner date bring? And was it too much time together? Would he grow tired of me?

Since I was going to be coming directly from Nora's dinner I told Marco I'd meet him at dinner. He was not happy about that, finding it lacking in courtesy. He wanted to pick me up from my room but I insisted. It would save us time.

When the time came, I wished I'd had time to go up to the room and freshen up. This was going to be an important night, I hoped.

As I approached, I saw him standing at the entrance to the restaurant, wearing the most beautiful suit I had ever seen. He could have easily been a superstar. Almost too handsome to be real.

He beamed at me as I got closer. I supposed he approved of my choice for that night, a burgundy silk crepe with a bit of flounce and a requisite display of leg. I wore my lucky shoes. I felt good.

"It has only been a few hours, Bella, but it feels like a new day to see you again. And again more beautiful than the last time. I believe you must be magical."

"Thank you." I moved toward him and offered two lingering kisses, one on each cheek. You look wonderful," I added as I gently stroke the lapels of his suit. All I could think about was taking it off him. Yes, tonight was going to be our night.

12

DINNER DATE

The restaurant was breathtaking. Sleek and modern, in just my aesthetic, while still being utterly romantic. This was an inspired choice and was nearly impossible to get a reservation, I had heard. Emile had mentioned this place, and apparently told the chef that I might be coming. He'd set up an introduction, if I chose to pursue it. I wasn't sure tonight was the right time to engage with the chef and do some networking. My other needs were currently taking precedence over my career.

Dinner was nearly flawless. I laughed so hard that I literally cried. The conversation stopped only when a moment of silence is what we wanted. We talked about family and pleasure and beauty. He talked about his kids - they sounded like amazing men - and I offered funny stories about my girls.

I even told him about the reality of my career. How I was at a crossroads and had been dishonest about what I said on the plane. "I used to be a chef," I told him apologetically. "Now, I'm back to being an apprentice."

"No my dear, I don't believe you. You are a chef. It is clear in every cell of your body. Maybe that is not what you are doing now, but it is always who you are being."

He took my breath away. I wanted to say, let's get out of this fabulous restaurant and go up to your fabulous room. There I want you to take me completely and listen when I tell you that I love you. You are too good to be true and yet here you are. With me.

Nothing came out of my mouth. What could I say?

"Did you talk to your sisters about the wedding?" A welcome change of subject.

"Yes, and it works out perfectly."

"Yes, Nora's ceremony ends at five and the wedding starts at six. You will all come. I think Lizzy already accepted Esteban's invitation."

"Yes, my baby sister is smitten."

"They both are."

This was wonderful. I was dying to go the wedding, wondering what Marco would be like in a sea of eligible single women, as can be found at most weddings. This was good. Really good.

"Marco, this is so generous of you, to invite us all. Are you sure it's ok… all these extra guests at the last minute? I know what it's like to plan a wedding."

"Remember, it's Las Vegas, Bella. They expect to invite most of the hotel."

"Thank you. Now I have a purpose for the inevitable shopping trip tomorrow."

"I suppose that means no silver shorts?"

"Correct. They've had their one airing, and will now be permanently retired."

"Maybe I can negotiate a private viewing?"

Now it was my turn to change the subject. "Will you be stuck in the rehearsals all day?"

"Part of the day, yes. But I will still have plenty of time for you, don't worry." A wink and that smile again. "Then we have the rehearsal dinner but I don't think it will go very late. Is that okay?"

"Of course it's okay. You are free to do as you wish, as far as I know. And I do realize that your sole purpose for being in Las Vegas is not actually my entertainment. I'm fine with it. Really." I hoped he got my humor.

"Thank you for being so considerate and understanding." His sly smile indicated he was in on the joke. "I promise to make it up to you. In whatever way you wish."

This was getting juicy. "Well there's nothing to make up, but I appreciate the offer, which I might accept anyway." Hot. Very hot. All the innuendo tickled the middle of my body again.

Dinner was coming to an end and I needed to decide. Would I reach out to the chef while I had the opportunity, or would I bypass it to stay present to the man in front of me? I was torn. And then the door opened.

Marco called our server over and started to transmit a message to the chef about his enjoyment of his dish. How tender the lamb was, and the perfection of the accompaniments. His eloquence and grace made an impression on the waiter and me.

I hadn't told Marco about my connection, but when the server was about to walk away with the message, I stopped him. "Actually..." I said, "would you mind telling the chef that Monique Malone is here? Oh, and that I really enjoyed my meal as well. It was spectacular."

"Does Chef Turot know you?" the server asked with raised eyebrows.

"Yes, he is expecting me," I responded.

"Yes, yes I will tell him right away."

I turned to find Marco staring at me.

"You are remarkable."

"Why?"

"You know the chef and you didn't say anything. What else are you hiding from me? You are really some celebrity chef, and probably have your own restaurants around the world. And a reality show, right?"

"Very funny. Marco, I'm sure you are much more famous than I will ever be. It's just that my old friend Emile, who is nearly a celebrity, wanted me to meet some people while I was here. To further my reentry back into the wild world of food. He is the well-connected one, not me."

Marco shook his head at me, thinking I was being falsely modest. But I wasn't. I really was a nobody.

Out came the chef, out to prove me wrong. A jovial round man, who might have been Santa Claus in a previous life, came barreling toward us all arms and smiles.

"Monique, Monique, I am so glad you came! What a wonderful surprise! How is Emile? That rascal still causing trouble everywhere he goes? Oh my goodness, this is so wonderful!"

I had just assumed he was French, like Emile, but the accent was definitely Spanish. He picked me up out of my chair and gave me a great big bear hug. For a moment I thought he might not let go. What a warm wonderful man, so different than the typically manic and antisocial chef.

"Emile tells me you are thinking of going back into the fire. Brave choice! I don't know that I would do it," he laughed and patted his significant belly. Definitely Santa Claus. "Anything I can do to help, I'm happy to. But I will miss your articles in the magazine. You are such a good writer. If you wrote a book, I would read it. Maybe you can still write on the side, even though I know already that is ridiculous. To be a chef takes a whole life!"

"Thank you so much, Chef. Your restaurant is beyond description. And everything was perfect. My friend Marco also sent you a message about his dish."

Marco stood up and greeted the chef in Spanish. They kissed on both cheeks, in that way I found so sexy. I was quickly left behind in the trails of Spanish. They spoke as if they were long lost friends, so happy to meet another Latin comrade. I could decipher only a few words of each sentence. Perhaps they were talking about the towns they came from. Or not. My Spanish was abysmal.

They both turned to look at me and continued speaking. Uh oh, I didn't like this, but I did hear something about beautiful woman, talented chef. They were having a Monique adoration society meeting. This was getting embarrassing. Marco took my hand and kissed it. What the heck was going on now?

Another flurry of words, followed by laughing and hugging. I really better get my Rosetta Stone Spanish lessons out of the closet again. Or maybe I will have my own private tutor? Hopeful again…

Marco took my hand, and said, "Yes, I know I am a very lucky man."

"My dear, I am so glad you were able to come in. We might not have time tonight but I would love to talk to you anytime. I really mean it. The way Emile speaks of you, I know you have something special. You need to be in a major kitchen feeding the people!"

I was stunned. I didn't want to overreact in front of either of these men, but I was all shrieks and celebrations on the inside. I felt like some switch had been turned on in my life, and all of a sudden amazing men and world-class chefs found me fabulous. It was almost too much for me to take in.

I promised to re-connect with the chef and felt incredibly grateful to Emile. It was a pleasant surprise to hear how well Emile thought of me. And I knew it wasn't because I was a great lover.

"Tell me about Emile. He is a friend of yours?"

I had to be strategic about answering. Our history was complicated.

"Emile and I met my first day in culinary school. Our new class was being shown around as he entered one of the rooms, and the head of the school stopped mid-sentence to hug and kiss him. They were both quintessentially French.

Apparently, he had funded part of the newest wing, and was a regular fixture in the school. He noticed me right away, claiming I was one of the few attractive women in culinary school."

I averted my eyes, realizing the conceit in my statement.

"I have no idea about how the women look in culinary school, but you, Monique, stand out in any group."

I gave him a slightly embarrassed smile and continued.

"Emile sat with our small group at mealtimes, and we fell into an easy friendship. He became my mentor, my confidante and my greatest cheerleader. I never really understood what he saw in me in those early days, but he claimed he had a nose for genius and he could smell it on me. As I finished school, and embarked on my career, our relationship changed and we became more like peers. He asked my advice on chefs, restaurants and investments. Even personal stuff. We hung out like old friends or family. People often thought we were related. Emile is one of the most important people to me, and I'm so grateful for his presence in my life."

I left out an important part and it sat uncomfortably on the tip of my tongue.

"Was he ever more than a friend?"

The question I'd been dreading. *Be honest, or keep it clean?*

"When Jeff and I split up, and he began his very public affair, Emile and I... well... we started sleeping together. He provided a sexual outlet for me when I needed one."

I really didn't want to continue. This was too much.

"How long were you together?"

"Not very long. It was fun, at first. Our friendship made it easy to be lovers. His bright star in the food world gave us access to all the best restaurants and a social calendar to fill all my nights. Both of us knew, but never said, that this was a fleeting moment, but we took full advantage.

Then I saw him with a young waitress at a trendy cafe. I knew better than to think I was the only one for him, but the idea of my sharing myself so freely with him and him sharing himself so freely with whomever just grossed me out. He was sad when I told him we were back to being friends but he understood. That, and I'm sure he had better, and younger, fish to fry."

"There weren't any hard feelings?"

"I was sore, I guess. But I knew what I was getting into with him. It wasn't like Jeff's betrayal."

I needed to swallow, but didn't want to look like I was getting emotional. Even though I was. Marco's next question got my immediate attention.

"Are you seeing anyone right now?" He wrapped his fingers around my hand and squeezed.

"No. Not at all. As single as a girl can get."

Of course I wanted to ask the same question, but I was scared. I did it anyway.

"How about you? Anyone in your life?"

"No. I... haven't... I'm not seeing anyone."

Underneath the implacable look I tried to keep on my face, I grinned from ear to ear.

Marco led me out of the restaurant, and I held my tongue from asking where we were going. We got in a taxi. Were we going back to his room? Did he have another event planned?

I felt unexplainably secure, even in my complete ignorance. I trusted him and this was a very unusual feeling. Some other activity to continue our night would have been nice, but I didn't need or expect it. We were pretty good at entertaining each other even with nothing else.

We'd spent nearly the whole day together. I shouldn't have been worried he'd grown tired of me, at least not in the short term. He liked me, and I could clearly feel his attraction.

Marco directed the driver to another hotel. We weren't going back to the Wynn, which meant it wasn't straight back to his room. Part of me felt silly for being disappointed, but only just slightly.

I turned toward him to say something, I wasn't quite sure what, but found my lips on his. It was our first kiss that night and it felt wonderful. We were getting used to each other and finding our rhythm. Marco's attentiveness reached every interaction we had, and I felt him trying to understand what I wanted. He lingered in the right places and grew stronger and more insistent as my breath quickened.

We arrived at our destination, leaving me embarrassed and annoyed. I just wanted to keep kissing him. And more.

I sat in the cab as Marco walked around and opened my door. I felt like a woman around him – not a mother, not a middle child, not a struggling chef. It wasn't an issue of shying away from my power, but of embracing the delight in being treated a certain way. He kissed my hand and arm and neck as we strode across the casino, never once losing contact with me. Everything around me faded into the background. All I knew was the two of us.

The sound of a beautiful voice caught my attention. Exquisitely beautiful. No cheesy lounge singer. Something exemplary. Marco turned to me as we stood at the entrance of a small club and said, "I know you must have been curious about where we were going, and what we were doing. I really appreciate that you trusted me. It means a lot to me."

"I heard what you said about your wife's interrogations. I know that really hurt you. I didn't want to do the same thing."

I smiled, relieved that I'd followed my instinct and kept my mouth shut. It was a very lucky break on my part, given my tendency to want to know all details at every moment. Not knowing and just trusting was feeling remarkably good.

"Besides, I trust you." I hadn't meant for that to come out. I didn't trust anybody, betrayal oftentimes the air that I breathed. What was happening to me?

Marco appeared touched but he said nothing. Instead, we followed the sound of that magical voice. I thought of my mother, who'd spent her youth singing and performing. Maybe she would have been in a place like this, if it had existed. I missed her so deeply.

"Where are you, my dreamer?"

"Sorry," I said sheepishly.

"No need to be sorry. Let me join you."

We sat down and I told him about my mother. I hardly believed how honestly I spoke to him, even about things that were very personal. My typical way was to conceal and withhold. None of that was possible with him. It crossed my mind that maybe I no longer needed all the protection that secrecy afforded me.

He reached his arm around me and gave me a big squeeze. "I can't imagine how magnificent she must have been. Would you like to tell me more about her?"

"Our mother was the most beautiful woman I have ever seen, with this other-worldly quality. She and Dad were so happy, for so many years, and they ended up leaving this world together, which was pure romance for them, but pure tragedy for us. Mom was so full of love but there was something about her that you could tell held some sadness. As if she was missing something or someone.

We would often catch her daydreaming - probably where I got my own habit - but she would never talk about it. Instead she would make up these fantastical stories about other worlds and creatures. And she would sing. My gosh, our mother could mesmerize any human being with her voice. Her famed career all happened before we were born, but none of us questioned that it had been remarkable.

When it came time to raise her kids, she dropped everything and devoted herself completely to us. Danny's death nearly killed her. She could not believe her little boy was gone, even though he was a grown man and had lived a beautiful life. Then she and Dad disappeared in that boating accident, which nearly killed the rest of us."

Marco exhaled deeply. He clearly didn't know what to say.

"Enough for now. I just want to enjoy being here. With you." I leaned over and kissed him. My body moved toward him of its own will. This taking it (relatively) slow was fine most of the time, but occasionally I felt crazed with desire. Like a fire that needed to be tended immediately.

All of me. Why not take all of me.

I began to sing the melody, one of my very favorites, while Marco watched me with great amusement. I didn't have the musical talent of my mother and sisters, but I could hold a tune. And it wasn't an area around which I have a lot of self-consciousness so I sang freely. He smiled at me, that mesmerizing smile, and I enjoyed his pleasure.

"You didn't tell me you could sing."

"That's because I can't. I am the only non-singer in my family."

"You call that not singing? Hmmmm. I am just noticing that the more I know you, the more talents I discover. Where does it end?"

"Oh, probably in about one minute. You've seen everything. It's all downhill from here."

"Isn't downhill a good thing?"

"I guess. I always forget which is the good one, uphill or down-hill. It never really made sense to me."

We shared a laugh and I snuggled into his shoulder for the next few songs. He ordered an extravagant bottle of champagne, which I drank with great enjoyment. There was nothing in my life, at that moment, that wasn't absolutely perfect.

Fatigue began to overtake me, but I didn't want that to end the evening. I was feeling the effects of our previous night out.

Marco let the first few yawns pass, then took my hand. "Let's go."

Before I knew it we were in the elevator at the Wynn, headed up to the penthouse. The decision was made with a silent look - he asked me with his eyes which button to press and I nodded yes to his choice. Sleepy or not, I was going to be with this man tonight. We were quickly running out of time in Vegas.

I walked straight toward the window for that amazing view. Still mesmerizing. He stepped lightly behind me, brushed my hair to the side and kissed the back of my neck. This was my favorite move of all time. I let him linger there for some time, giving soft sounds of positive feedback to let him know he should continue.

"Bella, what do you want?" he whispered.

Without turning around I answered, "I want you to ask me again." I was being subtle, obtuse even. Would he understand what I was saying?

He spun me around to face him and looked straight into my eyes. I could only imagine what he saw with his penetrating gaze. My sly smile revealed my question, and his eyes demonstrated under-standing.

"Will you stay with me tonight?"

He got it. He really got it. I realized how much I expected him to fail the test, to not understand my subtle reference.

"Yes," I said with my eyes and my lips. Then I leaned toward him and offered him my mouth, which he took willingly.

He led me to the bedroom, which was as magnificent as the rest of the suite. They were serious about making people feel like royalty up here. I stopped him before he got to the bed and kissed his face, then down his neck. I stroked his shoulders and arms as I peeled off his jacket. I moved slowly, partly out of building anticipation and partly out of my own nervousness. I wasn't going to blow this one.

I lingered on each button of his shirt, taking my time to reveal his phenomenal body, adorned by a small patch of hair that began in the middle of his chest and ended at the top of his pants. Dark black hair, interspersed with gray and silver, was perfectly set off by his tan skin. When his shirt fell to the ground, I let go of my own need to be composed.

He tried to pull me in close and I edged him backwards, toward the bed. "Sit down," I told him.

Ordering him around was giving me a warm rush of excitement. I knelt down in front of him, moving in slow motion, and I looked up to see him catch his breath. I knew this looked sexy, and he must have been wondering what I was going to do down there. Had I mentioned this was fun?

I ran my hands down his legs, filling him with anticipation, then picked up his right foot and took off his shoe. He watched me like a hawk, perhaps not believing his eyes. Off with the other shoe and for the briefest moment, I thought about having him in my mouth. No, that was going to have to wait for another time.

I stood up halfway, kissed him intensely, then knelt astride him, one leg on either side. He couldn't hold himself back any more and pulled me in. My legs opened around him, which lifted my dress above my hips, revealing the entirety of my lower half.

He slipped his hands around my hips and pulled my buttocks in to him. His erection pressed against me, pulsing, while he rubbed our bodies together.

"Why are you still fully dressed?" he asked.

All I had on was my dress and my underwear - a very skimpy, very sexy silk thong. Not even a bra with my form-fitting dress.

His hands were deliciously warm on my bottom and up my back. Those amazing hands took my dress, now covering only half of my body, and peeled it off the rest of me. A moment of self-conscious terror filled me. Okay, this was it. This was the moment he decided I was horrifying and left in disgust. The body I worked pretty hard to maintain was still that of a 40-something mom. Not perfect, to say the least. Everything my swimsuit cleverly concealed was now on full display.

As if he read my mind, he said, "You are the sexiest woman I have ever seen. I want every part of you."

I reached for his belt buckle and fumbled. Buttons and ties were okay, but buckles left me clumsy and un-coordinated. Instead of taking over, he left me to sort it out.

I moved off of him to take his pants off and there we were left with just his underwear, my skimpy thong and miles of skin. How would this proceed? I was considering what I would do next when Marco took over.

He moved me onto my back and caressed my body with his hands, and explored with his mouth. His pace was just right for me, taking his time despite both of us being so aroused. He started out very gently with my breasts, my abdomen, my legs, always leaving me wanting just a bit more. He formed a spiral of kisses starting around my navel and broadening out to cover my entire torso. Every time he approached the top of my thong I started. It was like a small electric shock.

And there he lingered, going back and forth, moving the silk band just millimeters down at a time. I knew I wasn't going to let him go all the way down, (much too intimate for this stage), but the way he was playing with me was really working.

I brought his head back up to mine, and kissed him like I meant it. His body slid on top of mine and I exhaled, letting the weight of his body settle. It had been so long since I felt a man on top of me. I wanted to stay there for a long time. Then I thought about slowly lowering his underwear, followed by a pang of uncertainty. Would we proceed right to intercourse if I did that? Would these explorations that I was enjoying so much stop? Was I having second thoughts about having sex with him?

His hands stroked the length of my body, this time moving underneath my panties. I was already so wet that his fingers slid easily between my folds. And there he began to own me, slowly, delicately, with complete focus.

A flash of recognition and surprise came to me as I remembered a book Lizzy had given me about the female orgasm. I had unfortunately never been successful in convincing my partners to learn the particular technique, which was an issue for me as no man had been able (or willing?) to bring me to orgasm for a very long time. Marco was doing it now, whether he knew it or not.

His lips found my mouth, my face, my neck, my breasts while he continued to stroke without urgency or impatience. He seemed completely content just to watch me and touch me.

The climbs and falls grew stronger and stronger until fear arose instead. This was too vulnerable - here with this man I hardly knew, completely exposed and about to release myself into pure pleasure - and I stopped myself. Tension replaced the heat.

His face moved to my ear and he whispered, "I am here, Monique. Let yourself go and I will catch you. I promise."

He increased the pressure, of his mouth and his fingers, until I was pushed to the top. I stepped off the edge of the cliff and fell deeper and deeper into the sensations. Waves of orgasm rolled through my body as I wondered if time had stopped. I wanted to mentally chronicle how indescribable and unexpected this was, but my body refused to let my attention go. I could hardly look at him, although I knew he was trying to catch my eyes. It was just short of too much for me.

When the physical sensations dampened, I rolled toward him, and curled my body into his. He held me while I fought the overwhelming urge to cry. If I could have stood up, I would have gone running out of that room. But I couldn't move. I was scared and naked and certain that the higher I ascended, the more devastating the inevitable fall would be.

I couldn't have imagined his thoughts, the woman in his bed having gone fetal and fighting tears. He said nothing but kept his body wrapped around mine.

13

SHOPPING CURE

And then I woke up. The room was filled with light and it took me several moments to understand where I was. The evening recreated itself until I remembered why I was in this strange room, in an empty but disheveled bed. Soft clanging outside the door reminded me I was not alone.

As soon as Marco entered the room, wearing low slung bottoms and carrying two large white mugs, my humiliation bloomed. He'd taken care of me and instead of reciprocating, I'd fallen asleep. Crying. Could I have summoned any magic to make myself disappear? What must this man think of me - selfish and weepy? Trying not to appear shell-shocked and ashamed, I looked at him and smiled.

"Good morning my beautiful Monique." The sound of his voice melted me again. "Tea, darling? I hope that's what you wanted."

"Yes, yes, that's perfect. And so thoughtful. Thank you."

"How did you sleep?"

"I don't know. I mean... I must have passed out. I'm so sorry. I didn't even drink very much..."

"There is nothing to be sorry about." He sat next to me on the bed. "I am so happy you stayed with me. It was wonderful to be with you."

His face was full of contentment, but my mind could only go to one thought: Was it? I knew he thought I was a horrible person and was plotting how to drop me as soon as he could. There was no doubt in my mind.

"I have a fitting in about half an hour, but I want you to stay here as long as you want. I think you need some rest."

Aha! He was leaving! Ample evidence of his disgust with me.

"No, no, that's okay. I should be going." I tried to wriggle myself out of the bed, while staying completely covered with the sheets. It was an exercise in clumsiness and awkwardness and immaturity. I didn't care.

"Why do you hide yourself from me?" He furrowed his brow in confusion. "And I don't want you to leave right now. Please, have your tea. Stay here. I am not ready to say goodbye."

He tenderly moved the hand that held up the sheet and let it fall, revealing the extent of my nudity. He moved in toward me and wrapped his arms around me.

"What a beautiful night I had with you. Thank you for sharing yourself with me. It was... well... I hope it was okay for you."

I couldn't believe what I was hearing. This man was thanking me for letting him pleasure me. I froze, unable to make this situation make sense. He was either the greatest playboy ever in the history of time, or... something else too much for me to imagine. The love of my life?

"Marco, I'm so embarrassed about what happened." I didn't want to talk about it and yet there I was, doing it. "I can't believe I just fell asleep. You must think I'm so rude and selfish. And I am. I just don't know what to say. And how emotional I got. You must think I'm a complete lunatic."

"Aaah. I understand. That is why you want to cover yourself and leave quickly?"

I nodded.

He looked away as he moved his head almost imperceptibly up and down. "It does not happen very often in my life that I connect with someone like this. I did not come to Vegas to hook up. Quite the opposite in fact." (*What did that mean?*) "Monique you are unlike any woman I've ever known and I certainly don't think you are any of those things you said.

I don't really know what happened for you last night, although I would love for you to tell me, if you want. What I know is that I was so happy that you stayed with me, and that you opened yourself to me, and that I was able to be a part of something that was enjoyable for you. It was wonderful for me and I don't feel like I missed anything."

I was going to cry again. *NO Monique, keep it together*, I screamed in my own head. You do not need to keep falling apart in front of this guy. He is not the recipient of all your pain. He showed up in your life, has been awesome so far, and may or may not betray you like the others. You do not need to expose yourself any more.

"It was... unexpected... for me. I haven't had so many good experiences lately and it brought some things up. It was really nice for me, no doubt, and I don't want you to think otherwise. You have been absolutely wonderful." Clearly I had lost any control over what came out of my mouth. As if I had drunk a truth serum or something.

"Thank you for being honest with me. And trusting me too." He slipped under the covers, brought me to him and kissed me. Softly at first, then passionately. Our bodies intertwined and everything from the previous night rose in me again. He could have anything, anyone he wants, and just kept choosing me. I didn't get it.

I wanted to explore his body, magnificent as it was, to take my time, and feel him and taste him. I wanted to show him that I could give as well as receive, that I was intensely attracted to him. But he just wanted to give to me. He took charge in that beautiful bed and the small part of me that wanted to resist, to be in charge, was consumed by all the pleasure I experienced.

He took the covers off of me and looked at my fully naked body. He refused to let me avert my eyes. He implored, *Look at me. I want you to see me looking at you.*

The time passed too quickly and he was going to be late for his appointment. We left the suite in a flurry, promising to keep in touch during our busy days. His was filled with wedding activities, including the rehearsal dinner, and mine with my sisters, shopping for dresses, then taking Nora out for a family dinner.

"Will I see you tonight?" he asked.

"You mean you haven't had enough of me yet?"

"Actually, I haven't had nearly enough of you."

The way he said that nearly buckled my knees.

"We will have an early night tonight - the bride's orders - so I will be here. In the room. When you get back from dinner."

His hinting was much more charming than subtle. This ability to be so direct and commanding, and then sweet, like a bashful boy, dissolved my heart every time.

I didn't want to answer directly. Some ridiculous vestige of playing hard to get, so I said, "I will let you know what we decide to do."

"I'll be waiting for you."

He walked me down to my room, even though I told him he didn't have to. "Chivalry is not optional," he declared.

I opened my door to find Lizzy going through my clothes.

"Hey Nik! I need to borrow your white t-shirt. Mine's dirty."

"Hey Lizzy. Thanks for asking."

"Hey Marco! Where are my kisses?" We laughed as he entered the room and gave Lizzy her two kisses. What a good man...

"Oh, you've decided to grace us with your presence." The haughty voice from the other room was unmistakable. "Shall I assume you've not come back a virgin?" Nora opened the door and nearly jumped out of her shoes when she realized that Marco was also in the room. I shook my head in disgust at her, but didn't speak.

"Good morning Marco," she said in a tone that was sheepish and defiant at the same time.

"Nora." He kissed her on both cheeks. Lizzy stood frozen, unable to speak, perhaps waiting for Nora to apologize for her rude remark. I knew better than to expect an apology coming from our sister.

"Have a beautiful day ladies." He strode toward the door,

holding my hand. "And don't worry Nora, I have returned her as intact as she came to me. For now."

He kissed me at the door, handed me his key and said, "Use it."

It felt as if we'd condensed six months of relationship into two days and I'd just been asked to move in together. For a moment I forgot my sister's awful behavior and giggled like a little girl.

"See you later," was all I could manage.

As soon as the door closed, I turned to glare at Nora. Sometimes she just went too far.

"He told *you*!" Lizzy scoffed at Nora.

"I didn't know he was in here! No need to make such a big deal about it. The real question is how come you're still *intact*. Is he a monk or something?"

"No, he's not a monk, not that that's any business of yours anyway. God, Nora, is it really that hard to not be offensive every minute of your life?"

"That was harsh, Nik," said Lizzy.

"I deserved it," Nora said, which left us both open-mouthed and stunned. "Let's start over, okay? I'm so glad we're spending the day together. And Nik, I really want to hear about your night. You two are looking like the king and queen of Vegas. Is there going to be a double wedding tomorrow?"

"Shut up," I said with a girlish grin. "Let me get ready so we can get this day started, okay?"

"Okay," they said in unison as they sat down on the bed and watched me expectantly.

"Boy I'm really glad we paid for three rooms here," I said sarcastically.

"I'm sorry, *who* paid for three rooms?" asked Nora, who was bankrolling this particular jaunt.

"Fine." I resigned myself to an audience while I got ready. An audience that plied me with questions faster than I could answer them. Why didn't we have sex? What did we do, exactly? What did we talk about? Did I meet the chef? Am I going to sleep with Marco tonight?

I answered what I could and didn't withhold much. I down-played my crying stint, although they could probably tell I was doing that. My sisters were well aware of both my emotional nature and my sordid history with heartbreak.

We were in disbelief that not even 48 hours had passed. I knew this was a recurrent pattern for me – falling hard and fast. Lizzy too, although the inevitable crash always left her a bit less scarred than I'd been. Even Nora and Sam wasted no time. I wondered what it was about us that made us so vulnerable? Able to fall in love so quickly.

These two days had been a surprise for me, certainly, but I under-stood this pace. Perhaps we were each trying to find our version of our parents' love-at-first-sight magical story.

The three of us skipped out of the room, credit cards ready for some major damage. There were no shortage of shopping opportuni-ties and we planned to take advantage of most of them. Dresses topped on the list, but shoes, handbags, even lipsticks filled much of the afternoon. We giggled most of the day away, giddy with the experience of being together, and our respective recent excitements. Amazing men and a prestigious award kept us in broad smiles.

I could tell from Nora's face the few times that Sam's name came up that she missed him. She would never have admitted it, of course, but she wanted him here, with her. Nora had such an obsession with independence that she kept the people she loved the most at arms-distance. It gratified her ego but I knew her heart suffered. I hatched a plan as I watched her pretend she didn't miss him as much as I knew she did.

I made an excuse to back-track to a shoe store we had seen earlier, while they were still trying on dresses. As soon as I was free, I dialed my phone.

"Hi Sam, it's me. Listen, I need you to do something."

14

A GUIDE AND A PLAN

The teacher Lalune was looking for found her. Actually, they found each other. Lalune accidentally barged into a meeting of the high elders, being held in her father's chambers and heard Avanora speak.

Lalune had always been fearful of and mesmerized by the old mermaid, who spoke with such reverence about their ancient customs that it made Lalune want to know more. Avanora described the magic that only the oldest of the mermaids still had, and all the traditions that had become uninteresting to the new generation. The young ones seemed only to be concerned with treasure and fun, she said.

Avanora, whose eyes reflected something Lalune had never seen in the ocean, looked directly at Lalune when she asked the question, "What can we do to bring the passion back to our youth, instead of placating them with these all-too-easy lives?"

"You can let them pursue what they love and be who they want to be." It tumbled out of Lalune's mouth before she knew what she was doing. The council, including her father, rose in an uproar at her discourteous addition to the conversation, and she was hastily escorted out of the room.

"Who was that young mermaid?" asked Avanora.

Embarrassed and angry, Lalune's father admitted, "My daughter. Who should know better. I do apologize…"

"No need to apologize. She spoke bravely and wisely. These are the qualities I speak about. So rarely seen in our community of youth anymore."

Avanora made a point to discover where she might find the young mermaid, and came across Lalune daydreaming near the surface.

"It is not safe for you here. The land-walkers often bring their boats to this area and go diving."

Lalune was so shocked to have been found, that she could not speak for a moment.

"How did you find me?"

"You have not kept your hiding places secret." Avanora smiled, with a disconcerting familiarity.

"I did not realize… I just love the light up here. The constant darkness below makes me… sad."

"I see that, child. Your sadness has also evaded secrecy."

"I am sorry for barging in on your meeting. Are you here to scold me? I'm sure my father is preparing my punishment as well."

"I have no intention of scolding you. Or punishing you. I am here to help you."

"Help me? With what?" Lalune had to watch herself. These old mermaids had stronger magic. Maybe she was able to read her mind.

"Your heart's desire."

"I do not know what you are talking about." Lalune could hardly hide the fear and excitement in her voice. Could this really be the mermaid who would help her? She had to be careful. Maybe this mermaid was a spy sent by her father.

"I see." Avanora's pause lasted an eternity. "Well, my dear, you can find me at the blue cave whenever you are ready. Be well, child."

Avanora swam away, with Lalune's eyes wide, following every move. There was no time to process what had happened as Lalune's sisters swam by with their friends.

"What are you doing here?" they asked her, accusingly.

"I could ask you the same thing."

"Are you in one of your moods again?"

"No, Adina. I am not in any mood. Just minding my own business."

"You should not be up here. It is too close to the surface."

"Then why are you here?"

"We are headed toward the island, if you must know. Not hanging around, waiting to get caught. You are one fishing net away from being gone forever."

"That is an awful thing to say, Adina!" At least her younger sister was more compassionate.

"I am not planning on getting caught in any fishing lines. Thank you for your concern."

"We should go. Before the seals make a mess of things." Adina looked back at her sister with an expression that might have been remorse. If Lalune chose to see it that way.

"Bye Lalune," they all said.

"Bye…"

———

It took days before Lalune mustered the courage to go to the blue cave. She realized that even if it was a trap, it was her only option at this point. More punishment could not be any worse than the imprisonment she was already experiencing.

"I am so glad you have decided to come see me, Lalune."

"I do not really know why I am here."

"I think you do. But we do not have to talk about that just yet. Shall we go for a swim? I would like to show you one of my favorite places."

They headed off in a direction Lalune did not recognize, away from the small island and most of the mermaids' activities.

They arrived at an outcropping of shimmering rocks that reached all the way to the surface of the water.

"It is beautiful here. I can feel… something."

"You have not lost your sensitivity. That is good. This is a special place, where our kind have come for millennia."

"What happens here?"

Avanora told her the story of a mermaid who had lived her life never feeling like she belonged in the ocean. She studied the land-walkers so closely that she eventually fell in love with one and decided to cross over.

"She did what?" Lalune could not believe her ears.

"She decided to leave us, child, and join the other world."

"What happened to her?"

"She lived and died many years ago, after a full and beautiful life as a land-walker. I knew her quite well. And although I miss her terribly, I know she had to leave us. This was not her true home."

"I do not understand…"

"Lalune, there are few creatures as blessed as we are. Our ocean kingdom is bountiful and beautiful, and brings most of us the greatest joy. But there are some, who are born… different. They do not belong here. What the Great Mother has given them belongs in the other world. If they do not heed this call, it will consume and destroy them."

"You are scaring me, Avanora."

"You are afraid because you know this is your journey. It happens rarely, but only to those who have the strength to survive the trans-formation, and to survive out there, where things are very different."

"I want to go back, Avanora. Please take me back."

"Of course, child. But first, I want you to feel where you are right now. The magic is strongest here, and a bit further toward shore as well. You can feel it, can you not?"

Lalune was too shaken to answer.

The old mermaid relented. "Follow me."

Lalune found it difficult to follow the old mermaid, so absorbed in the swirl of her thoughts. When they had returned to the cove, Lalune was still unable to formulate a coherent response to what she had experienced.

"Do not worry, Lalune. This is much to process right now. I know you have been holding this in for a long time and you need time to understand. You know where to find me. I can help you."

For days, Lalune swam past the old mermaid's cove, then turned back before being seen. The fear was too much.

Then Avanora appeared at her home, again, for another council meeting. Before leaving, Avanora found Lalune, and said only these words: "The world will be changed by your voice. Let it be heard."

No one had ever spoken to Lalune so directly before, as if the sound had come from inside her own heart. It felt like a current she could not fight, and it shook the unrelenting despair from her soul and turned it into hope. She could not hide any longer or let the fear stop her.

The two mermaids began to meet every morning. Avanora shared all she knew about making the transition and they worked together to get Lalune ready for the biggest event of her life.

Time, fluid as it was in the underwater world, began to move much more quickly for Lalune as she immersed herself in her preparations and lessons. There were materials to collect, rituals to learn, and spells to practice so that she could walk, talk and think as the land-walkers did.

The most difficult incantation would reorganize her skeleton so she could stand and walk, but Avanora assured her that she would be fast asleep and feel no pain. There were the communication spells, so that their language would make sense in her ears and her mouth would form the correct sounds.

Finally, there was the issue of covering her new body. The land-walkers were almost never bare, as she had been her whole life, and she had to be prepared with material to conceal herself. The details revealed themselves with each passing day.

"This is how it is done," Avanora said, weeks into their lessons. "You must arrive at the smaller rock patch, a few leagues past the area I took you, undetected, and bring your whole body out of the water. Leave plenty of time so that the full moon does not catch you too soon.

With the shell placed on your tongue, lie as still as you can until the sun rises. Repeat the spell, only to yourself, but do not let even a whisper pass your lips or the energy will not be sufficient for the transformation. Do you understand, Lalune?"

"Yes."

"Good. You are learning quickly. There are very few I would trust with this information. It could be dangerous for all of us."

"I understand." Lalune wanted to leave. Be done with the work of the day and be alone.

"I understand why your heart brings you to this crossroad. And why you want to run away from it."

"I must go now, Avanora." Lalune did not want to be sharp or impatient with Avanora, she had done so much for her, risked everything to teach her the secret. But she needed to see the place with her own eyes. Where she would leave this world behind.

She traveled slowly toward the magical spot, to see for herself how it would feel, when the time was right. Upon arriving at the larger outcropping of rocks, still a distance from her ultimate destination, Lalune felt unable to continue. She decided she was not yet strong enough, and would double her efforts in completing her studies.

She knew this was exactly what she had to do, yet grieved all she was giving up. She could not dare ask, "What if it won't be worth it?"

There would be no one to take care of her, Lalune realized, which meant she had to master the intricacies of survival as a land-walker. They lived highly individual and transactional lives, compared to the mermaids, so she would have to be very clever. The sea would no longer offer her everything she needed, nor protect her from harm.

The first few days would be the most difficult, Avanora warned her. This was when her adaptation skills would be weakest and the land-walkers would be most suspicious. The exact steps for interaction and assimilation had to be executed perfectly. There was no room for error. Or even for enjoying her new state as a land-walker until she had found safe shelter, and stayed out of the water for one entire earth cycle.

Occasionally, Lalune wondered how it was that Avanora knew so much about life on land, but those questions never had time to root with the enormity of information that filled her mind.

Avanora spoke freely about Lalune's dream of singing, and for the first time in her life, Lalune felt sure that it would happen. Only in the quietest moments, when the flurry of activity stilled, did the vast array of doubts float to the surface of Lalune's thoughts.

"What will everyone think of me for leaving our paradise?"

"You must let those thoughts go. They are fear speaking. You know what your life is supposed to be. No one's dissent can change that."

The surprises came fast and frequent in the discovery of an entirely new way of being. Lalune dedicated herself to this process like nothing she had ever attempted before, being very careful not to attract unwanted attention for her secretive life.

She did not think there could be anything more that she did not know when Avanora halted their lessons one day to speak about love.

"Today, we are going to learn about your life as a woman, a female land-walker. You must know about love, dear one. It will feature prominently in your future."

"I do not care about love, Avanora. I just want to sing."

"These desires are not so different, my dear. It is important you understand what will happen to you. You will have a woman's body, but you will always have a mermaid's heart. We are unlike them, on the inside. Our feelings are more intense. You will have to be careful to see things clearly." Avanora felt from the look on Lalune's face that she had to repeat herself.

"Always remember you will never be exactly like them. We cannot remove or transform the inner spirit. It will make you softer than them, so please, be careful.

Even as a land-walker you will retain your mystical beauty, so the males will be very drawn to you. You must be cautious and use your intuition. When you find the right one, it will feel as if you have come back to the sea. Your body will feel more alive and the human world will look as beautiful as our undersea world. You must wait until that happens."

"What do you mean, the right one?"

"We love freely here, but on land it is done differently. The land-walkers search for the one true love. Many do not find each other, but you will. All your feelings will be directed toward only one man."

"Really, Avanora. I am not interested in the land-walker males. They are odd and... scary."

"Yes, I understand, my dear. But when you change, your feelings will change."

Lalune was almost embarrassed to ask this. "Will I mate with this male?"

"Yes, with one you love. It will bring you enormous amounts of pleasure. Do not fear it. You will marry and start a family, a beautiful family. They will be land-walkers and never need to know your past. Unless you tell them."

A flash of darkness crossed Avanora's face, which Lalune noticed.

"What is it? What if they come out with tails?" Lalune was honestly worried.

"They will not, but they will surely carry some of our magic, which will be wonderful for them, if they use it well. Sometimes... the offspring will need to adapt... differently. It is not something you should worry about now."

Avanora did not want to continue on this subject.

"You and your family will lead blessed lives, Lalune, if they open their hearts. The children will love in the same way we love, but their guidance might be muddied by their land-walker bodies. They may falter in a way that will not happen for you, but they will find their way. As you will find yours. Do not be afraid."

"But I am afraid."

"I know. That is how you know this is important."

"Maybe I will not be able to do it, Avanora. Maybe it will be too hard of a life for me, so used to the simplicity of our kingdom."

"I know why you say that. Your soul has not chosen the easy path, Lalune. But your calling to live a different way indicates your ability to succeed. The seed of your new life is embedded in your visions and fantasies of it. Trust that what you have been feeling your whole life holds the truth. It is the fear that is an illusion."

"What if I cannot do it? Will I ever be able to return?"

"That is much more complicated, dear. I would not make the transformation if you are not sure. Returning is not easy."

"Please tell me. What would happen?"

"If you return, it is irreversible. You only get one chance. You would be gone from the world of land and the ones who love you would be very sad."

"Could I bring them with me?"

"Only the one true love would be able to come with you."

"Would he become one of us?"

"Yes. He would fully transform. But this would also be irreversible. Please understand that."

"Yes, Avanora. I do," Lalune said, not quite sure if she did.

It was overwhelming, but the certainty of her decision filled her as soon as she remembered the dreams she had been carrying her whole life. There was no way to guarantee that any of it would work, from the transformation, to the life she would build as a land-walker. The only guarantee was the impossibility of her continuing life as a mermaid.

"I will do my best, Avanora. I know what I have to do. I will make my way in that world, I will be a great singer. Love or not. I must go now. See you tomorrow."

Over the next few days, Lalune could tell that something was bothering Avanora, but neither of them spoke of it. Lalune worried that perhaps Avanora disapproved of her progress.

"We have spoken of many things, my dear. You have been a good student," Avanora said.

Lalune was relieved.

"There is one last piece, however, which I must tell you. I do not want this to frighten you."

Lalune's heart gripped. Had there not been enough to take in?

"I want to know, Avanora. I must know. Whatever it is."

"You will be given something greater than any other mermaid." Avanora paused, trying to find the right words. "Changing worlds is a grand act. One which does not come without a price. In your life as a land-walker, you will have to return the gift."

"Return the gift? I do not understand."

"Something… someone very dear to you will be taken away. One life for another. Loss is a normal part of the other world. But you may feel it much more deeply than your new kind. You will experience something painful. We never know when or how. But it is inevitable."

All the possibilities flashed before Lalune. Would she lose a child, or her true love, or someone else in her life?

"You are very strong, Lalune. That is why you were chosen. You will recover."

Lalune did not know what she should be thinking, or asking.

"I do not want you to worry about this. It is woven into the material of a land-walker life. I… I did not want you to be unprepared."

"Oh, Avanora. I cannot think about this. I want to have a life in the land-walker world. I am afraid of the pain, of the difficulties. But I cannot let it stop me."

"Exactly, my child. I knew you would understand."

Lalune did not know whether she did or did not. Regardless, the plan would go forward.

"The other issue is much smaller."

Lalune was surprised that there was more. Was this not enough of a price?

Avanora continued. "Your offspring will carry something from this world."

"Yes, I know, Avanora. You told me that. But you said they would not have tails."

"Yes, that is true. Physically, they will be like all the other land-walkers."

"Then, what is it?" Lalune's voice shook.

"You will have an easy time knowing what is in your heart when it comes to love. Your senses will still be as sharp as they are here. But the children... they may falter."

"Yes, I remember you saying that as well."

"They may make poor choices. This is also normal. And carries consequences, just like it does for any creatures, on sea or land."

"Then what is the issue?"

"Should they make poor choices in love, it will be much more difficult for them. They will feel the pain more intensely, and the Great Mother will often take drastic measures to reassure balance is restored."

"This does not sound so bad, Avanora." Lalune was not sure if she had understood completely.

"No, it is not so bad. But their lives may not be free of painful situations."

Lalune felt tired by all of this information. She found it hard to not allow defeat into her heart.

"No lives are free of pain, Avanora. Is that not true?"

"Aaaah, yes, you are correct." Avanora smiled at Lalune's wisdom. "Teach them to choose wisely, Lalune. Then, it will be easier for all of you."

"I must go now, Avanora. There is too much for me to think about. I will return tomorrow, ready to begin again."

"As you wish, dearest one."

Avanora watched Lalune swim away, with a heart full of excitement and sadness.

15

UNIONS AND REUNIONS

The nearly perfect day of shopping was topped off by a surprisingly quiet dinner. Cruising around Las Vegas searching for the perfect gown had tired us out enough to dissolve any snarky attitudes. Nora picked from the list of restaurants to which I was given a special invitation, and we got the royal treatment. The magnificent meal, and my loving sisters, formed a delicious experience.

We were giddy with excitement about the next day's events and ecstatic over the food. Our connection created a smile that circled the table throughout the entire meal. Even though I often found them ridiculous, and impossible, I adored my sisters. They taught me dedication, commitment, and joy.

I didn't worry about Nora – she'd created a near-perfect life for herself, which included her true love. The possibility that Lizzy just might have found the man of her dreams this weekend gave me the chills. It made no rational sense, but I couldn't deny what I saw. She was one of the most loving people I had ever met, just like Dad and Danny, and deserved nothing less than to be swept off her feet by a true prince charming.

My fate was still in question. Did I dare let myself acknowledge what had been happening with Marco? He wasn't perfect, but he appeared to be as perfect for me as any human being I'd known. All evidence pointed to *too good to be true* but I wanted to believe that there was no cruel twist waiting for me. *It's so fast*, I kept telling myself. *Slow down*.

My inability to trust a man, and to trust my feelings, would have to shift if I wanted to create something with Marco. So far, I was the only obstacle in this potential relationship.

I left my sisters after dinner, none of us able to put into words all we were feeling. The walk to the penthouse elevator stretched to fill a surprising amount of time. I must have been walking slowly although I was vibrating with anticipation and nervousness.

As I stood outside his door with the key inches away from the lock, I breathed deeply to gather my strength. I was crystal clear on my intention for this evening: to demonstrate to Marco the woman that I wanted to be - sexy, confident, generous, and loving. The kind of woman this man deserved. I desperately wanted to be her.

My key slid easily in and out, and the unmistakable click let me know it was time to enter.

I walked past my favorite view of the Vegas skyline to his bedroom, where I found Marco sitting up in bed with his reading glasses on, and a book in his lap. I watched his surprised expression change to glee as I sauntered toward him.

"You made it." He smiled so broadly I thought his face might split.

"I missed you," I said as I sat down next to him, removed his glasses and relocated the book. I was determined to be courageous. And I did miss him.

In between the kisses I lightly planted on his face, he asked, "You did? How much?"

"You're about to find out," I replied.

For the next hour my mouth made it to nearly every inch of his body, moving with infinite patience, and saving the best for last. I should have predicted that he would have a beautiful cock, but it still surprised me as I remove his pajama bottoms. Straight and hard, with skin so soft I wanted to rub it against my face. I'd been thinking about having him in my mouth almost since the moment we met. My oral fixation, more often satisfied by the creations of my kitchen, was undeniable.

I licked him like a lollipop, slowly and firmly, as he grew more and more excited. He gasped as my warm mouth finally surrounded him. Stroking him with my hand, I brought him in and out of my mouth, passing over my wet lips then filling to the back of my throat, over and over.

He was generous with the guidance I needed to get it just right – a word here, a gentle movement there, helping me know what was working. I enjoyed him like the dessert after my delicious meal and wanted him to feel as loved by me as I had by him.

I invited any thoughts of self-consciousness and inadequacy to float away. Watching him experiencing so much pleasure filled my own body with the same.

Increasing the pace, I sensed his climax approaching, while his arms gently pushed against my shoulders, trying to move me away. I caught his eye and smiled, letting him know it was okay to keep going. This was nearly the best part for me.

His groans became more insistent as he held my shoulders strongly. He was on the verge of orgasm as I teased him with my tongue on the tip of his cock, then took him into my mouth again. He couldn't hold himself back anymore.

"Bella, I'm coming," he growled. His head arched back and his groans filled the room. The pulsing of his cock undulated through his whole body and then mine. I held him until my mouth was full of him.

I didn't move until he had completely finished, lying quietly with his eyes closed. He looked a bit stunned, so I moved slowly off of him and slid up until we were face to face. Without opening his eyes, he took my mouth to his and kissed me deeply. His hands slid under my dress and slipped it off in one move. We flipped over and he was on top of me.

We paused there for a moment, contemplating the implications of what might be the next step. There wasn't a single article of clothing between us. Was I ready for us to consummate our relationship? Was he, especially since he just had an orgasm?

I didn't doubt his desire for me in that moment, but I could sense resistance, and wasn't sure if it was coming from him or me. I was scared, even after the intimate moment we'd just shared. I did much better when the attention wasn't on me.

We gazed at each other while our bodies found their way. The gentle rise and fall of our breath, with a tender urgency, accompanied the communication between our eyes. I wanted to say something but didn't know what. I wanted him to make the decision for the both of us.

He moved my legs open with his thigh as he kissed my neck. "That was amazing, Monique. You are a woman of so many surprises."

"Glad you liked it," I said cheekily.

"I'm so happy you came here tonight. I was worried you'd had enough of me," he said, recalling what I'd said to him earlier. Our bodies were grinding. The smallest move and he would have been inside me.

If only he knew how much I wanted him. How I'd spent the whole day thinking about him, imagining what this night would be like, and fantasizing about our lives together. I was infatuated.

But I didn't want to get hurt and even though it had only been a few days, I was already too invested in the relationship. Would it end in heartbreak, as all the others had?

"Why would you think that I'd had enough of you?"

"Everything has been so perfect. It's easy to think that it's too good to be true. And you... well, I feel you pulling away sometimes. I don't really know what that means." He laid the truth before me. Would I honor it?

"I see... You're probably right."

I wasn't not sure, from the look on his face whether he was surprised or relieved. "What are you afraid of, Monique?"

A ball of defensiveness rose to the back of my throat and forced the words out. "What makes you think I'm afraid?"

"I can feel it. In your body. Maybe I'm wrong."

"Well… it's… I… just want to make sure that I'm doing the right thing."

"Do you know what the right thing is?"

"I don't know. I feel confused with you. I mean I think I do, but I'm not sure."

"What if I told you that I am afraid? I feel disoriented and… we could easily just sleep together but it feels like something more important is happening."

His clarity and honesty prevented me from continuing the charade any longer.

"I *am* afraid, Marco. You're right. I'm trying to appear much more together than I am. Inside it's a whirlwind and I can't find my legs underneath me. I'm trying so hard to make a rational decision and it's impossible. I don't understand why."

"I think it's alright, Monique, that we feel this way. I think it's exactly as it's supposed to be. We can decide to slow down and see if the fear works its way out, or just move forward. We're in charge of this situation. Do you agree?"

"Yes I do. It's just that my body is feeling such desire for you. It's my heart that… is feeling vulnerable and my mind is spinning with all the reasons this can't actually be happening."

"But it is happening. I'm right here, with you. I'm not in your imagination. I'm right here next to you. Feel me. Let's be in this together."

His gaze turned directly to me as he softly asked, "Will you tell me what you want?" I remembered that same question in front of the window, our first full night together. Last night. It felt like months ago.

"I want to be happy," came from my lips, which I regretted almost immediately. *What a banal thing to say.*

"What will make you happy?"

The heart of the issue revealed itself. "Maybe I don't know."

Everything was getting too raw, then the perfect diversion

popped into my head. "What do *you* want?" Turning the question around might have given me time to get myself together.

"I want you to be happy."

That was tricky, really tricky. "That's not fair," I said, unable to stop myself from smiling.

"These past few days, with you, have been remarkable. Really. I don't know if I've ever experienced anything like this, connecting with someone so quickly and on so many levels. I am very attracted to you, Monique, as I hope you have seen. I don't want to presume anything. Although in our current state..."

Of course. We were naked, together, in his bed. I felt foolish. And childish. And overdramatic. I was making a mess of an otherwise perfect situation. I wanted to vanish.

"Does what I said upset you?"

"No," I lied.

"I don't want to upset you, Bella. I want you to feel comfortable with what happens here. And I see you are not comfortable."

Snap into shape Monique! Put on your grown-up panties, and be a reasonable adult. Right now.

"I'm not upset," lying again. "It's hard for me to tell what's really going on. It does feel too good to be true, for me too."

He moved his body completely off mine, then wrapped his arms around me. The heat of the previous moment began to fade. He looked tired. I was frustrated by my own ineptitude.

"Do you think I am not who you think I am, or this is not what you think it is?"

"It's always so hard to tell, don't you think? Or maybe it's me. Always over-analyzing and over-complicating everything. Not wanting to trust when something feels too good. I don't want it to be this way. And yet, it's what I do. I'm sorry I'm being like this. I'm sure you just want to have a good time and I'm being so fucking dramatic about everything."

He nodded, but didn't speak. Self-consciousness crawled across my bare skin. I wanted to hide.

"I don't know if you are being dramatic or not, but there's

nothing here that is not as I would want it to be." The seriousness of his voice pierced my worry. "We both have pasts, Bella. We're old enough to not have escaped unharmed from love's little adventures. I'm not just looking to have fun. It would be much easier, sure. Also meaningless."

He lifted my face to see his. "We get to choose what we want Monique. You and I. Maybe there are other people or circumstances outside this room, but right here and right now it's just you and me in this bed with absolute free will."

I felt as if I was being schooled, full of discomfort and humiliation. Why was this such a big deal for me? I'd had casual sex in my life, and yet this was so intense. I couldn't tell if it was a sign of danger, or a sign of importance. I was trying so hard to be logical, to get my head clear. It was as if I was swirling underwater and couldn't find the surface. What was happening to me?

"I know that," I mumbled.

"So let's choose." He kissed me. I kissed him back. I closed my eyes and realized how nice it was to be in bed, with that man, making each other feel good. If I could let myself be in the amazing moment I was currently living, none of the drama would be necessary.

His hand gently stroked my belly, grasped my hipbone, then slipped between my legs. The fire lit, once again.

We spent the few remaining hours of the night exploring and enjoying each other with our hands and our mouths, without crossing any lines, or triggering any more drama on my part. He studied me, and my reactions, just as he had mentioned at the pool, and I did the same for him. I plied him with questions about his likes and dislikes. The connection between us deepened even though the relationship remained unconsummated. Joyful satisfaction made a rare appearance as the anxiety took a brief hiatus and I fell asleep in his arms.

We woke in a tangle of bodies and sheets. It took me some time to figure out where my limbs ended and his began. When I inched toward his body, he instinctively pulled me in even closer. His *good morning* to me pressed against my leg. Our mouths met and the heat built very quickly. I pulled him on top of me and opened my legs. He slid between them and I knew this was it.

I was completely ready for him, after a night of arousal and pleasure, almost not awake enough for the neurosis to begin. He responded with a thrilling urgency.

"Please get a condom," I whispered. He moved swiftly to the side of the bed, and easily back into position. He paused to look at me, asking me with his eyes if this is what I wanted.

"Yes," I said out loud, and moved his hips over mine.

The initial sensation of him entering me was transcendent. This was my favorite moment of lovemaking, anticipation and recognition meeting in a delicious flash. I could hardly contain myself as he slowly filled more and more of me. Both of us moved in slow motion. I closed my eyes and floated in the sheer pleasure of him on top of me, inside me, breathing on my neck, kissing my face, moving with me.

He stopped for a moment when my body had taken him in completely and we both caught our breath. My resistance, my uncertainty, and my denial dissolved. I just wanted this man to continue lighting my body on fire.

He slid his palm underneath my lower back, changing the angle of my hips and entered me even more deeply. The animal-like groan from my lips was hardly recognizable to me.

"Does that feel good?"

I couldn't speak. Only moan. I danced with him, surrendering to his lead, and allowing myself to be free of anything other than what I was experiencing in the moment. The truth was clear - I was loving this man and he was loving me back. I let myself fall completely into his strong arms and the power of his body. He knew the way.

It was so hard to keep my eyes open, immersed in the remarkable sensation of his rhythmic stroking, but I forced myself to look at him. The pleasure in his eyes was undeniable.

Despite the fact that it had been a very long time since I'd had an orgasm from intercourse, I was currently feeling the possibility.

Without a doubt. Would this man break my frigid spell? Would I be able to relax enough, to not get tense and try to force things along, to let my body do what it supposedly knew how to do?

Marco had already shown me patience and skill, taking me there with his hands, but I wasn't sure if I could break my own pattern. My body wanted to release into him so badly, but fear kept me away. I repeated to myself, *let go, let go.*

"I have you. Nothing to hold onto, Bella. Let yourself go. With me."

His words entered from a place beyond hearing. Was it possible he understood the jumbled mess that was happening inside me? He kept proving to me over and over that that was true.

Marco lifted my thigh toward my chest, opening me up even further and sped up. His breath made it clear he was moving closer to climax and I opened my eyes to watch him. For the next several minutes we were connected in every way. I watched him growing more excited and my own body responded. As he slowed down, I drew him in deeper and whispered, "Don't stop. Please."

He resisted, so I wrapped my legs tightly around him, bringing his face to mine and said, "Yes."

I wanted to feel him come inside me. I stopped worrying about my own orgasm and focused on his.

He struggled, wanting to wait for me. I kept pressing him, intent on bringing him to orgasm. The conflict created even more heat between us, and I pulled his mouth to mine. And then everything slowed down.

"Mi amor," he groaned. Loudly. Something electric filled me as I felt him climax. The heat ignited the deepest part of my body, transforming me into something other than flesh. There was no question that I was in the right place with the right person and that I no longer needed to explain what was happening between us. Some primordial part of me knew that he was the one. It was nothing short of magical.

I didn't orgasm; I woke up to a new world. The room filled with the first light of day and everything shimmered. I didn't breathe or need to breathe.

He continued to pulse and shake for some time, whispering, "Mi amor, mi amor."

"Si, si. Muy bien."

He laughed at my childish Spanish and the spell was broken. We were back to being a man and a woman in a bed in Las Vegas. But it was different. All my fretting was gone. I felt wonderful and beautiful and loved. No doubts could live in the bright light of that morning.

"Buenos dias, Marco."

"Buenos dias, Bella. Mi amor." I closed my eyes and let him hold me as we slipped into sleep again.

I woke up with my back to him, his arms wrapped around me, like tangled spoons. He was stroking my face, my breasts, my belly, and then below. He found me wet and ready and exhaled deeply. "Monique..."

His fingers glided over me, just like the first night and I knew what would happen next. Or was I dreaming? No, the electricity in my body told me I was very much awake.

I moved his hand and rolled onto my belly. He understood, bringing my hips back to his, and entering me from behind. His hand reached around and began to stroke me again. This combination, his fingers and his cock caressing me at the same time, was going to take me completely over the edge, my thoughts of frigidity a distant memory. "Marco," I thought and spoke and felt.

"Si, mi amor. For you."

Patiently, he moved my hips to find the right angle to touch me the way he knew would work, and to keep entering me a bit at a time. He knew exactly when to speed up and when to slow down, when to press deeper, and when to back off. I floated on the edge of orgasm for what felt like days, with no interest in pushing or pulling anything along. I let myself sink into the ocean of pleasure I was experiencing. When my body began to buckle with the intensity of it all, he held me up. It was happening.

A cry from the bottom of my being rose out of my mouth. My body was white hot flames and the crack of electricity. But I was underwater, in another world. He held me as I came and came and came. I didn't think it would ever end and I had no interest in stopping it.

My body collapsed, sprawled out on the bed, face down, unable to move. His hands stroked my back, soft kisses caressed my shoulder. He moved my hair to see my face. It took everything I had to open my eyes and look at him. *I love you* filled my mind. I wasn't sure if I'd said it out loud.

Marco beamed at me. His face was in soft focus. "Are you happy?"

"No." His face changed. "I am ecstatic." The smile returned. "You are an amazing lover," I told him, looking straight into his eyes.

"You are the source of all this, Monique. It's not me. It's you..."

16

WHITE WEDDING

W hen I woke up again, it was afternoon. A glance at the clock shocked me awake.

"Holy shit!"

"What's wrong?" I'd frightened him awake.

"We overslept. Nora's ceremony is in a few hours. I have to go! She's going to kill me!"

"And maybe me too!" He sprung out of bed and began to gather my belongings. We were both dressed and out the door in minutes. Since it was Vegas, no one gave us a second look in our clearly disheveled states.

He insisted on walking me to my room again. This time I gratefully accepted. Every moment of this time together was enhanced. The way he held my hand, the way he touched my back, the way he kissed me. The world had gotten brighter and more luminescent. I glided more than walked.

At my door, he said, "These next few hours without you will be like I am underwater, unable to breathe."

"Grow gills, darling. I'll see you very soon."

I watched him as he walked away, then tore myself away from that beautiful sight to enter the frenzy I was sure was happening in my room.

The girls stopped when I entered, saying nothing. They were looking for Marco.

"He's not here."

"Oh my God! What happened? You look like a total mess, Nik. You did it, didn't you? The slutty dress worked?"

"Let her get a word in will you?" implored Nora.

"I love him." I couldn't believe I said it.

"No, sweetheart. You are just flooded with some biochemicals that feel like love. It's just lust."

"I love him, Nora. I'm serious. Something happened up there that I've never experienced. Never, in my forty plus years as a woman. I don't even feel like the same person anymore."

"Oh my God Nik!" Lizzy exclaimed. She had to sit down. She might have been crying.

Nora was unconvinced. "You just got properly fucked my dear. That's all. Okay? That's what a really good screw feels like. Don't confuse it with love. That's trouble in the making."

"Shut up Nora! Look at her? Doesn't she look different to you? I think you do, Nik. I think you look like a woman in love."

"Thank you sweetie. I feel amazing. Absolutely amazing. I swear to you something magical happened. I wish I could explain it."

Nora sighed deeply, exasperated by her romantic and foolhardy sisters. "No time for that now. It's a big day, if you happened to remember. Time to scrape your lover's stuff off your dirty body and get ready."

"Yes, boss," I said as I give her a hug.

"Love you," she said.

"Love you too."

"I guess you two will continue rummaging through my stuff while I'm in the shower?"

"Yup," they said in unison. "I might ask Lola to take me shopping. She did a really great job with you," Lizzy added.

I returned to find Lizzy doing Nora's makeup. They were such beautiful women. Sometimes it surprised me, even though I'd been looking at them my whole life. Nora had dark eyes and hair, like our mother, and Lizzy was all gold and pink, with Dad's blue eyes. With me in the middle, we made a perfect progression from one parent to another.

It was half an hour before we had to be downstairs. I was finishing up my own hair and makeup when the knock on the door startled all of us. Lizzy, aware of the surprise, jumped up to answer it.

She greeted Sam with kisses on both cheeks.

"Well that was nice!" he exclaimed.

Nora must have heard a man's voice. "No more lovers in here, ladies. It's time to go!"

Sam opened the door wide and said, "No more lovers? Not even just one?"

Nora stood stunned and silent. This had happened so rarely in my life that I would have hardly recognized her expression, but it was becoming a habit in Vegas. Was she mad? Was I going to be in big trouble for arranging this? We all stood completely still, waiting for Nora to react. No one breathed.

"You're here," she said in disbelief.

"Of course I'm here sweetheart. Where else would I be?"

She ran to him and wrapped her long body around his. "I can't believe you're here. How did this happen?"

Instead of answering, he kissed her. Passionately.

Lizzy and I were mesmerized by the scene of our sister expressing her adoration of her partner, and Sam reciprocating even more back at her. They were captivating to watch – beautiful, strong, completely enamored with each other. I drifted to the possibility of Marco and I ever having even a small piece of this. My heart beat faster as I thought about seeing him in a few hours.

"Okay, you two. I need to finish getting dressed. Get out of here." They went off to Nora's room, hand in hand. It looked like I was safe.

Lizzy jumped up and down, "You did it, you did it! Look Nik, did you see how happy she was? You really did it!"

"Yes, baby girl. *We* did good."

My mind was filled with my unusual big sister as I got myself ready.

Nora reminded me of Mom, but in a strange way. Their personalities were nearly opposite, but they looked exactly alike. And then there was the sadness that no one could name or fix. The one I shared, but Danny and Lizzy seemed not to have inherited.

I wondered what would fill that hole for Nora. I couldn't imagine that there was anything she wanted that she didn't already have, or have plans to achieve. It had always been no nonsense with her.

Sometimes, I watched her stare off into space, like Mom used to, and like I still do. I understood the source of my sadness and yearning. At least I thought I did. But Nora's was unclear. What was she dreaming of? What was she wishing for? And what could we do to help her get it?

I didn't think it was an issue with her career. Nora loved what she did, although still blamed our parents for forcing her into it. She was right. She was the good girl who did as she was told. But there was nothing else that she would have wanted to do, whether she admitted it or not.

Nora even liked the politics of getting ahead in academia. She played the game better than anyone I'd ever seen, stopping at nothing short of success at every goal she created. Thinking about it, I realized that's how she'd always been with relationships as well. She'd never been the victim. Always the victor.

Even after Lizzy and I were both ready, the conspicuous sounds continued from Nora's room.

"Nona, do you want us to wait for you?" we asked, cautiously, using our pet name for her, invented by Lizzy when *Nora* had been too hard to say.

"No," she answered breathlessly. "Don't wait!" We fell into the silliest, girly giggles, knowing exactly what was going on next door.

The two of us walked hand in hand, as we'd been doing since we were kids, all the way to the ballroom. Lizzy updated me on her adventures with Esteban, describing the double wedding we were going to have, our matching dresses and how the wedding band would only play Salsa.

She'd fallen hard for Esteban, although they were taking it slower, sexually, than Marco and me. She wanted to know everything that happened between us, and I obliged. Lizzy was the better listener of my two sisters, less inclined to analysis and more open-hearted.

When dinner was about to start, and we still didn't see Nora or Sam, Lizzy and I smiled at the thought of their surprise reunion. Both of us knew we would be lucky to find as much love as they shared, even in their unique way.

If Nora ever gave Sam any indication that he wouldn't get horribly rejected, he would have been on his knee in a flash. They adored each other in this crazy meant-to-be way. Neither Lizzy nor I could imagine anyone else putting up with her. It was nothing short of miraculous.

The reunited couple arrived at the very last minute and the awards ceremony went beautifully. Nora was softened by Sam's surprise visit, thrilled with us that we had arranged it, and came off as beautiful, brilliant, and charming. Her acceptance speech was funny, humble and she thanked each of us individually. She and Sam never stopped beaming at each other.

Marco never left my mind. If I had to describe what happened to me that morning, that weekend, magical would be be the best word I could find. It had elements of fantasy and wonder and utter incredulity. But it was actually happening. At least I hope it was.

The audience rose to their feet for Nora, applauding wildly. Lizzy started to whoop and others joined her. My sister was one of the most difficult people I knew, but there was no doubt that she was a rock star in her field. I was so immensely proud of her and wanted her to have everything her heart desired.

She hugged and kissed each of us two or three times.

"We love you, Nona. And think you're the best!"

"I couldn't have asked for a better family."

Were those tears in her eyes?

A substantial crowd, eager for her attention, but polite enough to wait for her to finish up with her family, began to form a circle around us.

"Nora, there's a crowd of people waiting to talk to you. Your adoring fans I believe," Sam informed her.

We waited as she effortlessly thanked and greeted those awed by her presence. There was going to be a small reception that we assumed she'd wanted to attend, but she said, "Let's go party at the wedding!"

Alright! We all agreed. I had filled Sam in beforehand, and gotten him an invitation, so he was ready to go.

"Whatever you want, my love," he said to Nora. "You keep getting more and more amazing every minute I know you. However you want to be celebrated, sweetheart, you get it."

"I love you so much, Sammy. Thank you for coming, even though I forbade you. This is the best surprise I have ever gotten."

"Nora the ice queen has soft spots. Who knew?" I couldn't help myself.

"Shall we?" she said to change the subject.

"Yay!!" squealed Lizzy. "Let's go get ready!"

The transition to wedding garb didn't take long. We had all laid out our new fancy dresses and just had to slip them on. A refresh of the face and hair completed the look. Lizzy insisted we take pictures. We did make a rather stunning group - Sam in his tux, us in our gowns, surprisingly no legs showing, if you didn't count the slits in our dresses.

Nora chose a deep violet, Lizzy was in bright pink and I wore a silvery blue silk sheath, that made me look like a mermaid, they said. I liked the compliment.

Our mouths dropped as we walked into the first room, where the ceremony would be held. We had left Las Vegas and entered heaven, apparently.

The room was bathed in white and silver, so meticulously done that it was impossible to imagine that this had been a hotel ballroom the day before. A flamenco guitarist filled the room with romance and each guest was more beautiful and elegant than the next. My concern about the formality of our dresses vanished as I noticed everyone in their finest, having taken *black tie* very seriously.

Esteban saw us first, even with a room full of guests. He ran over to Lizzy, who was already hopping up and down, and swung her around as if she was a small child. He gave her a dramatic kiss on the mouth and then bends down and gave her belly a gentle little kiss.

"How is my hot mama?"

She giggled. "Missed you, baby. This room is so beautiful, Stebby. Oh my God, I feel like I'm in heaven."

"Aah, not as beautiful as ours will be."

Nora, Sam and I froze. Had he really just said that? It would have been just like our sprite of a sister to get herself engaged this weekend. The funny thing was that we didn't worry about her. Well, not too much. She always ended up on the right side of things, even with this pregnancy. It was turning out to be the best thing that had ever happened to her. And maybe to all of us.

Sam put his hand out. "Hello, Esteban. I am Sam, Lizzy's..."

"Brother-in-law," I offered.

"So nice to meet you. Your family has made this an extraordinary weekend. We are so honored that you wanted to share my brother's wedding with us."

"Oh, Esteban, it was so kind of you to invite us. This is absolutely amazing," I said.

"I am so rude, I am sorry." He proceeded to kiss Nora and me, on both cheeks. Lizzy stuck her face out, waiting for her turn. He obliged.

"Are you ready for tonight?" he asked.

"Absolutely!"

Nora and I looked at each other. What was happening tonight? Should we have been worried?

They both looked at us with mischief in their eyes. I had to admit they made a great couple, and his generosity with her pregnancy cemented the deal with me. Even if they announced their engagement, I would be perfectly happy for them. Maybe even a little bit jealous.

"Excuse me, but I have to get back to my brother now. I just wanted to make sure you were all here."

"Can I come with you?" Lizzy asked tentatively.

"Of course, mi amor."

"Okay, we'll see you later," she said as he whisked her off.

"And where is your Romeo?" asked Sam.

"I don't..."

"Hello." Marco's voice came from behind me. How long had he been standing there? I turned around slowly, knowing how amazing he was going to look and wanting to savor every moment.

He didn't take his eyes off me as I faced him. He reached for my hand and kissed it lightly, still keeping his eyes locked on mine. He moved toward my cheek, I assumed for a kiss, but instead whispered in my ear, "You take my breath away." And then he kissed my neck.

I wanted to swoon. I forgot there was anyone else in the room, or that time and space existed. This man awakened something in me that was beyond desire. It was like the feeling a plug must have when it entered a socket.

He stepped back, introduced himself to Sam and kissed Nora. Sam had studied some Spanish and was excited to use it. Beautiful words rolled off his tongue, to Marco's delight.

"Now you are the only one, my darling, who needs to learn Spanish," he said as he squeezed my waist.

"Si señor," I responded.

"Let me not forget the deep congratulations for our next Nobel Prize winner, Dr. Malone. How do you feel?"

Even listening to him speak made me giddy.

"I don't know which was better... winning the award, or having my sisters and my partner conspire to have him here. It was all so wonderful, Marco. Thank you for asking."

"Of course," he said as he nodded gently. "Would you like to meet some people?" he asked.

"Yes," I answered for all of us.

He led us to the groom's family, which consisted of about 150 people as far as I could tell. They each hugged and kissed us, so pleased that we were there to celebrate their family's special occasion. Some of the English was quite good, some not so much. But everyone was welcoming and festive.

Sam and Nora got swept into the group, while Marco and I stepped away.

He stood in front of me and gave me a proper kiss. "Hello, Bella. You made me wait too long."

"Hello darling. You missed me?"

"I've been trying to grow gills all day. Haven't quite gotten the hang of it yet."

He was so clever and funny. "Don't you have to take care of groomsmen things?"

"All I have to do is stand here and look at you. And maybe some other things a bit later."

I couldn't stop smiling, so he continued. "All I could think of today was you, and our wonderful morning. Was it a dream?"

"Yes, I think it must have been." Heat filled my cheeks and I glanced away, hoping to cool down. "Thank you again for inviting us. We are so excited. And it seems that Esteban and Lizzy have something planned for later. Should I be concerned?"

"I wish I knew, but I wouldn't be worried. I will have to stand at the altar in a few minutes, but for now I am all yours. And I'd like to just parade you around the room for a bit."

"Am I just arm candy? Is that all I am to you?"

"Actually, I prefer my arm candy unwrapped."

"Hmmm. I'm afraid this will have to do for now."

"I suppose that's fine," he said, mocking disappointment.

He introduced me to many more people, whose names I forgot

almost as soon as I heard them. He enthralled me as he moved through the room like royalty, so charming and elegant. How had I landed this guy?

Esteban's other brother found us and let Marco know they were starting.

He kissed me. "Until I can breathe again."

17

TAKING A BITE

I couldn't move for a few moments, so entranced by him. I looked up to find my family waving wildly at me, beckoning me to the seat they'd saved. I floated the whole way over.

The wedding was as expected. The crowd gasped as the bride entered, looking like a cake topper - petite and perfect, bejeweled from head to toe and beaming like a little girl. Her husband-to-be cried as she walked toward him. Marco never stopped looking at me, even as tears ran down my cheeks. I didn't mind one bit.

The wedding party left the room together, and the guests were ushered into the grand ballroom, which made the ceremony hall look like a dingy closet. The decor transformed from pristine white to a festival of colors. Everyone stood awe-struck, just for a moment, at the entryway, disbelieving the grandeur of what they were seeing. Thankfully the ushers kept people moving along.

The four of us exchanged glances of disbelief.

"I can't believe we're here," mouthed Lizzy.

"I know."

I was fully expecting to sit apart from Marco, understanding the tradition to have the entire wedding party together. But we entered and saw a special table for the bride and groom, on an elevated stage, and no other specially designated table. This was a newfangled approach to weddings, I thought, but I liked it if I got to sit next to my man.

My thoughts were confirmed as we found our names on the table. The four of us, plus Marco, Esteban and Esteban's other brother and his wife, made up the table. The men had not yet arrived, so Sam was our token date for now.

But his attention was only for Nora. Her response to his arrival, which really could have gone either way, changed something in him. In them. Maybe all this love and lust around us was making all the relationships better. Not that they needed any help, other than my sister being so demanding.

Even that thought made me laugh, as I remembered her puppy-dog face when she saw Sam in the room. And how they were so blatantly having sex, which my conservative sister would have never done with us so close by. Nora looked nothing short of blissful. I gave myself a mental pat on the back for orchestrating this surprise. Not bad, Nik.

"Daydreaming again, Bella?" I heard to my right, and there he was. My beautiful man coming to be with me. Things could not have been any better.

The evening passed too quickly. We ate and drank and danced to the wonderful band, playing a variety of Latin music and contemporary dance tunes. Sam was eager to show off the ballroom dance lessons he and Nora had taken, and Lizzy was happy to be swung around by her Prince Charming. I just wanted Marco to hold me, and that he did.

"I'm so sorry I had to rush off this morning," I told him.

"Yes, that. It's fine, but only just this once." He flashed me that smile again.

"It was a bit frantic and I didn't tell you what an incredible time I had last night. And this morning." We both smiled remembering how we had woken up.

"The way you share yourself... how honest you are, even when it's hard... I want you to know that I don't take it lightly."

I didn't know what to say. If only he knew how much I was

concealing, how the rush of emotions I had around him nearly drowned me every time I saw him. But I'd never heard a man say the things he said to me and I wanted to let myself take it all in.

I let the part of me that wanted to say, *He's too smooth! You're being played! Wake up!* make it's way out of my system. Then I closed my eyes and enjoyed him holding me.

"I feel the same way Marco. It's been wonderful, these days with you. Maybe I'm just having one of my famous daydreams?"

"Maybe we both are."

We were a well-matched couple, not only in the bedroom, but also on the dance floor. He was the perfect height for a partner, standing just half a head taller than me when I was in heels. Our bodies fit together like puzzle pieces.

I realized that I didn't worry about who was leading when I was with him. Being in charge all the time was exhausting, frankly, and this was a breath of fresh air. I released myself into his support, his guidance, and gave him my trust. This was working on and off the dance floor.

We spent most of the evening dancing, sometimes switching partners. My turn with Sam consisted of us doing the most dramatic moves he could think of, steps that Nora would never have let him get away with but ones he knew I'd be willing to do. We laughed, strutted, dipped, and spun.

"You look so happy, Nik. It's about time. And Marco can't stop looking at you, like he can't believe his eyes. You know you've totally got him, don't you?"

"Don't you think it's just too good to be true, Sammy? I mean he's too fucking perfect!"

"No, he's not perfect. But he might be really, really good. You deserve a man who is going to worship the ground you walk on, and also not let you get away with any shit. He might just be it."

"Don't say that Sammy. You're going to jinx everything!"

"Do you know who you remind me of?"

"You and Nora?"

"Nope. Even better. Claire and Peter."

Remembering my parents brought an ache to the center of my chest. It was impossible to not feel the hole they left or to imagine ever having a love affair like theirs. Could what he was saying be true?

"I miss them so much, Sammy. I can't really believe it..."

"Me too, Nik."

Sam knew the easiest way to distract me from my painful memories was to move my body, so he spun me around until I crumbled with laughter. I missed my brother too, as if one of my limbs was gone, but Sam was a priceless gift in our family. The older brother we needed. I gave him a huge kiss and told him how much I appreciated him coming.

"If not for you, sweet Nik."

We walked over to the table arm-in-arm, ready to sit and catch our breath. Marco and Lizzy were doing the twist on the dance floor, seeing who could go lowest. Despite her recent top-heaviness, she won by quite a bit. Esteban and Nora, who stood about a head taller than him, appeared to be having a serious conversation. She might have been interrogating him. Uh oh.

Sam and I had the same thought. "I better go save that poor young man before Nora castrates him," he offered, while I laughed.

Marco saw me sitting by myself and came over to grab me. He, Lizzy and I finished the song doing the 3-way bump. I couldn't remember ever having so much fun, feeling so free, and loving a moment so dearly.

The announcement was made that the speeches were going to begin and we should take our seats. I was grateful for the break. A girl who lived in clogs and sandals had a hard time in the stilettos I was pretending I could walk in.

"I would tell you that you can really move, but I've seen you at your best, and know that this is nothing."

"Marco!" I was concerned that someone had heard us, but pleased to receive his compliment. "You better stop that, mister. We have to make it through this wedding."

"Do we?"

"Ughhh," I said, feigning exasperation.

The speeches were heartfelt and beautiful. The fathers, both of whom spoke, had the whole audience in tears. Apparently, they were childhood friends, reunited when their own children fell in love. I couldn't stop crying, which left Marco searching for tissues. By the look on his face, he was touched and entertained by my emotional outpouring.

The speeches seemed to be coming to a close when Esteban escorted Lizzy to the microphone. Nora and I looked at each other, horrified. *What is that crazy girl going to do?*

"Hola mi amigos! Me llamo Elizabetta. Sorry but that's all the Spanish I know," she said with a sweet laugh.

I didn't blink or breathe, so surprised and concerned about what was happening. Everyone else seemed fine, but I couldn't understand. Lizzy didn't know any of these people. What was she doing up there?

"I just met the bride and groom recently, but I have to say they define love. This whole room is so full of love. I can't even describe it well. Maybe if I were a poet... but I'm not." Again one of Lizzy's signature giggles.

"Since I didn't know them that well, I had a hard time picking out a wedding gift, so I thought something else might work. When I was growing up, my sisters used to dance around the house and sing to me. It kept me from crying, I guess. Since they have shown me what love is I guess this song is for them too. And of course, my Stebby," and she blew Esteban a kiss.

She looked over at the band and gave them a 4-beat.

I couldn't believe what my baby sister was doing. How had my sisters gotten such balls? Both of them. I must have gotten all their share of self-doubt.

Nora certainly received a less than normal share of insecurity. She'd been sure of herself for as long as I could remember. When she and Sam met, it was as if they both fell under the same spell, simultaneously. There was no doubt that they would be together. She never appeared in any way uncertain that their feelings were real or that they were meant to be together.

In stark contrast, I'd questioned every relationship I'd ever had. Either thinking it was more than it was, or downplaying it if it was too intense. I'd never gotten it quite right. Would this be my time to know? Could I let go of all my mental gymnastics and use my instincts to experience this man? The magic of our night together filled my thoughts. This was indisputable.

All of me, why not take all of me.

Lizzy was singing our favorite song. Tears pressed against my eyes, again. Of all of us, she had inherited the most of Mom's talent and the crowd couldn't believe what they were hearing. Shocked delight filled the expressions of everyone in the room. She could easily have pursued a professional career, but chose not to. No interest, I supposed. But singing made her happy. And now it was making all these people happy too.

I glanced over at Esteban, who I thought would start crying, even before me. That guy had fallen for my sister, hook, line and sinker. Whatever her spell was, it landed on the right guy. Without knowing the words, he was even trying to sing along.

Nora and Sam were happily singing. She and I knew this song forward and backwards, and Sam had been the unwitting recipient of our many impromptu song and dance concerts.

The bride and groom rose to dance. They extended the song out, and Lizzy did some amazing jazz riffs. That girl was killing it.

I turned my gaze slowly to Marco. Instead of watching Lizzy, he was looking at me, smiling.

"This is your song. I remember from the other night. How wonderful."

"Yes, she's amazing, isn't she?"

"Yes. Both of your sisters are superstars. It must be hard."

I didn't quite understand what he was saying and gave him a confused look.

"It must be so hard to be as nearly perfect as they are, and still pale in comparison to you."

"Aren't you overflowing with compliments tonight?"

Marco tenderly swept the hair off my cheek and held my face.

"I'm overflowing... yes... with something..."

His expression was very serious.

"What is it?" I was terrified to ask but did anyway.

"You don't know? I thought you would."

I was sure I stopped breathing. "Tell me... please."

"Yes. I will..."

The room erupted in applause, shocking both of us back into the moment. I could only imagine what he was about to say to me.

Marco, Esteban and the groom's other brothers invite everyone up to the penthouse after the reception. The guys had ordered a beautiful spread of snacks and champagne, expecting a significant crowd. At least fifty people, mostly family members, came up, and the party lasted until the wee hours. I was greeted as if I was the woman of the house, and I played the part. Marco and I were the consummate host and hostess.

His friends were wonderful to me, treating me as if I was already family, and forgiving my terrible Spanish. Apparently Marco had told them a bit about me, or the news had spread some other way, and there was a great deal of interest about me and my sisters.

Lizzy received the most attention, after her superb performance, and loved every minute of it. She would have made a stupendous celebrity.

As the crowd began to disperse, Lizzy disappeared first - I'm sure she was absolutely exhausted. She let me know that she'd be staying a few extra days with Esteban. Then Nora let me know that she and Sam were going to take a few extra days as well, maybe going up to the Grand Canyon or Hoover Dam.

I wished I could have stayed too but I needed to get home to my girls. I missed them so much. And Marco had to be in New York the rest of the week, so I would have been on my own anyway.

Nora and Sam slipped out, followed by a slow trickle of the remaining guests. There were a few stragglers left as Marco took my hand and led me to the bedroom. We turned to face each other and he wrapped his arms around me, holding me securely, swaying slightly as if the music was still playing.

"Thank you for coming with me tonight."

"Thank you for inviting me. Inviting all of us. It was a spectacular wedding."

"Because you were there."

"Marco, you say the most beautiful things. Sometimes I just can't believe my ears."

"I know you doubt me."

"I don't... that's not what I meant."

"You doubt what is happening here, between us. But what will you do when I have fallen in love with you?" Out of left field, this one stopped my heart and froze my body. "Will you believe me then?"

I buried my head in his neck, afraid to look at him. I couldn't speak.

"I know... it's not a question you can answer, is it?"

There was nothing I could say.

Marco stepped behind me and began to slowly unzip my dress. His hands, breath and mouth filled the spaces where the shimmery blue fabric had fallen away. He moved down my body, until he landed on his knees.

"That ass of yours, Bella... it's quite miraculous, you know."

"Glad you like it." I was surprised at my ability to be humorous considering all that was happening in my body.

Then he bit me. The sting mingled with the pleasure and I gasped. He was biting, licking and sucking me like a peach. "You are going to let me have it one day, aren't you?"

It was my intention to answer, but then he slipped one of his fingers between my cheeks and began to slide it along the length of me. A shiver covered my body.

"Marco..."

His fingers kept moving, eventually finding the warmest, wettest part of me. Just a few strokes dissolved me, but instead of lingering there, he began to move his finger back toward my bottom, and paused.

"You can have anything you want, Marco. Any part of me you want." He could have entered me right then, no part of me off limits to him.

"I'm so glad you said that, Bella." Instead of pressing the finger that was massaging my bottom, he removed his hand completely. I gasped again, because of its absence.

He took my hips and spun me around, so that his face was now directly in front of my pussy. I began to understand what he was referring to.

He ran his nose and lips down the small line of hair that ended at the opening of my lips. My knees buckled and I realized I was still in my heels.

"I can't stand up, Marco."

"Yes…"

He moved the pooled fabric of my dress away from my ankles and helped me out of my shoes, kissing my feet and ankles. It gave me time to contemplate what he wanted to do, the one thing I'd stopped him from doing. Before now.

As he rose off his knees, and kissed me, I knew I couldn't possibly resist him, no matter how self-conscious I felt.

We moved to the bed like a couple approaching the shore, stepping in with anticipation, enjoying every wave and tickle of the warm water.

I laid myself down, knowing I was going to allow him where I previously had not. Beginning with my toes again, he kissed, licked and sucked nearly my entire body, until landing between my legs. My hands instinctively began to push him away, even though my body was on fire for him.

"Let me taste you, amor. Let me please you…"

I released the tension in my arms, and his head descended. All I felt was the warmth of his breath, as he kissed me lightly. This was such a scary, vulnerable place for me – I hardly allowed any men there – and I couldn't bear to look at him.

"I knew I would love how you smell and how you taste. I imagined being with you, like this. Look at me, amor."

I opened my eyes to see him smiling, with his eyes. His tongue moved over me, slowly, like a child with an ice cream cone. I wanted so much to turn away, to stop the rush of what I was feeling, but I couldn't. He continued to stroke me with his tongue, as he had done with his fingers. It was working. My body responded, despite the situation in my mind.

He increased the pressure, and drew me strongly into his mouth. His tongue pushed inside me while the brush of his whiskers tickled my skin. Then somehow his thumb replaced his tongue, and he was sucking on me tenderly and insistently. When his thumb pressed upward, from the inside, I knew what the outcome will be.

"Marco! Oh my God!" Was it really possible that I was coming like this?

Not only possible, but undeniable. I found myself floating in some other world, unable to stop the waves of pleasure coursing through me.

He nuzzled the inside of my thighs as I recovered, whispering 'Mi amor' between each kiss. I was incredulous when I felt the heat rise again. His slick thumb moved downward, now between my cheeks where he had begun this exploration.

"Do you like me touching you there?"

"Yes, Marco. I do." It was very hard to speak.

"Good," he said as gently pressed the tip of his finger inside me.

My body, which he seemed to know better than I did, had left my domain and become his instrument. Layers of self-protection and shame dissolved under his hands and mouth.

And then he spoke the thoughts in my head.

"I want to be everywhere in your body at the same time."

He rose onto his knees and wrapped his arms around my waist to pull me up to him. When I reached down to wrap my hand around his cock, he closed his eyes and moaned. He sat back onto his heels and placed me astride him, as I had been the first night we stayed together. He expertly guided my body onto him, and moved me, with his arms around my back. The shock of feeling him enter me had not faded at all since the first time, and watching him try to manage his arousal nearly brought me to the edge again.

We were face-to-face, as bare as two people can be. There was nowhere I could look other than his loving eyes.

He stayed present and patient as I found my way, battling my demons and letting my body experience him.

My moans grew louder, as he remained quiet and controlled, waiting for me.

"Tell me what I can do for you, Bella. What makes you happy?"

"You seem to already know what to do."

"Let yourself go, amor. Let yourself hear what my body is telling you."

We rolled in an orgasm that moved back and forth between the two of us for minutes. When I wanted to break contact, he took my face and made me see him. This was an intimacy I'd never experienced.

We filled the night with an entire sexual repertoire, finding each other over and over again. My previous difficulty with orgasms during sex faded into memory as he showed me how easy it could be.

He succeeded at demonstrating with his attention and passion what I couldn't hear in words. I trusted him with my body, and now my heart.

"I believe you," I whispered as he drifted off to sleep.

18

SHAKY GROUND

The morning came in a flurry, with both of us flying out, him to New York and me back home to San Francisco.

In the limo to the airport, a whisper of insecurity filled my body. Would this be the end?

I was compelled to ask. "What's next, Marco?"

"What's next... hmmm. Well, we spend these next few days apart, which will be terrible, then I return home on Friday and we... begin."

"We begin?"

"Yes, Monique. We begin the rest of our lives."

This was utterly romantic, but I was looking for something much more concrete.

"Marco, perhaps it's too soon to make declarations, but I kind of need to know what... what's happening with us."

"What would you like to happen with us, Bella?"

"I should have known you would turn it around." I sighed. "Fine, I'll go first. I want to see you, to be involved with you. I am... not interested in seeing anyone else." That had been excruciatingly difficult.

Marco smiled. "That was hard for you. Thank you for doing it anyway."

I wish I could have controlled how transparent I appeared to be. "And you?"

"I am yours, Monique. There is no one else in my life. Just us."

I let myself exhale, happy that the moment was over.

The scene at the airport unfolded like a bad romantic comedy, neither of us wanting to let go of the other's hand. I spent the entire plane ride reliving my fantastical weekend. Could this really have happened? It didn't seem possible.

It didn't matter that I was alone - no sisters, no Marco - I was plenty busy with my thoughts. Landing home began the frenzy of real life, and my arms filled with my beloved girls before I knew it. They wanted to know everything, and I told them some. They knew me so well, I couldn't hide anything. But I did try to tone it down.

I told them about Nora's wonderful award ceremony and how we got invited to a wedding and how aunt Lizzy sang in front of everyone. I only mentioned that we had met some nice people – men – briefly.

Marco called as soon as he landed. "I miss you. I can't believe you were in my arms just a few hours ago and now we are thousands of miles apart. How are the girls?"

"Happy to see me. And I'm happy to see them too. We have a very full and busy week."

He had to run off to a dinner meeting, and we promised to talk the next day. "Buenos noches, mi amor."

We spoke every day, sometimes several times a day. He asked about my progress in my restaurant endeavors and I asked about the big project he was working on in New York. I couldn't wait for him to get home over the weekend. We had a big date in the city all set up.

On Friday afternoon, right before he was supposed to get on the plane, he called. He sounded terrible, and there was quite a bit of background noise. Like a train station. Or hospital.

"Where are you?"

"I'm sorry Monique, I won't be able to fly back tonight."

He sounded awful. As if he was in shock. "Are you alright?"

"Yes, but there's something here I have to take care of. I need to call you back later, okay?"

"Are the boys alright?" All these thoughts were running through my head: There has been an accident. He was in trouble. Something really, really bad had happened.

"Yes, they're fine. I'm sorry, I have to go now."

I didn't hear from him for two days. The nightmare began to take shape. He was a criminal, a drug lord maybe. He had a wife and children in New York that he neglected to tell me about. The stories came nonstop from my vivid imagination. I couldn't understand what would have caused a man to completely disappear.

I felt as if I was losing my mind, filled with desperation and rage. A burning ache blossomed in the middle of my body where I antici-pated his disappearance would live. All I heard in my head was, *You knew this was going to happen. It was all too good to be true. He's probably some sort of psychopath, on the run from the law, and you just got dumped.*

When I saw his number pop up on my phone, I was honestly shocked. I was sure he had disappeared.

"Hello," I answered in as neutral a tone as I could muster.

"Mi amor. I'm sorry I haven't been able to call."

"What's going on, Marco?" *Stay calm, stay calm.*

"I can't really talk now. It's okay. Please don't worry."

"I wish you could tell me. I don't understand."

"I know. But I have to go now. I will try to get home in a few days. Then we can talk. Goodnight."

A few more days of stewing and I started to unravel. My sisters asked me what was going on and I couldn't even tell them. I had no idea, except that my magic carpet had been brutally pulled out from under me. I could hardly do anything but worry, projecting the worst possible scenarios.

It was two more days before I heard from him again. I tried very hard not to sound crazed on the other end of the line.

"How are you doing?" I asked.

"I'm alright. I'm coming home tonight."

"Oh, good. Have a safe flight." I knew he could hear the sharpness in my voice. Anger was the only thing holding me together at that point.

"I know you are angry darling. It's just... we will talk when I get home." I heard the flight announcement. "I will call you. Bye."

I couldn't tell if it was rage or despair fueling the breakdown I was destined to have. Something big was going on. I knew it. I cried the rest of the night.

I didn't want to fall asleep, afraid of missing his call, but it was unnecessary. I didn't hear from Marco again until the next afternoon.

If I ever see him again, I screamed at no one, *I am going to let him know exactly how unacceptable this behavior is! I will not tolerate being treated like this!*

Part of me wanted to believe that he would stroll into my house with a perfectly good excuse that would inspire my immediate forgiveness. The rest of me knew that something traumatic was about to happen. I prepared myself for the worst and began to justify the whole experience.

The story I rewrote sounded like this: It was a fabulously romantic and sexy affair. Like a summer fling, but shorter. I couldn't expect that someone would fall in love with me that quickly. What I was feeling was just lust. Just like Nora said. It had been a long time, and I just wasn't used to having sex. Great sex. It was all merely an excess of hormones causing my delusion, which would soon pass. He was not the man for me, especially if he had all this drama in his life. No, certainly not. I had more than enough drama already.

I told myself I wouldn't take his call, if it ever came. I'd make him wait and see how he liked it. Then he would know. Then he'd come running back. The irrationality of my theory made no difference to me.

There was no way I could keep myself from picking up the phone when his number appeared.

"Can you meet me this afternoon? I can be at your house in thirty minutes."

"I can't. I have the girls."

"Please, Monique. I really need to see you. Just for a little while. Please."

I wanted to lash out and scream at him, all the awful things I'd been thinking. I wanted to say *NO, I won't! I am so angry with you I don't think I could even look at your face!*

Instead I said, "Fine. Meet me at the Colonial Cafe on Sutter. You said half an hour?" There was no way I was going to let him in my house.

"Thank you my darling. I'll see you then."

Was I about to be dumped to my face? What do you wear to a dumping? Or was I about to find out that he was a serial killer? Time moved like cold molasses.

The girls were fine with my heading out for a little while. In fact, they were a bit frightened by my state of mind, and suggested I take a walk. Brilliant idea.

The cafe was only around the corner from me, but I walked for nearly the entire thirty minutes, talking to myself, getting stared at by the homeless people, and praying. Praying that the worst that I had imagined wouldn't come true. It couldn't.

Marco was already in the cafe when I arrived. His normally disheveled hair was especially so. He looked tired. And sad.

He popped up when he saw me and wrapped his arms around me. Funny greeting for a dumping, I thought. He looked at me and tried to kiss me, but I turned my cheek. He lingered there, and then crossed to the other. All the while searching my face, my frozen face, for any signs of what to expect.

"How are you?" he asked.

"Well... how I am is not really the subject of this meeting, is it?" Crushed glass poured from my throat. I couldn't help myself from trying to hurt him.

He dropped his head and took several deep breaths. It was killing me, waiting for him to say something.

"Are you going to tell me what's going on?" That sounded a bit hysterical, I had to admit. I was on the verge of bursting into flames.

"Yes." Then nothing again. For too long.

I closed my eyes and breathed. I had to keep control of myself. I wasn't going to show him my weakness, my hurt, my longing. I was not going to be afraid.

"There's a situation in New York that I haven't told you about. It's a bit strange, and hard to explain, and I was afraid you wouldn't understand. I know you've been feeling… uncertain about me… and us. I didn't know how you'd react over the phone. I was afraid…"

His pauses were killing me.

"But now something has happened. And you deserve to know." He ran his fingers through his hair, trying to get it out of his eyes. Then he reached for my hand, which I pulled away.

I couldn't let him touch me, as that would've cracked the whisper-thin container holding me together.

He looked at me to say something but I stared straight ahead. Cool and composed. Yes, that's what I was.

"A few years ago, I was in a relationship with someone. We were together for about two years. It was fairly serious, but we broke up. It was-"

"Why?"

"Why?" He seemed to not understand my question.

"Why did you break up?"

"It was complicated. I knew how I wanted to feel but I didn't. Feel it. And she wanted to get more serious, have children. I knew I did not want to have children. With her. But we loved each other." He looked at me, perhaps regretting that statement. Did I flinch? I kept building up my container.

"We separated. It was very hard at first, but eventually we were on good terms again."

"How long ago was that?"

"The breakup?"

"Yes." You asshole, I wanted to say.

"Just over a year ago. And then, Carla, that's her name, got sick. She was diagnosed with bone cancer. And it was very bad. They said she only had a few months to live. She was very scared and asked for my help. I agreed.

So for the past several months, I've been spending time in New York, helping her with everything. And she had been doing remarkably well. Everyone thought she would recover. It was a real miracle. And then, this week, it got bad again. The cancer spread everywhere, even though we all thought she was doing so much better. Really it was getting much worse.

Carla's in the hospital and we don't know what will happen. It's not good."

I realized I was hearing about another human being's life and death situation, but all I could think of was one thing. "Did you become lovers again?"

"No. Not in that way."

"Not in that way?"

"We still had love for each other, have love, but it is not in that way... it's hard to describe."

"It sounds like you are having an intimate relationship with her."

He was growing frustrated at my responses. "Yes, Monique, nursing someone to their death is an intimate relationship. But it is not as you think."

This man magically knew exactly what would trigger me – betrayal, half-truths, infidelity. "How do you know what I think?" The seething and toxicity sprayed out of me. I was about to boil over.

"I don't," Marco said, the exhaustion spilling from his words and his body. "I don't know what you think. But I know you are angry. And perhaps you have a right to be. I just didn't know how to explain this to you. Do you see how complicated it is? And when we were in Vegas, I still thought that Carla would have a full recovery. Then the situation would no longer be an issue."

"So you would have never told me about it?" I was incredulous. The leaking grew faster and stronger.

"I just knew it would not go over well. I know you were scared about what was happening with us. This would be too much to handle."

"You have no idea what I can handle. I'm very strong you know!! And I REALLY don't like being treated like a child, or being lied to."

"I wasn't trying to do either of those things. And now I'm telling you everything, in the hope that you can just hear me. It's been very difficult..."

"You didn't go to New York on business at all, did you?"

"Monique, that's ridiculous. Listen, I don't know if I can handle any more but I have to go back in a couple of days. I just wanted you to know."

I took this as a personal offense. He should have been groveling at that point, begging me to take him back. Instead he was basically telling me to back off and let him do his thing with his dying girl-friend. I couldn't stand one more minute of it.

"You don't have to worry about me. I'm fine. You don't owe me anything either. Best of luck with your situation in New York. I hope Carla gets better. And don't worry about leaving. There's nothing more for you here."

I walked out the door, giving a brief glance back through the glass in the front of the cafe. Marco sat, mouth wide open, like a little boy who had just lost his puppy. I wished him nothing but suffering.

19

LOCKDOWN

My phone began to ring before I even walked in my front door. I didn't answer it.

I kicked myself that I didn't follow my first instinct that this man was too good to be true. He belonged in the same category as all the others – liars, cheaters, the ones who claimed to love me but never did.

I went into full lockdown, beginning a period of survival living, taking care of only what absolutely needed to be done, for myself, for my career, for my family. It was nose-to-the-grindstone time, with clear goals always in sight, and the fortress fortified. I would not let this destroy me.

I had to tell my sisters and Sam, so that they would know not to ask about Marco. They couldn't understand what had happened and I couldn't explain it. I forbade them from talking about it. I had a feeling that Lizzy was getting information from Esteban, but it didn't matter. The subject was closed.

The reality was that I was so ashamed at how I behaved in front of them, when we were in Las Vegas, like a lovesick teenager. It was embarrassing to completely lose myself like that. I would not let it happen again.

Marco continued to call and text and email, and I refused to respond. My anger grew a life of its own as his messages accumulated on my phone. I was determined not to be felled by this monster again.

Until the nights, when I listened to his messages and cried myself to sleep. Every night. I thought I'd never reach the bottom of my sadness. I wanted to be swallowed whole by the darkness of what had been lost. I could find no way out of it or through it, so every night I just sat in it.

I listened to his false protestations of love for me and his insincere apologies for not telling me what was going on. He became more and more angry as I refused to talk to him. His messages became more desperate and accusatory. And finally, there came resignation. He sounded desperately sad, and it made me happy. I wanted him to feel even just the smallest part of the agony I'd been through.

Time passed because it had to, not from any will on my part to move on. I went through the motions of my life, working day and night, taking care of my family, not taking care of myself. I felt empty and broken, like scraps of garbage floating on a dirty stream after a storm.

My body carried me around, but other than that held no use for me. It was cold, dry and empty. Maybe I looked the same on the outside but it was just the shell of me. I felt both untethered and heavily weighted down. There was no place that didn't hurt.

I relived our moments together over and over until I wasn't sure if the memories were real or rewritten. I'd been betrayed in the most poignant way for me and I couldn't let it go.

Looking at my own behavior, how irrational I was, made me feel even worse. I'd only just met this man and spent a few days with him. That was all. It wasn't the ending of a ten year marriage, or the loss of a beloved brother and parents, all of which I'd survived. But this felt impossible to transcend. I couldn't decipher the intensity of my response.

The day finally came when I was brought face to face with something behind the impenetrable wall of my anger. With the help of a friend, my own bad behavior was revealed.

Emile did not ever spare me the truth, no matter how difficult, and this situation was no exception.

"Monique, you are behaving like an insane woman. You must put your head back on if you want to get anywhere."

"I've just been deeply hurt, Emile. Give me a break. I think I'm actually doing pretty damn well, considering."

"You are wrong. You are not doing well at all. You look like shit. Are you even sleeping?"

"Thanks a lot."

"What did this man do that was so wrong? He exhibited his humanity? He revealed that he is just as flawed as the rest of us? I don't understand why you won't even speak to him. I think you are being ridiculous. You are a grown woman, for god's sake. Start acting like it."

I was actually shocked by Emile's accusation. "I can't believe you're not supporting me here, Emile. Especially you. Especially after what happened with us."

"Marco is not me, Monique. Don't blend all your relationship experiences into this one situation. It sounds like he's trying to be a good guy. Don't punish him for the mistakes the rest of us have made."

I'd been so mired in my own suffering that my pettiness and cruelty were invisible to me. Until I heard what Emile said to me, then my anger turned into shame, and I realized how badly I behaved.

My disgrace, instead of creating an opening, kept me even further from any possibility with Marco. My deep humiliation at making a situation that must have been grueling for him all about my own selfishness and insecurity now pointed to my current unworthiness. This was the final turn of the sword.

I couldn't find my way around this new set of emotions, so I kept pretending he was a monster - a liar, cheat, manipulative, deceitful, terrible person. This story kept me just within the line of complete collapse.

I had big work to do and couldn't afford to be taken down by another failed love affair. I'd gathered more and more evidence that the world of the heart was not a safe place for me. It was best for me to stay in the world of logic and work, not feelings and emotions.

I couldn't ignore all the love around me and all these nearly perfect couples - Nora and Sam, now Lizzy and Esteban. I was the only one who kept failing, who couldn't find the love I wanted. Or singlehandedly destroyed it.

But I did have my daughters. I told myself that maybe that was the love I would experience in this lifetime. Maybe it wasn't for me to be loved by a man in the way of my dreams because I received so much love from my children.

Every day there was a new theory as to why I'd ended up in that situation, alone. With Marco, I experienced something completely different. It was nearly impossible to admit that now, as I tried my best to discount the experience. I used my intellectual prowess to explain my feelings away. I'd succeeded before in my life by turning off the feelings that were too much, or not right. I could do it again.

This went on for weeks, until the tears became less frequent. The shell I had built was getting stronger. I made good progress in my work at the restaurant, feeling confident again. Marco's calls came less and less frequently, allowing the wound to heal. Or so I thought.

I received an invitation from Nora. I wasn't strictly in the mood for a family dinner, but I supposed it beat sitting at home alone. My social life had shrunken back to nothing after the debacle with Marco. Even thinking his name brought sharp pains to the base of my throat, as if I was being drowned. Still, being with my family could be nice. They were worried about me and I wanted to show them that I was just fine.

I entered the house, tired and defensive. "Hey, girls. I'm here."

I heard voices in the living room and headed that way. Everyone was standing up, and as I scanned the room I noticed an extra person. Marco.

It took a minute to compute what was going on.

"Monique..." he said softly.

"What the fuck? What are you doing here?" And then it dawned on me that my sisters had set me up. Again. They had invited me over to trick me into talking to him. Rage filled my body.

I looked right at Nora. "Are you kidding me? You are doing this to me again? I can't believe you." I turned around for the door. Sam and Marco ran right behind me. The girls were too scared, I supposed.

Sam caught my arm first. "Listen here young lady," he said in that fatherly tone he sometimes adopted with us. "You aren't going anywhere. You are going to sit your ass down in there and listen to us. If you don't want to listen to Marco, you're going to listen to me. This has gone way too far and it's time that somebody did something about it. And that somebody is me."

He brought me back to the room and sat down next to me on the couch, holding my hand the whole time. Marco sat across from us, sandwiched between Nora and Lizzy.

"I'm so sorry, Nik. I know this is really hard for you. We didn't want to make it so hard. But we didn't know what else to do. We just want you to be happy again. I want you to be happy. Like me." Lizzy spoke between deep sobs.

I prepared my response to my sister. Something angry and accusatory. Even insulting. The words were brewing, but Nora cut me off. She wasn't nearly as soft or kind as our baby sister.

"You can't keep running away every time something important happens to you, Monique. Your life will continue to be a series of things you did not do and did not try. You can be with him or not. It really doesn't have anything to do with me, with us. But you can't just hide and pretend that you're done. Just listen to him. That's all we're asking."

"Really Nora? I thought it was just a good fuck!"

I didn't let her answer as I continued.

"I know you're always so interested in demonstrating to me how shitty my life is, but you didn't have to do it in front of him. Since when did shame and ridicule become part of the plan to make some-one's life better? I can't believe that you would do this to me. I've been taking care of myself all along here. You act as if I'm a child that constantly needs to be redirected. What gives you the right? I get to choose who I want to be with. Not you!"

Nobody spoke. They knew I was right. But Sam still held me in my seat. I was not allowed to go.

Softly, quietly, Marco spoke. "I asked them to help me. I begged them. I was desperate and didn't know what else to do. I know how close you are with your sisters and Sam. You trust them. And they trusted me. Maybe I could convince you too, if I had a chance. That's all I wanted Monique. A chance to be heard."

"They trust you because they don't really know you."

"Do you really believe that I am some sort of monster? That nothing was true?"

I couldn't answer that.

"Regardless, this is not about you. It's about my family's need to interfere in my life. And now to humiliate me."

"They are not here for YOU Monique! They are here for ME! I am the one who needed the help, whose life is in a shitpile right now. Don't you get it?"

"No, I don't get it."

"You wouldn't talk to me."

"That's because you're a fucking liar and I don't talk to liars."

Marco's head dropped and the air left his body. "I'm sorry," he said just above a whisper.

Looking up, he said it a bit louder, "I'm sorry. I fucked up. I should have told you from the very beginning. But how? It's just such a strange situation and I was sure you wouldn't understand and I was right. I was so fucking scared Monique that you would do exactly what you did - walk away from me."

"I didn't walk away Marco. You abandoned me."

And there it was, the steaming hot mess of my fears, stinking up the middle of the room. My weakness, my neediness, my shame.

Sam looked at me understandingly, nodded, then stood up. "We're leaving now," signaling to the girls. "We'll be upstairs. Please take all the time you need. We love you very much, Nik." He kissed my forehead.

I watched them all shuffle out of the room. The only one looking back was Lizzy whose face was filled with pleading and despair.

"Please, Nik. Just listen to him."

I had to look away from her, in order to stay calm.

We didn't speak for several minutes. A torrent of emotion on the verge of breaking pressed me and I just needed to keep the whole thing contained. I'd shed so many tears over this man already. No more.

Marco stood up, walked around the table and sat next to me. Where Sam had been.

His voice shook as he began to speak. "When I saw you at the airport, just smiling and daydreaming, something happened to me. And then our weekend together was something out of a fairy tale. I still don't understand how it was all possible but I couldn't deny it. And I was going to do everything in my power to keep you around.

I didn't abandon you, but I know why you say that. You thought I lied to you, and chose someone else over you. I didn't handle the whole thing well. I know. It was stupid and I made this happen. This whole mess.

But I can't accept that you don't want to be with me. I think that's a lie. You're scared. I get it. But everything that happened between us was true. Everything I said to you about how I feel, is true."

I looked up at him for the first time. Was he crying?

The dam broke and all my composure washed away on a river of tears. All the hurt I'd been trying to contain, just to keep going, flooded out of me. I couldn't even think about composure. I was taken down and under.

He tried to put his arms around me, to comfort me, but I pushed him away. I couldn't get up, but I moved myself to the far end of the couch away from him, put my head down and cried. I imagined he would just tire of this scene and leave. But he stayed, inching himself closer to me.

I was so tired, drained by the act of holding up an empty body all this time without him. I was tired of pretending that everything was fine and I was just as competent and content as ever. I was tired of being the liar.

Marco put his hand on my back, then slowly moved it around my waist and pulled me into him. I was too exhausted to resist. The tears kept flowing as he whispered, "I'm sorry. I'm sorry, Bella. I'm so sorry."

Although pain still coursed through my body, I finally felt like I could breathe again. As if I had come out from dark cold water into the warmth and the light. It felt right to be in his arms. I couldn't deny it, even though I want to.

On a stream of tears, the words began to flow. "It *was* like a fairy tale, Marco. How we met and the time we spent together. It was perfect. But nothing's perfect and all my ideas about it being too good to be true were right. You have this whole other life, with another woman and you didn't tell me. You let me believe that... it was something else with us. But it isn't. You are with her in a very intimate way."

He moved me slightly away from him so he could look at my face. Shaking his head, he said, "I am with Carla because I promised. And I want to be there for her. I am with her as you would be with Emile, if he needed you."

"Emile and I did not have that kind of relationship."

"But you were lovers. And you love each other. What's the difference?"

Nora had said the same thing to me, and I hated hearing it then as much as I hated hearing it at from him.

"I told you about Emile, even though I didn't have to. My relationship with him was never a threat to you."

"*You* know that, but did I? All I could see was this man, who you call your best friend, who you had also been sleeping with. How do you think that sounds, from my perspective? Quite bad, right? But you know that it is different than how it sounds. And I trust you."

The sword entered and turned an inch. I had to close my eyes to absorb my foolishness. He was right. And yet when we were arguing he never threw that in my face, my blatant hypocrisy. Another quarter turn of the blade.

I needed to go somewhere else. Away from this disgrace. "How is Carla doing?"

The question surprised him. "Things are not going well. But she is so strong. I don't really know what to expect, and the doctors don't have anything useful to say. How are you doing? How have you been?"

Strong Monique was finding her way back. I sat up straighter. "I'm okay. It's been very busy, with the magazine and the restaurant and the girls. We're getting Lizzy ready for the baby, too. But that's been nice. Something to look forward to."

"And how are you?" he asked again.

His voice was like a truth serum. "It's been... very hard, Marco. I couldn't believe that my worst nightmares had come true. It was devastating. But I'm strong too, and I can just keep going."

"Without me?"

20

TRUTH PREVAILS

"Yes." I steadied my voice as well as I could.

"I see."

Silence.

"What if I can't keep going without you? What if I just don't want to? What if I know that we are supposed to be together as clearly as I know this is my right hand?" His voice cracked. "What can I do so you will believe me? How can I convince you that... I love you?"

My heart skipped several beats.

"And I believe you love me too. I can feel it in your body when we are together. We are like magnets, Monique. Can't you feel it?"

"You don't know me. You don't know how I feel."

This made him angry. He got up off the couch and started pacing.

"Maybe that's true. The way you're acting toward me now, certainly doesn't make sense. Are you really so scared of having someone know you and love you that you would push me away? You are foretelling your own fate."

"I didn't ask for this!" I yelled up at him, across the room.

I heard myself speak and was disgusted by what was coming out of my mouth. When had I become such a victim? So pathetic?

He stopped pacing. "Don't we all ask for love?"

"I don't know."

"Yes you do! Monique, don't you think you were part of this? That your heart was part of this? Am I that crazy that I imagined what was happening between us? If you were not asking for my love, what were you doing? Playing with me? Just having a bit of fun?"

"That's not fair."

"No, it's not. None of it is fair. We're not here because life is fair. We're here because we experienced something that happens so rarely among two human beings that it's nearly impossible. You make me feel like I made the whole thing up in my head. That it didn't really happen."

"Maybe it wasn't what we thought it was." The lies continued to come out of me. Was I testing him, or myself?

He sighed. "I can't make you love me. I can't make you be with me. You don't have to convince me how strong you are. I get it. You can do anything you want, you can have anything you want. What will you choose?"

I looked at him. What would I choose? I knew that there was still anger in my face. It probably hurt him to look at me, but he held my gaze. He was strong, but I was stronger. I could make him suffer. I could make both of us suffer.

Or I could choose something else.

"I'm sorry," I said.

His face completely changed from anger to shock. "Why?" he asked.

"I got blindsided by the situation with Carla. I don't blame you for not telling me. All I've shown you is what a hysterical woman I am, from the very beginning. Marco, I feel so ashamed at so much of what I've done. I was out of my mind, maybe. But that's no excuse. I wanted to punish you for not choosing me. For choosing her. And no matter how much it hurt me, I was going to hurt you back.

I feel so vulnerable with you. And it scares the shit out of me. I made myself ripe for betrayal. Everything was surreal, and my reactions were not reasonable or rational. I just couldn't reconcile our time together in Vegas, then what happened when we came home.

It's all so humiliating. That's the best word I can think of. The situation with Carla was the perfect excuse."

"For what?"

"For me to convince myself that I couldn't possibly... that I had to leave before getting left. I just couldn't believe this would have a happy ending."

Marco listened and watched as he stood in front of the fireplace with his hands in his pockets. He looked like a confused little boy. My heart melted.

"What do you want me to do, Monique? Just tell me. I'll do it."

"I don't know."

"Please tell me."

"I don't know, Marco."

"You don't know? Really?" He was exasperated. For good reason.

"I want you to be honest with me." This was a good start.

"I can do that. Even when it's hard."

He walked toward me. I stood up, not sure where the courage was coming from, but I said it – "I want you to love me." There it was. Out in the open. Finally.

Marco took a long slow breath. I hoped he was taking it in. "Do you want to love me back? Do you... love me back?"

"Yes." It had to come out. I couldn't stop it.

Neither of us moved. He put his head in his hands. I could hardly look at him, so scared of what his reaction would be. I was glad his face was hidden.

"My God," I heard him say. What did that mean? Had he not expected me to say yes? I wanted to dissolve into myself. Where could I hide?

"Please don't hide. Not now." I looked up to find him watching me. I couldn't read what was on his face. Was it... sadness?

"I'm not hiding Marco. I'm talking to you."

"Why does it scare you so much?"

"Because it's overwhelming. And it's fast. And it's undeniable. Because I can pretend, but I can't hide."

Then it came rushing out of him. "I am so in love with you it intoxicates me. I walk around in this new world where everything is different, better, because of you. I miss you when we are apart and don't want to let go of you when we're together. If you just let me love you, and I promise I will do the best I can, I won't give you anything to be afraid of."

I walked over to him. He took my hands and put them to his chest, over his heart. "If we need to start over, I can do that."

"We don't need to start over. I don't want to start over. I want to start from here."

His lips lingered as he kissed my hands. "I was scared too... to tell you how I felt, because I knew it would scare you away. But I love you Monique. I love you..."

I kissed his lips as he spoke. It felt like an eternity since I'd had his mouth on mine. The electricity was still there, just as I had remembered it. My body and my heart said yes to him, loud and clear. My mind whispered, love him.

For a long time, we held each other, afraid to move too much. I missed him so much I could feel it in my bones and my flesh, as if blood began to flow again through my body. I wanted to stay there, in his arms, for the rest of eternity.

Footsteps, then a small voice. "Can we come down now?"

"Yes," we said simultaneously.

Lizzy saw us together and instantly started to cry. "Oh Nik, you did it! I'm so happy for you. You belong together. Everyone can see that. I love you too, Marco. I'm so glad you asked me for help. You two apart is like the sun and moon not speaking or something."

"I'm not sure the sun and moon have a speaking relationship, Lizzy," from the voice of logic.

"Nora!" scolded Sam.

"Okay, okay. Just a joke. Who's hungry?"

I wasn't hungry for food. I was full from the certainty of my being with Marco. Everything he said was right. Everything. I'd been too much of a coward to say, but knew was true.

"You two might not be hungry now. But you should eat anyway.

You might need a little cooling down," Nora said with a raised eyebrow.

"Yes, ma'am," Marco said, obediently. Everyone laughed.

It was nice to be together. All of us, except for Esteban, still in Los Angeles. Lizzy was going to see him in a few days and she couldn't contain her excitement. I kept waiting to hear that they'd eloped, but they were actually taking it slow. Relatively for Lizzy, our ultra-romantic sister.

Unlike my impetuous plunge, they'd not even slept together, and were waiting until after the baby was born. I admired the maturity of their relationship. I was supposed to be the big sister, but I'd acted the most childishly.

We sat at the dinner table for hours, enjoying each other. Marco touched me the entire time, and didn't let me out of his sight. Even when I had to go to the bathroom, he wanted to come in. I refused. He was seriously trying to make up for what happened.

We didn't talk about Carla, or what we were going to do about it, but I knew we could work it out. Together. That was a conversation for another day. That night was about enjoying our reunion.

My sisters and Sam each took me to the side to apologize for what they'd done. They felt desperate and sad for me. My anger had dissolved, and I apologized for making it so hard for everyone. They promised no more interventions, and I promised no more cause.

"Are you guys going to stay over?" asked Lizzy excitedly. "I am! You definitely should. Then Nik can make us her famous breakfast in the morning."

"Oh really?"

"I think it sounds like a great idea. It's late and who wants to drive all the way back into the city?" said Marco.

"Yay!" Lizzy exclaimed.

"I suppose," I said, pretending resignation. "Sam, did you stock the fridge?"

"What do you think? I knew you were coming."

"I really wish you guys weren't so sneaky. It doesn't suit you," I said with a smirk.

We settled back into the living room, the men built a fire and Nora whipped up some hot chocolate with and without fortification.

As the evening came to a close, the reality of the night brought back a nervousness I hadn't felt in so long. I led Marco up to the guest room, the one I always stayed in, my body shaking as I thought of being with him. I hadn't thought I would ever feel him next to me again.

"Are you cold?"

"No. Not really. I think I'm nervous."

"Me too."

I was shocked to hear him say that. I'd been so absorbed in what a big deal this was for me, that I'd forgotten that he was going through the same thing.

"I missed you so much Monique. I felt like a broken man. And I didn't know how things were going to go tonight. I didn't know if you would ever forgive me, or want to be with me again."

"I didn't either. Thank you for not giving up. I know it would have been so easy to walk away from me – all my messiness, and craziness. To imagine yourself so much better off. I wouldn't have blamed you."

"I wish you could see what I see, Nik. I don't see a crazy lady. I see someone whose heart is so big that sometimes it feels like too much. But it's not too much for me. I want all of you, remember?"

It was going to take me a long time to unravel what happened that night. How I cracked the armor around my heart and began to feel again. Maybe it would remain a mystery, like the magic that happened in Las Vegas.

I wrapped my arms around him. "Let's go to bed."

"I thought you'd never ask."

We moved as if for the first time, tentative and watchful. Marco spoke to me the whole time, making sure I was okay. When he entered me, we both stopped.

"Monique, my love, I need you to trust me, okay? I know I screwed up, and gave you reason to doubt me, but I promise I will do everything to make sure that never happens again. But I need to know you're with me. I don't think I could take…"

"I know, Marco. I know." I could hardly stand to see the sadness on his face. "I love you. And I trust you. With everything I have."

He moved gently, and the shell broke irreversibly. *Don't be the idiot that ever lets this man go again,* I heard inside my head.

We were clumsy and silly and in love. There was nothing perfect about our lovemaking other than that we were sharing the experience together. We fit together like magnets, just like he'd said that day at the pool, so long ago.

I thought I would have been the first one up, but I found Sam already in the kitchen, making coffee.

"Good morning sleeping beauty. Feeling better?"

"Yes, thanks for asking. And next time you want to stage an intervention as an excuse for my sister to let you stay over, please use somebody else's life."

"Clearly, I'll have to. I don't anticipate you're going to have any family-worthy drama anymore. But knowing you…"

"You're such an asshole."

"That's why you love me."

"Somebody's got to."

"Yes, yes, I suppose that's true."

I did adore Sam. How straight he was with us and how kind.

"Stop daydreaming, missy. You know how your family gets when they're hungry. You better start cooking."

"Ay ay, cap'n. Are you on toast duty, as usual?"

"You got it."

Sam loved to cook and we made a great pair in the kitchen. He was also one of my biggest fans.

The next set of footsteps - was it Nora or Marco? Definitely not Lizzy as she would easily sleep until the afternoon.

It was Marco.

"Good morning, mi amor," he said after a lingering kiss. "Sam, how are you?"

"Very well, my friend. Very well. And you?"

"Aaaah, I believe somebody turned the world right-side up last night. Everything is perfect."

A smile took over my face. He always had the most beautiful things to say.

I knew I still had some healing to do, and some forgiving of myself and Marco. I had behaved abominably. I accused him of all sorts of monstrosities but it was me who had grown the fangs and the tail.

I got back to my cooking, but found it hard to participate in the festivities. Everyone was so happy that Marco and I had found our way back together. I was too, even though I knew we had a long way to go. *I* had a long way to go.

"Another amazing breakfast, sis!"

"This is amazing. I really love the eggs today, Nik."

"Thanks guys. It's my pleasure."

Marco beamed at me. Perhaps he thought I would have never forgiven him. How foolish I was, to let my perceived rejection taint everything. Thank goodness for his persistence, and my family's intrusiveness. I was immensely grateful.

21

CALM AFTER THE STORM

Marco and I began again, this time more carefully. Over the weeks that passed, we revealed our lives to each other, discovering everything left out in our fast and furious love affair. I happily spent time at his beautiful apartment, when he was in town, and tried not to lose my mind when he went to New York.

He invited me to accompany him, to meet his boys, but I couldn't get myself to go. The idea of meeting Carla, the poor dying woman on whom I had wished such ill will, was horrifying to me. Apparently, she was doing very poorly and wouldn't make it much longer. She was back at home, with the little family she had, and was as comfortable as could be expected.

Marco was infinitely patient with me. I didn't know how he did it. I was unreasonable and demanding and sometimes just plain crazy. He let me be however I needed to be and just held me. I understood why Carla wanted him. He was the perfect companion in times of stress or hardship.

Life seemed to take a turn for the better, in so many ways. Crisis no longer felt imminent and I settled in to a period of contentment. It was an ordinary day when I got the call from my sister.

"Hey No-"

"Listen. I'm on my way to the hospital with Lizzy. She's bleeding. Get here, okay?"

"What?"

"Just get here!"

The phone went quiet. I couldn't believe what I'd just heard. Lizzy had not been feeling well all week. We figured a bit of rest would do her good. What was happening?

I grabbed my headset, got in the car and started making calls. Jeff needed to pick up the girls. I had to call the restaurant about not being able to make my shift. And I called Marco.

"It might be nothing. These things happen all the time and it turns out just fine." Was I trying to convince myself?

"I'll be right there." I knew he would come, and I wanted him to.

Nora texted me that they'd gone to the emergency room, so I stopped there first. Nora stood at the reception desk, speaking to the attendant.

She grabbed my hand when she saw me. Fear clouded her eyes.

"They're taking her up to a room."

"What's going on, Nora? What happened?"

"It was so bad, Nik. She was bleeding all over the place. I have never seen that much blood. This can't be good, Nik."

"You can come with me," said a man in blue scrubs.

We clutched each other's hands as we were led to the main part of the hospital.

"You can go up this elevator to the 14th floor. There is a waiting room just opposite the elevators. Wait there until the doctors are done examining her."

"Thank you."

Neither one of us spoke during the ride up, perhaps imagining the worst and not wanting to share it. The whole situation with Lizzy and the baby had been so strange. How the father was such a jerk and yet she wanted to keep the baby, and then meeting Esteban who was more than happy to help Lizzy raise the baby. I didn't know what to think now, except that I needed my baby sister to be fine. To be perfectly fine.

Nora and I held each other, until Sam joined us. Those few minutes felt like hours passed, and none of us could speak. We all jumped when the doctor finally entered the waiting area.

"Can we see her?" I asked.

"Shortly." He looked too serious.

"What's going on?" Nora asked.

"Your sister is having a miscarriage. It appears there were some serious congenital issues with the fetus, and it spontaneously miscarried. Because it is relatively late in her pregnancy, it can be quite traumatic, physically and emotionally."

"Oh my God!"

"She lost a great deal of blood, so we are going to keep her overnight for close observation."

"Is she in pain?" I asked hesitatingly.

"There might be mild discomfort, but no pain. It's important that she stay calm. This can be a very emotional event, but for her own health, she needs to stay calm."

I hated doctors. What a stupid fucking thing to say to someone. You've just lost your baby, maybe almost your life, but the important thing is to stay calm. I wanted to hit that man.

Sam took us both by the hand and led us toward Lizzy's room. Before we entered, he looked straight at me. "Nik, we don't know how she's going to react. We want to be there for her, okay?"

"Okay." I didn't want to understand why he was saying that only to me, but I knew. I needed to be strong for my baby sister.

We opened the door slowly, to find Lizzy typing into her phone, and crying softly. She smiled when she saw us.

"Hi guys."

"Sweet girl... how are you feeling?"

"Been better. But okay, I guess. It doesn't hurt that much, when you have a miscarriage."

I caught my breath, closed my eyes and composed myself. I stroked her soft golden hair.

"Esteban is about to get on a plane. I told him he didn't have to come up, but he insisted."

"He loves you honey. Of course he's going to come."

"I appreciate you all coming too. I'm glad you're here."

"Of course we would be." I didn't know what else to say.

"I guess it wasn't my time to be a mommy yet, huh?"

Nora began to sob. We all looked over in shock.

"Nona, don't cry. It's okay. Really it is. I'm sad I didn't get to meet this baby, but he was very special. He taught me so many things in his short little life. Maybe he'll come back again, when I'm more ready."

"Sweetie, you would have made the best mommy we've ever seen. You **will** be the best mommy. You didn't do anything wrong."

"I guess. But Mom always told us we have to know when it's right. With a man. And I knew it wasn't right with Mike. He was an asshole. And maybe this baby didn't want to have an asshole for a father."

"Maybe," was all I could say.

My baby sister was the craziest, zaniest and in some ways the least mature of us, but sometimes she was like a wise old woman. She could see a world that most of us didn't have access to, except when we saw with our hearts. Anyone else might have been inconsolable, but she saw something completely different in this horrible experience. She was like a creature from another world.

We all stood quietly around the bed and held Lizzy and each other. No one moved when the door opened.

"Hola, Elizabetta."

Marco.

I turned to him and all my composure vanished. I stepped aside so he could move in toward the bed. He leaned over and gave her two kisses. Her favorite double-cheek kisses. He spoke to her in Spanish. "Como esta?"

Lizzy had been furiously studying Spanish, to surprise Esteban.

"Bien. Et tu?"

"Muy male. I am worried about my sweet little sister. Is she feeling okay?"

"I am fine Marco, really. It doesn't hurt nearly at all. And all my family is here. And Esteban is coming too."

"I know. I will go get him from the airport. He is trying to get here as fast as he can."

"I know. I wish he wouldn't worry. I'm going to be just fine."

"We know, sweetheart. We know."

We all sat with Lizzy through the rest of the afternoon and night, taking turns crying, and soothing each other. We sang together and watched terrible movies on the hospital TV.

When Esteban arrived, he looked as if he'd been crying. He passed the group of us Lizzy and grasped her. "Mi amor, mi amor," he said.

The rest of us stepped out to the waiting room to give them some time together. What must he have thought?. This wasn't even his child, but he had taken Lizzy and the baby as a set. He'd been more than willing to raise another man's child, just to be with the woman he loved. He was a hero.

After some time, I went in to check on them, and found them in the tiny bed together, sleeping. Esteban had himself wrapped completely around her, as if he was her protective blanket.

We all stayed in the waiting room in various stages of sleep and wake. I kept trying to tell Marco that he didn't have to stay, but he insisted, and I was glad to have him there.

We woke up with stiff necks and sore backs, but happy to have stayed. Lizzy teased us all for looking so disheveled. We were told that she could go home later that day, but would have to come back for more tests in a day or two.

She decided to stay at Nora's, after we all insisted, and we promised to take turns nursing her back to health. She swore that she was fine. Esteban never left her side for the entire week. Anytime Lizzy wanted a drink of water or a snack or even to just walk around, he was there, waiting on her hand and foot.

We had a small ceremony for Baby Boy, and Esteban proposed to Lizzy as soon as she recovered. She was as healthy, physically and emotionally, as I'd ever known her to be, and she was deliriously happy with her new love.

My ideas about an elopement ended up completely wrong as they planned an extravagant Las Vegas wedding. Lizzy gave up her San Francisco apartment to move in with Nora, but spent more and more time in Los Angeles with Esteban. We expected to hear that she was moving down there anytime, but I believed she didn't want to tell us quite yet. Her work required her to be in town every week or so, which kept her close enough to us.

I began to settle back into normal life, when I was reminded about events happening in threes.

Carla died. Marco needed me to be there for him, and I agreed. I let go of all the ridiculousness and decided to just love my man and appreciate this amazing thing he had done for another human being. He insisted I come to the funeral with him, which I really didn't want to do. I thought it would be too awkward, but he wanted me there and I went.

It was a beautiful ceremony, serene and intimate. Marco's eulogy was remarkable and I understood why she needed him. I was so proud of him, even as he broke down in my arms. If I could help from thinking about how odd it was to be at my boyfriend's ex-girl-friend's funeral, then it would be fine. I would be fine.

He was appreciative that I came, perhaps not believing that I would agree. I had spent so much time hating him for what he did, all I needed to do was be there for him, and that would have changed everything. Would have prevented those weeks of abso-lute misery we both experienced. If only I could have turned back time.

Instead, I had to let go of that terrified woman who created her own tragedies. I had to be the woman who was strong enough to step fully into her dreams. I had to trust in what my heart had been telling me all along.

I returned home to find that I'd been fired and replaced at the restaurant, event number three. I wasn't aware you could be fired from a job you did for free, but apparently it was possible. Between the time I took off to take care of Lizzy and the time to go to New York, it was apparently deemed unacceptable.

Perhaps I'd learned all I needed to from that place. Perhaps it was time to put myself out there for real, doing what I was meant to do. I buckled down to create the next step in my journey back to my beloved kitchen. This time, on my terms.

I'd been holding back on one aspect of my relationship with Marco, and it was finally time to turn the page on the painful events of the past few weeks, and move into a new intimacy. I hadn't yet introduced him to my girls.

I was highly protective of them and never wanted to bring anything into their lives that could cause them any pain. They'd heard about Marco, mostly from their aunts, and were dying to meet him, but I stalled. I'd been stepping very carefully, but Marco eventually got his invitation to my house, to meet my children. We were all excessively nervous.

We planned a full evening of cooking and movies. The girls sensed this was important, but being so young, didn't strictly know what to think. This was a big step for me, bringing a man home. I hadn't allowed any other men since their father into this part of my life, except for Emile, who they knew as only a friend.

Marco arrived fully loaded with gifts and goodies. Not having girls of his own, he was clearly unsure of himself, so he overdid it. The girls, of course, were terribly impressed. Who said the key to a girl's heart wasn't shiny things?

Attempting to draw attention away from the extravagant gifts, I moved us all to the kitchen to finish our dinner preparations. The girls were thrilled that I'd fallen in love with cooking again. Food had become a source of joy to me, as opposed to a place of constant soreness. The life of a successful chef might have been (temporarily) behind me, but feeding my family with love was again an important part of my life.

The girls had always been adept in the kitchen and loved to take responsibility for their parts of the menu. I put them in charge of guiding Marco.

The kitchen was small, so we had to work together. With the three of us, we'd figured out a system, but an extra set of hands, and a large unfamiliar body, threw us off a bit. There was quite a bit of bumping into each other and dropping things, which led to great hilarity.

Claire and Lola reminded me so much of Nora and me when we were young. Claire was born serious, and very, very talented. She was a natural leader and got things done. Lola was my wild child - extremely emotive and eloquent, with an uncanny ability to see into people's souls. Her insights bordered on the psychic and I often wondered if she had some connection to a magical world we couldn't see.

Claire took on the task of directing Marco in the kitchen, and freely critiquing his work. Lola plied him with a nonstop stream of questions, relevance and appropriateness notwithstanding. He obliged both of them.

Every now and then I stopped and watch them. I'd had no doubt they would get along brilliantly, but was not quite sure what that would look like. What I saw was strong evidence that he was a very good father.

He was natural, easy, relaxed and honest. He never spoke down to them or tried to ingratiate himself. When Claire got a little too bossy, he told her. When he needed a break from Lola's questions in order to concentrate on his preparations, he told her.

I was impressed. He looked over at me and mouthed, I love you. He took every opportunity to brush against me, or touch my arm. We both pretended that the girls didn't notice.

The meal was imperfect in its preparation, but perfect in its enjoyment. Everyone offered to clean up afterward, which was a great surprise to me. The girls were then put in charge of setting up the movie, which left Marco and me alone, for the first time, in the kitchen. With my hands busy in the sink, he took my shoulders and kissed me passionately. The combination of this man, in my house, with my girls in the other room made everything more exciting. And scary.

We settled in on the sprawled-out floor cushions, at first a bit tentative about who was going to sit where. Normally the girls would each lay on one of my shoulders, but no one wanted to leave Marco out, so we created a new foursome shape. I snuggled under Marco's arm, and the girls fit themselves in around us. He held them as if they were his own. My heart warmed.

I'd chosen a comedy, so as not to have to cry in front of everyone... again. Whenever he could, Marco snuck in a kiss or a whisper.

Although the girls were too excited to sleep, having a new visitor over, I forced the issue. I promised a great breakfast, which everyone expected anyway, and ushered them off to bed. And then things got awkward. Or maybe just for me.

We had agreed that he would stay the night, but now that it was time to bring him to my bedroom, I felt uneasy. I didn't have men over, and now one was spending the night. I wondered how much the girls understood about what that meant. I knew Lola had a good idea about what happened between men and women. What did she think? Would she be her normal inquisitive self and ask us about it in the morning? I was feeling embarrassed already.

I wasn't sure I could be intimate with him, concerned about the girls so close by. What if they wanted to come into the room, which they often do?

"It's okay, darling. Don't worry. The girls will be fine. And maybe, so will we."

He read my mind again. "I know. It just feels strange to have you here. Doesn't it feel strange to you?"

"Not really. Maybe just a bit, because I can feel your nervousness. I don't want to make you feel uncomfortable. Do you want me to sleep in the other room?"

"Don't be ridiculous. I just... I don't know..."

"Didn't the girls see you and Jeff being affectionate?"

"No. Actually no one did, because it so rarely happened. Especially after the girls were born. That's pathetic, right?"

"No, not pathetic. Truthful. Now don't you want them to have a good example of what it looks like, an adult relationship? I mean one that's not on TV."

"They do, from their father. He and his girlfriend have been serious for some time, and I know that she lives there most of the time. I'm not worried about that so much..."

"So what are you worried about?"

"I guess I haven't really had to split my attention before. I want to make sure that I'm taking care of everyone."

"But what if I want to take care of you? Will you let me?"

"If you insist." We both laughed, but I felt the seriousness of his statement. Would I let him take care of me? Could I allow myself such an unlikely extravagance?

We laid down in my bed, breathing together. There was a softness to my desire, but I could tell he was waiting for me to make the first move. He was being respectful about my concern around the girls. It felt like the first time having a man at your parent's house. Something sacred was being transformed. Not necessarily broken, but evolved.

I wanted him to love me, here, in the bedroom that had never experienced that event. I turned my head to kiss his neck, and my hands explored his body. He relaxed and responded to me quickly. I slid my body on top of his and crouched above him. He held me and kissed me, not forcing anything to happen. But the heat built quickly for me, and I wanted to be with him. I slid him inside me, and he moaned. I closed my eyes and let him move the both of us.

I had expected to feel differently, less engaged, with him here, but our bodies connected as deeply as ever. We were quiet and gentle and just as electric. I raised and lowered my body on his, and he guided me with his hands. I knew he liked looking up at me in this way and I held his gaze.

"Mi amor, mi amor."

"Are you happy?" I asked him.

"Happy is not the word for this. Thank you for bringing me into your family. Your life."

"I love you Marco. Thank you for letting me love you."

I moved more vigorously and his excitement grew. I sensed his climax approaching. He always wanted to wait for me to orgasm first, and sometimes I wouldn't give him the chance. Tonight, he was being insistent on waiting for me, and tilted me forward, so that I could feel the extra friction of rubbing against him. With infinite patience, he took me to my climax, then turned me onto my side as my body softened.

"You loving me is more than I could have ever dreamed of," he said.

He held me so tightly while he came, I thought I might have broken. I loved that feeling, of his power and strength, even in complete surrender. He tried to keep quiet for the sake of the girls, but the vibration of his moans resonated through his chest.

"Now this bed has been officially christened."

Marco laughed. "The first of many."

We slept easily, although I woke up many times just to look at him, in my room, in my bed. I counted my blessings, then slipped back to my dreams.

———

The next six months passed like a sweet sigh. All the turbulence and drama of the prior two months dissolved, leaving only the petals of some especially beautiful blossoms.

Jeff's girlfriend gave birth to a beautiful baby boy, and they decided to get married. I was honestly happy for them, and the girls, although initially hoping for a baby sister, found their new brother adorable.

The professional awards continued to accumulate for Nora and she and Sam even talked about combining households. After almost twenty years of being in a committed relationship, this was a big deal for them.

I began a new job working in a downtown restaurant catering to the corporate lunch set. Most restaurants like that did boringly ordinary food, but this place prided itself on creatively healthful cuisine,

with a famous name chef at the helm. Since he was there infre-
quently, I had relatively free reign as Executive Sous Chef. I couldn't
have imagined a better situation that let me be home with my girls in
the afternoon and be in the kitchen during the day.

Marco and I settled into our own rhythm, spending several days
a week together, either at his place or mine with the girls. I traveled
to New York more and more frequently with him to visit his sons
who were kind and welcoming. We felt like a family to me.

22

ARGENTINA

We planned a trip to Argentina, for his father's 75th birthday celebration. Although Marco was both Italian and Argentinian, his closest family members were all in South America. I intensified my efforts to learn Spanish, afraid I wouldn't be able to communicate with his large family, and nervous about making a good impression. Apparently, he hadn't brought a woman home for a very long time, and my visit was anxiously anticipated.

I couldn't believe it was possible, but I loved him even more, as time went on. The more we were together, the more we enjoyed each other's company, which was such a change from my history. Being with Marco was making me a better person. He taught me how to trust by being a perfect steward of my heart. I let the scars from our past issues soften and heal.

We were both nervous before the trip. My anxiety revolved around meeting the family, and I assumed Marco's revolved around the same. He came from a very large, very prominent family and they had apparently not enjoyed some of the previous women he'd brought home. I found this out through Lizzy, who got the scoop from Esteban.

On the one hand, this man was an important part of my life. On the other, his family was thousands of miles away, so if we didn't get along, it wouldn't be the end of the world. Still, I wanted people to like me (one of my many flaws) and I wanted *these* people to like me.

During the long plane ride, I could see Marco was distracted. He told me he was thinking about the plans for his father's party, and the logistics of doing everything he wanted to do while we were there. His boys would be joining us in a few days, too.

I fell asleep on the long ride from the airport, and woke up to find we were parked in front of a huge, white estate. Maybe even a villa. Certainly one of the biggest houses I'd ever seen. Marco's father Andres, one of the most successful real estate developers in South America, lived a grand life, which I learned from Lizzy.

Since it was so early in the morning, Marco assured me no one would be awake, and I'd have plenty of time to rest and freshen up before the introductions began.

Andres opened the door, wearing a beautiful silk dressing robe. For a moment, he reminded me of Hugh Hefner, but much better looking.

Marco was surprised to see him there, at the door. Without pause, Andres wrapped his arms around his son and held him tightly. "My darling son, you are here, you are here." Then he kissed him firmly on both cheeks and looked him square in the face.

"Life is good, I see," Andres said with a sly smile.

"Papa, this is Monique. Monique, this is Andres, my father, who is never up at this hour."

I had completely forgotten myself and began to put my hand out to shake his. Not sure if he noticed or not, but he took me by the shoulders, and kissed me just as firmly on both cheeks.

"Buenos dias, senor Gonzales."

"Now I see why my son never comes to see me anymore." His English was flawless.

Uh-oh. In trouble already.

"I would not leave your side either. How wonderful to meet you, finally," he added.

"Can we go in, Papa?" We were still standing at the entryway.

"What a beautiful house," I said as I tried to take it all in. Like a cross between an old European castle and a funky modern museum.

"Gracias. It's home," he said with clearly false modesty.

"Why are you awake, Papa?"

"I wanted to be the one to greet you. And Monique. There is some coffee, and maybe even some pastries. I know it has been a long flight."

"It was very easy," I said. "Thank you."

"Leave your things here. Martino will bring them up shortly."

He escorted us to an impeccable sitting room, where a tea and coffee service fit for the queen was laid out. I looked at Marco in disbelief. He had greatly under-represented his family's stature. This was the big leagues.

"Thank you, Papa. You are looking very well, too."

"All is well, Marco. I continue to be the luckiest man alive."

Andres served us. Marco informed him that I didn't drink coffee, and he sent for a woman called Isabella to bring some lemons. I was embarrassed, already looking needy and peculiar.

"I hear this is very good for you, the hot water and lemon. Is that true?" This man was truly charming.

"Yes, that's what they say. Let's hope they're right!" Everyone laughed, and my discomfort faded.

Marco and his father begin to speak, very quickly, in Spanish. They were talking about the boys, I believed, and the business. I followed fairly well, but it was taking some serious concentration, which in my fatigued state, was not plentiful.

"I am so sorry, my dear. How rude of us to exclude you. We must speak only English from now on."

"It's okay, Mr. Gonzales. I have been studying Spanish..."

"She's doing very well," added Marco.

"I can usually keep up fairly well, but maybe not this morning, in my... state."

"Yes, you two must be very tired. We can finish up here, then you can go upstairs to rest. I am so pleased that you came. It means very much to me. And please stop calling me Mr. Gonzales. It makes me feel very old..."

"Don't worry Papa. No one would ever think such a thing."

"Thank you, Andres. It is really lovely to be here," I added.

When we arrived in the room, the luggage had been carefully arranged at the foot of the bed.

"This is like an opulent hotel," I said to Marco.

"Yes... it's a bit over the top, isn't it?"

"Not really. It is amazing though. Very beautiful."

He wrapped his arms around me and kissed my neck. "*You* are very beautiful."

I moved his head and kissed him, softly at first, then passionately. My feelings of fatigue began to melt under the heat of my excitement.

"Are you still tired?" I asked.

"No," he said as he pressed our hips together. "Muy caliente," he growled, using a euphemism for being turned on.

We peeled each other's clothes off, our mouths never losing contact. I was surprised to find myself so aroused, after being so exhausted just a few minutes before. The intensity of our connection had continued to build the longer we were together. Gone were the days of my frigidity and my insecurity. My sex vixen was running the show these days.

We never made it to the bed. Instead, I found myself pressed against a huge armoire. Marco lifted one of my legs and entered me. Things moved very quickly for both of us. As he slowed down, trying to cool things down, I pleaded, "Please don't stop." The intensity was intoxicating, and him taking me in this way was unbelievably exciting.

Our bodies knew exactly what to do, even though standing up was a rare position for us. Electricity filled my body and my legs buckled. Marco held me up, while still moving against me. I pressed one of my hands against the wall to steady myself, and keep from collapsing.

"Marco!" I exclaimed.

"Si, amor, si," he encouraged me.

A deep groan came through my body, out of my mouth. I tried to muffle myself by keeping my face against his body, but the sound filled the room. I was barely aware of how he did it, but he picked me up, laid me on the bed, and slid himself back inside me.

The heat rose again. I really loved having him on top of me, maybe more than anything else. I didn't care how traditional it was - missionary was very productive for us.

"It's your turn, my love."

"I think it's still your turn," he joked.

I grabbed his bottom and pulled him deep into me. From the tenor of his moan, I knew it wouldn't be long before he climaxed.

I held his face to mine as the pulses of pleasure beat through his body. That feeling never got old for me. Marco was such a generous and attentive lover, anytime I could give him pleasure was delightful for me.

He lay still for a few moments, and I thought he might have fallen asleep. I gently stroked his back.

"Thank you for being here with me," he said. "You don't know how much it means to me."

"Almost as much as it means to me that you invited me."

"Well, none of the others could make it," he said jokingly.

I gave him a playful slap on the bottom and we laughed as we moved under the covers.

"Is it nap time?" I asked.

"Absolutely."

Marco was still sleeping when I woke up, so I decided to quietly slip out and take a shower. I walked around the room in awe, admiring every piece of furniture and art. His family was wealthy, that was undoubtedly true, but they were also incredibly tasteful, which did not always go together. The mixtures of colors and textures, the use of light and open space, all made for a sophisti-cated, yet inviting space.

The bathroom was a showpiece, with an open shower area in the middle of the large room. It was larger than some of the apartments of my youth.

I luxuriated in the hot shower. It felt so good, removing the grime of traveling, and waking me up. I stood motionless under the warm spray when something made me open my eyes. Marco had come into the bathroom. I wasn't sure how long he'd been watching me - I didn't hear him enter. The broad grin on his face let me know he'd been enjoying the show.

He opened the door and asked, "May I join you?"

He'd already stepped in before I said yes.

"Good morning, darling," I greeted him.

"Yes. Yes it is."

I moved him under the spray of the showerhead and let him enjoy the hot water. Then I took the soap and began to wash his body. I knew he loved my touching him like this, and it wasn't so bad for me either.

It still took my breath away to look at him, such a perfect specimen of a man. Lean, muscular, and perfectly proportional. I loved the shape of his broad shoulders and strong chest. I often imagined him being carved out of a piece of light caramel granite.

My hands moved around his body, under the premise of cleaning him. I lingered in some areas longer than others. His excitement became obvious, but mine was just as strong. I couldn't get enough of him.

I moved him toward the cedar bench, and whispered, "Sit down," in his ear. He obliged. I knelt facing him, and took him into my mouth. The water and the heat made him even more delicious.

I didn't get to linger there as he pulled my body up to him. My legs straddled him as I lowered myself slowly onto him. The slickness of our bodies created a wonderful range of movement and pleasure. I felt especially playful and couldn't stop giggling, almost as if I was drunk. I was enjoying my lover in the shower of his father's immense house. I couldn't help but laugh.

We found our way to a passionate ending, but emerged waterlogged and pruney. He kept looking at me as if I had lost my mind, and maybe I had. I felt as free as I'd ever been, and as connected to another human being as I ever thought possible.

"Did I mention how much I love you?" I said as I ran the soft towel on his beautiful body.

"Not yet," he said teasingly.

"As much as all the marble in this house."

The rest of the day was filled with party planning and family introductions. Apparently, no one could wait for the official party to meet the mysterious woman Marco had brought home. Despite my concerns, everyone was kind and gracious and I felt welcomed at every turn.

We'd planned to have dinner at his sister's house, in a nearby town, that night, and left the large group assembled at Andres'. His sister, Carolina, had a large family, and Marco warned me to expect a bit more chaos and frenzy than at his father's house. I didn't see how that would be possible, but was excited to see what a female Marco would be like.

Dinner went flawlessly, other than my numerous failed attempts at Spanish. Everyone was patient and understanding, and the children all wanted to practice their English, all five of them. Carolina was an artist, like their mother, and their house reminded me of something from Gaudi, out of Barcelona. It was fun and light and sometimes downright silly.

Carolina's husband was a regular comedian, a soft round man with a belly that laughed with him. He was utterly charming and a consummate host. I could tell she ran things, and he was the entertainment, quite divergent from the typical Argentinian patriarchy.

After coming back from the bathroom, I found myself alone with her in the hallway. She stopped to look at me, as if something hovered on the tip of her tongue.

"Carolina, thank you so much for dinner. I love your family! It was so nice to have this night with you, without all the others around."

"You are quite welcome, Monique. We have been dying to meet you for too long. You know, I was supposed to be at the wedding, where Marco met you."

Although the details weren't quite right, I didn't feel any need to correct her. "Yes, it would have been wonderful to meet you then. But I was so infatuated with Marco that I'm not sure I would have given you proper attention." We both smiled.

"Marco and I have always been very close. We are almost like twins."

"Yes, I can see that. And he always talks about you with such love."

"He has been through so much in his life, all I want is for him to be happy."

I wasn't sure where this was going, and was starting to feel a bit uneasy.

She continued. "I know that you two had a difficult time not too long ago."

I gulped. "Yes. I was very foolish. And scared. The way we fell in love seemed to be too good to be true. I panicked. I feel very ashamed about what happened."

"He does seem like Prince Charming, doesn't he?"

"Yes. He does."

"And you are his princess."

I had no idea how to respond to that.

"I know you love him. I can see it in your eyes."

"Yes, I do Carolina. More than I could ever describe. I want him to feel that every moment of his life."

"Aaaaah, I think he does. I know he does, in fact."

She was silent for an uncomfortable amount of time.

I wanted to cut the tension. "Perhaps we should get back to the rest-"

"What I want to say to you, Monique, is thank you. Marco has always been my hero, and it has broken my heart to see him alone, or in relationships that did not make him happy. You have brought back the man I knew. The one whose heart is so full you can feel it in his presence. He deserves the best. I think you have given that to each other. And I am grateful. For you."

Tears pressed against my throat. This unexpected outpouring of love was too much for my emotional sensibilities. All I could do was wrap my arms around her.

"Thank you, Carolina. Thank you."

We walked back to chaos in the dining room, with the children climbing all over Marco, and the men having a heated discussion in Spanish.

Carolina admonished them. "No politics at the table."

"Yes, of course, my darling," her jolly husband responded.

Although they begged us to stay, Marco insisted that we had to return to his father's house that night. There was so much to do, he claimed. I didn't really understand, but I let him make the decision.

Saying goodbye was difficult. Every time I looked at his sister, and remembered what she'd said to me, I thought I might cry. I gave her a warm hug as we left.

She whispered, "We are so glad you are here. It is wonderful!"

I fell asleep nearly as soon as my head hit the pillow. The day had taken a lot out of me. I didn't have to work nearly as hard as I'd thought to impress everyone, but I was still on my absolute best behavior. Keeping up with the Spanish also fatigued my brain.

I woke up in the middle of the night to Marco, watching me.

"What are you doing sweetheart?"

"Just watching you. It's better than dreaming."

"You should sleep. It's going to be a busy day."

"I know. My head is just full. Actually I'm very happy. With you here, and my whole family going to be in one place. I can't really believe it yet."

"Are we picking up the boys in the morning?"

"No, they'll take the car. And they'll probably go straight to bed. My dad is taking them riding in the afternoon, with their cousins, which they will love."

"Okay, love, can I do something to help you sleep?"

"Just lay here with me. That's all I need. That's all I ever need."

"That and a nice clean shower every now and then," I joked, referring to our morning's activities.

"I'm so glad you enjoy being with me in that way. It is... wonderful. And not something I'm used to."

"Really? I don't think there exists a woman who could resist you. Don't you know you are the sexiest man alive?"

"Ha, ha. I'm not sure everyone received that memo. But I'm glad you think so. And the feeling is mutual, you know."

"You think I'm the sexiest man alive? Why thank you."

"Maybe the funniest one too."

"Yes, that I am. Now let's sleep." I snuggled under his arm and wrapped myself around him. The strong, regular thump of his heart escorted me into sweet dreams.

23

A SECRET SPOT

The knock on the door woke us up.

"Señor Gonzales. The boys are here!"

It was the maid, excited.

"Thank you, Isabella."

"I'll go down to greet them, and rescue them from my father's planned interrogation. Stay up here if you like, darling. Get some rest."

"No, I want to come down and see them."

We put on our robes and skipped down the stairs to see Andres holding each of the boys by the arm.

"Marco, you didn't tell me what men they had become."

"Papa!" They ran to their father with hugs and kisses. I even got a few myself. Andres couldn't stop beaming. Grandpa was clearly very proud.

"How was your flight, boys?" Marco asked.

"Other than Pablo thinking he had a chance with the flight attendant..." ribbed Diego.

"Shut up! You're just jealous that I got extra dessert."

"Boys," interrupted an amused Marco. "Don't you want to rest?"

"Actually, we're okay, Papa. We slept some on the plane."

"Between the fights?" asked Andres.

We all smiled. "Glad you're here, guys. Maybe eat something and then lay low. You know how much energy you'll need for riding later."

"Are we still riding later Grandpa?? We can't wait!"

All the men begin speaking in Spanish, hyperspeed. I had no chance of keeping up.

"I think I'll go for a run," I whispered to Marco.

"I'm sorry amor, are we leaving you out?"

"Not at all, sweetheart. I want you to catch up. All this male Gonzales energy, in one room, is too much for a sensitive gal like myself."

It felt good to get outside before the sun rose too high. Winter at home, it was summer here and the temperatures were scorching. Two of the grounds-people vehemently offered to accompany me, not understanding I was trying to exercise. I did my best to explain, but wasn't sure I did.

When I returned from my run, the main floor of the house was much quieter. The boys must have succumbed to fatigue and gone upstairs. But where were the older men?

A trip to the kitchen for some water uncovered the elder, having a heated discussion over the menu for the day, I believed. He stopped his conversation to offer me about ten different things to eat and drink. "Just water," I repeated, as kindly as possible. He didn't know where Marco was. Maybe working upstairs.

A search in our room came up empty, so I started peeking my head into random rooms. I found Marco in the library, nestled into a huge, brown chair, smiling down at an oversized book. He was looking at pictures.

"There you are!" I said.

"I thought you'd had enough of this craziness and ran away from me."

"Not yet, love. Not yet. What are you looking at?"

"Come sit with me and I'll show you."

"But I'm so sweaty."

"My favorite," he said with a grin.

It was true. Marco loved the way I smelled, no matter what. Sometimes I did believe he was intoxicated with me, as he often claimed to be.

"Is that your mother?"

"Yes."

"My God, she was so beautiful. Wow. She looks like Marilyn Monroe."

"Funny for an Italian girl, yes? Her family is from the North, and they look more Swiss than Italian."

"Either way, she is stunning."

As he flipped through pages of the album, I recognized some of the pictures from his house, and some of the people I'd already met. The pictures of him as a child were adorable.

He told me about all the people I'd be meeting at the party the next night. It was going to be a huge affair and I would likely forget most of the names, but it was wonderful getting a tour of his extensive family.

"What a wonderful family you have." I meant it.

"They are your family too," he said. I looked at him oddly and he turned away. I wondered if he was offended. I hoped not.

"Let me go get cleaned up, my love. What is the plan for the day?"

"I told them we'd like a late breakfast, then we have a couple of visits, and... another appointment this afternoon."

"An appointment?" That sounded strange, especially since he stumbled on the words.

"Yes, yes, don't worry. Nothing you need to worry about."

"Okay," I said, a bit confused as I headed toward our room.

We ate in the small room adjacent to the kitchen. Everything was delicious.

"I'd love to get my hands on that kitchen," I said over breakfast. It was a dream kitchen.

"I'm not sure that will happen darling. There is not a lot of acceptance for people crossing lines here."

"You mean because the help will not like me in their territory, or because the family will not like me consorting with the help?"

"Well, neither, I believe. But maybe we can arrange something."

We prepared ourselves for the start of the day and Marco let me know we'd likely be out all day. There was a dinner for only the immediate family tonight, as the kickoff for the major celebration tomorrow. The house was buzzing with preparations and I was not unhappy to be heading out away from the frenzy. Andres and the boys were leaving for the riding grounds shortly.

At each house we visited, we met more aunts, uncles and cousins, who each wanted to feed us more than the ones before. I had to learn more ways to say *no thank you* if I wanted to fit in my dress for tomorrow.

The family visits ended and off we went to the secret appointment. Marco was distracted, agitated even, but he wouldn't say why. I wondered if I'd done something to embarrass him or myself. I kept thinking that everything had been going so well, and didn't understand his strange mood.

Was he worried? Or upset? I tried hard not to take it personally.

I snuggled closer to him and whispered, "Hey."

"Hi, darling."

"Have I told you today how much I love you?"

His body softened. "Tell me again."

With small kisses between each word, I said, "I... love... you... so... much."

"Don't stop, okay?"

What a strange response, I thought. "I wouldn't think of it."

We were quiet for the rest of the ride through the congested city, but he never let go of my hand, holding it a bit tighter than usual. He gave our driver some instructions which I didn't understand as he pulled over near a small patch of green in between buildings. We were in a very busy part of the city. Downtown perhaps.

"Where are we, Marco?"

"I want to show you something, okay?"

"Of course."

We walked into what I initially thought was a small grassy area, and then was surprised as I rounded the corner and realized it was an idyllic urban retreat. Tucked away between skyscrapers, with an amazing view of the Buenos Aires skyline. I couldn't believe what I was seeing, and watched with my eyes and mouth wide open.

"This is incredible, Marco. What is it?"

"It's one of our many secret parks. My father's office used to be in that building," pointing to a shiny skyscraper, "and I would come down here as a child after school, waiting for him. I sat on the bench over there and watched the buildings and the people all day. I would look down here," pointing me toward the skyline, "and draw what I saw. It's where I first realized that I loved structures and shapes, not in an artistic way like my mother, but in a practical way. I wanted to build things."

I followed the images he created in my imagination.

"Let's sit down," he said as he guided me to the bench.

"This is so beautiful Marco. Thank you for bringing me here."

"It's an important place for me. When I think of my childhood, I think of this bench, right here."

I was incredibly touched.

"When I got a little older I started noticing the people a bit more than the buildings. The businessmen - it was only men back then - the families, the couples. That's when I started thinking about what I wanted my life to be. I imagined my career, how successful I would be, my family, who I would love."

"And who was that?"

"Well, back then it was Linda Sanchez, the tallest girl in the eighth grade."

"Did she love you back?"

"Unfortunately, no. She had eyes for my brother, who spent much more time wooing girls than... staring at buildings."

Despite the mention of his brother, I could see he was relaxing a bit. I was so happy that he was sharing this part of his life with me. Marco remained quiet for a moment, and then started again, this time more seriously.

"I didn't really know what love was, back then, but I knew what it looked like from all those hours watching the couples hold hands, kiss, and gaze at each other. I imagined what it must feel like, inside, to be that way, and I wanted it. I wanted to feel that."

He looked out in the distance, probably remembering those scenes.

"I've made so many mistakes in my life, Monique... done so many things wrong. But somehow it all worked out. I got everything I dreamed of, nearly. I've had such a wonderful life... the boys, my career, almost everything."

He smiled. "But that feeling... what I imagined those couples must be feeling... that one was... elusive. I thought I knew what it would be like, to be in love, but it was never as I imagined. Never that feeling..."

"Not even with Carla?" I wondered if it was awkward for me to bring up his late ex-girlfriend.

He shook his head. "We had great affection for each other, and so much in common. I think we confused friendship and familiarity for some other kind of love. It just wasn't... it."

I remembered him describing the relationship with his ex-wife Anna in similar terms.

"I more or less decided that what I imagined wasn't real. That I had just made it up."

I didn't know where this conversation was going, but I felt anxious, all of a sudden. And sad about his story.

"Then one day I saw this woman, this stunning woman, daydreaming at the San Francisco airport." He looked at me and smiled. "And then we spent the most magical days of my life, up to that point, together. And then she left me..."

I didn't like this new turn. "And then you found her again," I added.

"It was during that time that I realized that that feeling I had imagined, so long ago, here on this bench - it was real. I did not just make it up. It was real and I was feeling it. Or I was feeling the absence of it. I knew, Monique that I just wanted to love you. I knew that I would have to find a way to be with you. I knew I wanted to spend the rest of my days loving you."

My breath quickened and tears pressed against my throat. I couldn't take my eyes off him, although it added to my rising emotions. *Oh my God,* filled thoughts.

"I can't explain what happened, or what is happening, with us. It is our fairytale, amor. You have made this boy's dreams come true. Being with you is everything I dreamed being in love would be."

Marco slid off the bench and got on one knee. I couldn't process what I was seeing. He released one of my hands to reach into his pocket, removing a tiny red silk pouch, then used his other hand to open it. Out came a magnificent diamond ring. He turned to face me. I was crying and having trouble breathing.

"Monique, you are the love of my life. I don't want to spend any of it without you. Would you marry me?"

I felt paralyzed. My head spun and my heart pounded and I couldn't move or speak. My mouth was probably wide open. In my head all I heard was, oh my God, oh my God...

He tilted my chin so that I could see him. When our eyes met, the whole world dissolved. It was just us, me and my beloved, the man who captured my heart in a way I had never experienced. I wanted nothing more than to be with him... forever.

"Yes," I said between sobs. "Yes, of course. Marco... I can't believe..."

I stopped speaking as he slid the ring on my finger. In the sunlight it looked enormous, with a hint of pink. It fit perfectly, in every way.

"Oh my God," I kept repeating. Marco moved back onto the bench, took my face in his hands and kissed me. I melted under the heat of his mouth. My head was still spinning but I stayed connected to him, to keep me from floating off into space.

I moved slightly away, to take a breath, and I couldn't tell if it was my tears on his face, or his. He smiled that smile that had captured me in the very beginning.

'Did you plan all this?" was all I could say.

"Yes, for quite some time. I wasn't sure if there was going to be too much going on during this trip, this weekend, but I couldn't wait any longer. This ring was burning a hole in my pocket."

"It's so beautiful, Marco. It's perfect."

"I'm glad you like it."

"Of course I like it. I love it. Because it came from you. I can't believe it…" I tried to compose myself. "I love you so much Marco. I didn't need any of this, you know. You had my heart, regardless."

"I never thought of myself as old-fashioned. But I wanted to do this. I want our bond to be formal. And as serious as my commitment to you."

"I don't doubt you, darling. I don't doubt us."

When he kissed me again, I felt the relief in his body. I'd put him through more than he deserved. To make him happy was all I wanted.

"How long were you planning this?"

"About five and a half weeks. More or less." We both laughed.

"It sounds so trite, but it's true. You've made my dreams come true, Monique. I'm going to do everything I can to make yours come true too."

"You already have, darling. I never thought I would find love like this… I didn't believe it was possible for me either. And then you appeared, like a mirage. You have changed everything about what I see for my life. I… I'm just in shock right now. Sorry I'm being incoherent."

"You're never incoherent. Or maybe we both are."

"We belong together, I guess."

"You guess?"

"I love you, Marco," I stroked his face, "and I promise to keep loving you for as long as I breathe. And maybe a few lifetimes after that as well."

"Just a few?"

"Well it's already been several thousand! How many more do you want?"

"All of them. I want all of them."

As if on cue, we both started singing my favorite song. We sat on the park bench, singing and kissing and watching the buildings and the people.

As we walked back to the car, hand in hand, I said, "Look, darling. Now you are one of the people you were watching as a boy. Maybe we will inspire someone to believe in their hearts too."

"I hope so."

We hardly spoke on the way back to the house. I was still processing what had just happened, and hyper-aware of the new sensation on my ring finger. Empty for so long, and now full.

Marco held me. He was so much more relaxed, and I now understood why he had been acting so strangely. It must have been nearly impossible to keep it all in for so long. His thoughtfulness never ceased to amaze me.

I hoped that the house would be quiet, or everyone would be busy preparing for the family dinner so that we could have some time alone. As soon as the door opened, however, shouts of congratulations filled my ears and a glass of champagne appeared in my hand. Andres was the first to greet me.

"Welcome to the family, my dear. We are very happy to have you." He squeezed me so tightly I could hardly breathe, then kissed me square on the mouth. I didn't have time to be startled because the next family members had their arms around me. I kept trying to look over at Marco, to find out how he'd told everyone, but he was swarmed as well.

It looked like everyone had arrived early for the dinner, or maybe the dinner was just a ruse. I wasn't sure of anything at that point.

The boys each took me aside to welcome me to the family.

"We are so pleased you and Papa are together. We love you, Monique. Thanks for making Papa so happy. It's been a long time."

"I love you two very much, and can't believe I am lucky enough to be part of your family."

They wrapped around me like my daughters did, even though they were both taller than me.

The crowd moved into the ballroom, the music started and the party began. I finally made my way to Marco. "What is all this?"

"Didn't you realize how much my family loves parties?"

"How did they know?" I asked, suspiciously.

"I told my father, my brother and sister, and the boys. I guess they told everyone else. I didn't know they were going to do all this. I was hoping we could sneak upstairs..."

"Me too," I said with a wink. "I have an engagement present for you..."

He was definitely intrigued. "Do you think they will miss us?"

"Yes! You'll have to wait until later, I suppose."

"I am dying with anticipation..."

"Break it up lovebirds! Plenty of time for that on the honeymoon," said his cousin Juan. "When is the wedding?"

"We haven't gotten that far yet. Don't worry, you're all invited, of course," I said.

"Does that mean no romantic getaway to Bali, then?" Marco asked.

"We can do both, can't we?"

"You mean I get to marry you more than once? That's the most brilliant thing I've ever heard."

"And by the way Juan, there's going to be A LOT of this for... forever!" He then gave me the biggest, most dramatic, kiss. He nearly knocked me off my feet, which was how it felt to be with him. Hovering slightly off the ground.

24

THE MESS OF HOME

Then I remembered…
    "Oh my God! I have to call home, and tell everyone. I do have to sneak off."
"Yes, I'll let them know where we're going."

Marco told his father, who was busy dancing like a man half his age. "Si, si…"

We couldn't believe our luck, to be allowed to leave so easily, and skipped up the stairs.

I dialed my girls first, expecting this would be the more complicated conversation. How would I explain to them that I was marrying someone other than their father? I knew they loved Marco, but would they find it strange? Would they feel betrayed?

"I'm calling the girls now, sweetheart. I hope they will be okay."

"I think they will. Just call."

I remembered that their father is planning his own wedding. That might make things a bit easier to explain.

"Hi Mama!" They were on speaker.

"Hi sweet cakes. How are my love bugs?"

"We're great… watching a movie. What are you doing?"

"Well, I have some news…"

"Did you say yes?! Did you Mama? We both thought you would! Did you?" Both girls spoke at once, over each other.

I was confused about what I heard. How did they know? I looked over at Marco, who was grinning sheepishly.

"Yes, girls. I said yes."

I had to wait for the whooping and hollering to subside in order to speak again. "How did you know?" I asked them while looking at directly at Marco. He walked over to the phone.

"Hi senorinas. Isn't it great?"

"Hi Marco! We're so excited. Oh my God, can we go pick out dresses when you get back? We get to wear white too, right? Oh my gosh, we're so excited!"

"Me too, girls, me too. I'll explain to your mom about how you knew, okay? You can just catch up now. I'll give you some privacy," he said before walking toward the door.

I gave him a look the whole way out. The girls wanted to talk about the wedding, which I couldn't help with. Thank goodness they were happy. They wanted to know the details of how he proposed, and all about the beautiful house, and Marco's family. They say they were going to practice their Spanish tomorrow. I missed them and wished they were here. I could have used a family squeeze right then.

The call to Nora's was next. I wasn't sure how that one is going to go. Less whooping and hollering, I assumed.

"Hi, it's me."

Nora spoke loudly to whomever else was in the room, "Sam, Lizzy, it's Nik!" Then to me, "How are you?"

I could tell by the sound of her voice that something was up. "I'm great. How are you guys doing?"

"Great. Anything interesting happening down there?" Yes, there was definitely an odd tone...

I couldn't keep any suspense going.

"Well, yes, actually. Marco proposed. And I said yes."

Screaming filled my ear. I thought even Sam might have been screaming. Lizzy certainly was.

"So, you all knew as well? Was I the only one who didn't know?"

"Will you stop being such a pain and actually enjoy this moment?!"

"Yes, boss. We're having an amazing time down here. You would not believe how his family lives. It's something out of a romance novel. Seriously."

Lizzy's voice filled the phone next. "Nik, this is the most exciting thing ever! Can you believe both of us are getting married? We could do it in Vegas, together..."

"Hold up there, sweetie. We can work all that out when I get back. And I'm not quite sure I want to encroach on your first and only wedding."

"Okay, bridezillas. Let's not get carried away here."

"You're just jealous," Lizzy said.

"Not really. Not at all, in fact. Sam and I were first, if you remember."

"Now who's the party pooper?!" Lizzy said.

"Hey sweet Nik. I couldn't be happier for you. Maybe you'll trust me next time I tell you you've found a good one." Sam was right, but I couldn't let him get away with it.

"There will definitely NOT be a next time, Sammy."

"Fair enough, Nik. Fair enough."

"Let's all celebrate when we get back, okay?"

"It's a date. We love you so much Nik!" they all said in unison.

"Love you too. I'll talk to you soon."

The party was still in full force when I went back downstairs. Marco was spinning his nieces around the dance floor, while his sister took pictures. I just wanted to stand and watch them, all so beautiful and happy. I wondered if this was a consequence of all the good news and festivities, or if this was their way of being. I thought about staying there, for a long time.

Andres saw me and pulled me in to dance with him. He was definitely smooth and knew how to hold a woman. I could see how Marco became the man he was.

"Did you learn to dance like that in America?" he asked as I gracefully execute a spin.

"Yes, sir. My family are all very musical."

"We love to dance in our family, too. Your family now. I hope you will encourage Marco to see us more often. I miss my son very much. At least now I don't have to worry about his heart. It is in good hands, I see."

I smiled shakily, afraid I might start to cry. "Andres... I would love to spend more time here. You've all been so wonderful to me. Thank you for welcoming me into your home and your family. I didn't intend to steal all the attention from your celebration!"

"Aaah. This news is much better than an old man getting one year older. Anyhow, tomorrow night will be mine," he said with the smile I recognized from his son. Charmers, those Gonzales men.

I kissed him lightly on both cheeks when the song ended, but a new song began immediately and someone else's arm was around my waist. Marco's cousin was my next partner.

We all switched partners until only the kids were still standing. To think, this was not even the main event, just a warm-up party. I didn't know how I would have the stamina to do this all again the next day.

I finally got to dance with my new fiancé.

"I'd like to stay here for a long time."

"Where? In Argentina? In my dad's house?"

"Maybe. But what I really meant was in your arms."

"That is their sole purpose now, I believe. To hold you and love you."

One lifetime wouldn't be enough with this man.

"Take me to bed," I whispered in his ear.

"As you wish."

The night came in waves of delight. We drifted off to sleep while talking, and then woke up and found each other, ready to be taken and taken in.

"Marco, I am so happy. This is all so unbelievable to me. I feel like I'm going to wake up any moment now from this dream and..."

"You've made my dreams come true."

"I love you so much. I love every single thing about you," I said.

"Tell me," he teased.

"I love how you're kind and brilliant and strong. I love how you look and smell and taste. I love how you're not scared of how crazy I can be."

"Amor..."

"Let me finish. I love how you love your family, and my family, and me. I love how you treat my girls like princesses and my sisters like queens and Sam like a brother. I love what a great lover you are, and how I feel beautiful when I'm around you. I love that you're honest, even when it's hard. I love how safe I feel in your arms and how much I trust you. I love being in love with you."

"Monique..." he took a deep breath. "It is my dream come true to make you happy, to show you everyday how smart and beautiful and sexy you are. I love how you can feel everything, what someone is thinking across the room and the perfect thing to say to make anyone feel better. I love how your hands make magic food that heals the world. I love how you cry at everything, even computer commercials. I love how you cover your tender heart when you're out in the world, but you let it be bare with me, when we are alone. I love how fiercely you love your family, and what an amazing mother you are. I love that you show me your desire, and let me experience mine. Frequently.

I love how every man wishes he was me when you are on my arm. I love how you move your body when you dance, and how you follow when I lead. I love that you show off your superstar legs and wish I could make a mold of your butt that I could always have with me. I love that you pretend you're not ticklish, and how your hands feel on my body. I love your mouth, on my mouth, and on my body.

I love how you hold me, really tightly, when you are feeling pleasure. I love how you purr when you're sleeping. I love how you laugh and how you cry and how you tell me you love me. I love that you let me love you."

We looked at each other for a long time. This outpouring of love filled the middle of the night, bracketed by passion and a little bit of sleep.

We drifted off and I woke up with my hand on his cock. The gratitude continued, with a slightly different twist.

"I love how you're hard whenever I want you to be."

"I love how you're wet whenever I want you to be."

"I love how it feels when you're inside me."

"I love how it feels inside you."

"I love how you take your time."

"I love how time stops when we're together."

"I love how you know exactly what I need."

"I love how you let me explore your body."

"I love your cock."

This made Marco laugh. "He REALLY loves you!"

We became too absorbed by the building passion to keep talking.

"Thank you for finding me, Marco."

"Thank you for being, Monique."

Morning arrived in small streams of sunlight. A knock on the door confirmed the day had started.

"Señor? Your father wanted me to tell you there is a family meeting now. Thank you."

"Thank you, Isabella."

"Family meeting?" I asked.

"Yes. That's my father. He leaves nothing to the moment. We are going to plan the day, and the night. Perfection does not come easily, my dear."

"It does for some people," I said as I gave him his good morning kiss.

"Maybe we can stay here and miss the meeting," he suggested.

"No way. I'm not going to be the cause of your absence from the family meeting. I'll keep the bed warm for you."

"Nice try. You, my dear, are now part of this family, and are absolutely expected to be present."

"You're kidding."

"Not even a little bit."

We slipped into our dressing gowns and headed downstairs to find Andres, Marco's sister and brother-in-law, and his two boys in the sitting room. We were the last ones down. Embarrassment slowed my steps.

"Good morning everyone," I said, trying to appear cheerful.

"Good morning lovebirds," said a voice I didn't recognize. A man who looked exactly like Marco appeared from the kitchen.

"Sebastian. When did you arrive?"

"Very late last night. I believe you two had already... retired for the night." He stared at me intently. "Well, this is the future Mrs. Gonzales, I presume?"

"Hello, Sebastian. It is so nice to finally meet you."

"Yes, I understand why Marco was keeping you hidden, just for himself. Pleasure to meet you," he said as he kissed my cheeks.

This guy was as smooth as cream. Everything I heard about him appeared to be true. The word lothario immediately came to mind. Stunningly good looking, almost too pretty, I couldn't stop looking at him. He noticed.

As did Marco, who took my hand to sit down on the couch on the other side of the room.

"Papa, did the family meeting need to be so early?"

"Yes. We have much to do today. I know you are intoxicated by love now, but we have an important event, if you remember."

"Of course I remember, Papa. That's why we're all here. For you."

Andres reminded me of Nora, which meant I knew how to handle him. "Just tell us what you need us to do, Andres. We are at you service."

"I did not expect you to be so obedient..."

"Sebastian, must you be so rude already?" Marco's question, and the tone of his delivery, shocked me.

His sister began to speak very quickly in Spanish. She did not sound happy, but it put them all in their places. I'd never seen Marco get riled so quickly. It made me wonder if Sebastian's transgression has really been forgiven.

Andres grabbed the reigns from this small distraction, and

continued with the complex agenda for the day. Everyone's tasks were well defined and the day was scheduled to the minute. We dispersed to get on with our assignments.

Since I had the fewest obligations, Marco was able to slip me into the kitchen, where I spent the afternoon making Andres my famed chocolate cake. The kitchen was a real dream, even with the staff sneaking looks in every now and then.

One particular young man, who had apparently been assisting the chef, was so intrigued by what I was doing that he offered to help me. We could hardly speak to each other, but chose the world of food to communicate. Marco found us laughing hysterically at the funny face he had drawn in the spilled flour on the counter.

"Well, it looks like you are doing quite well in here."

"I think the cake is going to be great. Miguel was such a help."

Miguel, acting like he might have crossed some unspoken line, began to stutter and apologize. Almost bowing as he backed away from Marco.

"It's okay," I said to him. "No problemo. Bueno trabajo."

"Gracias, señora. Gracias."

Marco translated the next stream of Spanish for me: "He thinks you are a very good cook. And he is very happy you will now be coming here more often... now that we are getting married."

"Gracias," I replied.

Marco made his way over to me, and gently rubbed his thumb across my cheek, cleaning off a stray smudge of flour.

"I must be very messy right now," I admitted.

"Yes, a little bit." A smile rose from the bottom of my heart, as I acknowledged the love in his eyes. "Just the way I like it."

25

THE FIRST SONG

Lalune's lessons had been going well. She drank in Avanora's teachings with a newfound thirst for being alive. The darkness and despair that had defined her life until that point dissolved under the beam of her focus. The prospect of happiness fueled her efforts and dampened the fear.

In addition to her daily instructions, Lalune began spending time near the surface observing the land-walkers, to learn their ways and copy their manners. They continued to be as odd as they were enticing. She practiced her singing whenever she could, less afraid of getting caught, and gradually accepting the degree of her desire.

The island, un-inhabited by the land-walkers and regarded as relatively safe by the mermaids, became Lalune's second home. The large ship that had been slowly approaching that area stopped in the path directly between her home and the island. Lalune found it curious that it did not move for several days, but was so absorbed in her own world that she did not think more about it.

Although she could see and hear the land-walkers on the ship clearly, she was fairly certain that her body and voice were hidden from their detection. This strange event was not going to stop keep her from progressing towards her goal.

Something made her listen to them more closely on that cloudy day.

"We are shifting the location of the blasts, due to the oncoming weather system. Not going to take any chances."

Lalune was shocked by what she overheard, and began to study these boat-men carefully. She gleaned that they were planning a series of explosions to look for oil in the ocean that was her home.

She was too scared to warn her family because she should never have been around the land-walkers.

She went back and forth for days, trying to decide what to say, and if she should say anything at all. All of the anxiety about her transformation was dwarfed by the fear for her family, and her community, and she finally realized it was worth their inevitable anger to save their lives.

She decided to go straight to her father. He would know what to do and had the authority to lead the community. Lalune felt the first explosion as she entered his chamber. It was too soon! She thought there would still be days to inform everyone.

The bombing shook their home and sent the mermaids fleeing, hardly getting out in time. The sea creatures scrambled in a frenzy, trying to find safety from the deafening sound and their crumbling seafloor. The whales, the most sensitive, were driven mad by the vibrations, and sped toward the mainland shore.

Lalune knew that the vibrations confused their sense of direction, and they would end up beaching themselves in the shallow water near shore. Panic filled her body, but her instincts led her to follow a pod of whales racing inland. Not knowing what else to do, she began to sing.

She used all the power she could muster to reach them with her voice. Miraculously, they began to slow down, and then change direction. They were regaining their bearings, and swimming toward her. These enormous creatures, the most revered in her world, were drawn enough by her song to stop their fatal drive.

They floated in the calmness of the sea, away from the explosions, and listened to her. As they began to move back into the belly of the ocean, they returned her calls. Lalune trusted that they would now be safe, and their calls would protect any of the others driven mad by the explosions.

As her mighty friends swam away she realized that she had proven her voice could save lives, and could change the course of destruction. Maybe the whales would return and tell everyone her story, how she had saved them. Maybe the mermaids would forgive her her grave transgression. She could only hope.

The swim, trying to keep up with the whales, nearly all the way to the shore of the land-walker's island, left Lalune tired and disoriented. Her second realization came slowly as she recognized where she was - that magical place Avanora had taken her so long ago. Actually, even closer to the mainland but still dense with magic, and as close to the land-walker's home as she had ever been. This was the perfect opportunity to attempt her final move.

Lalune made the decision to complete the rest of the plan that night. She was ready to implement all her knowledge, and test the old mermaid's spells. Perhaps all this chaos and commotion was a sign from the Great Mother that it was time. Either way, Lalune was going to surrender to the opportunity as it lay before her.

The sun was low in the sky and the beach was nearly empty but Lalune had to wait until complete darkness to swim onto the shore and find a rock to block her from view. This was where she would spend her last night as a mermaid.

Lalune began to recite the incantations she had memorized what felt like ages ago, then removed the stone from the scales near her fin and placed it in her mouth without swallowing. This stone had not left her side since Avanora had imbued it with the magic of communication. This was nearly the most important facet of her transformation.

Lalune hoisted her body onto the sandy ledge of the enormous rock. Everything felt so dense and clumsy and it filled her with a flash of dread about her future. Would life lose its buoyancy? Did all land-walkers feel this heavy?

The waiting was killing her. Too many thoughts, both positive and negative, consumed her. There was nothing she could do but trust that her decision was the right one.

Lalune did not believe she would be able to sleep but the exhaustion from the day eventually overtook her.

Her instincts opened her eyes as the sun came over the horizon. It was so spectacularly beautiful, she almost forgot what she was doing on shore. As her eyes adjusted to the warm air, and the bright light, she realized her body was now covered in a green silk dress, and where her tail had been was now a set of legs, beautiful legs.

It did not feel any different than her tail from the inside, but stroking her hands down her new skin, free of scales, was a euphoric experience. A wiggle of her toes made her erupt in bubble-filled laughter, which nearly startled her off her precarious position on the rock.

This was what it sounded like to be on land. It was enchanting, like music, all the time.

She laughed even louder, and the buoyancy of her voice brought her to her feet. My goodness, the sand! What a feeling. Gritty and dry, almost dry, a little bit cold and a little bit warm. As if all of the universe was contained in those bits of sand.

Standing up straight was a revelation. The feel of gravity pulling strongly down on her body was unlike anything she had ever experienced. Instead of gliding gracefully, she clunked along like a tentative toddler. I will not fall, she told herself, even though there was no one there to witness it or laugh at her. Just one step after another, she thought.

It took four or five strolls along the shoreline, being careful to miss the water with her toes, until she felt more comfortable on the legs, her legs. Easier than I thought it would be, she thought. Maybe all those exercises the old mermaid taught me were worth it. She felt strong and tingled with excitement.

Lalune heard the sound of voices, deep voices. There were landwalkers coming, more than one. What were they doing here so early? And then she remembered the ones who rode the waves. Yes, they would come out before all the others so that they would have the ocean to themselves. She feared them, as they passed above her family's home on occasion and could have discovered her and her mermaid community. But now she was one of them, and had nothing to fear. What should she do? Was it odd that she was also there so early? Would they know that she was not like them?

There was only one way to know and only one way to go toward her dream. She would smile and she would sing. Yes, that was it. She did not care if they noticed her or not, but it was time to let her song find ears to land on.

She began very quietly, unsure of how to use her lungs to project sound after a lifetime of being used otherwise. The sound was sweet and soft and otherworldly. She had no words, only soft round vowels, imitating the beguiling sounds of her own language.

The noise of the land-walker males grew closer and closer. They were laughing and speaking loudly. No matter, she could continue singing and wouldn't mind if they paid her any attention or not. But they stopped. Nearly all of them. Perhaps shocked by the appearance of a lone woman on the beach they called their own. The old mermaid had warned her that they would find her irresistible. Was it true? Never mind. It was no concern of hers.

They stared at her, and she tried not to stare back. Just took small steps on her brand new legs and sang her soft sweet song. It made her happy to hear it, regardless of who else was around.

There were five of them, and they were putting on their black water suits and whispering. Perhaps about her. Yes, certainly about her. She smiled.

One of them began to walk toward her, and another followed him.

"Hey, wait for me! I saw her first!"

She understood them, as expected. Now, would she speak and test out her new language? Was it not too soon?

She was nervous. Very nervous. It was bad enough that her legs were a bit wobbly but now she may have to speak. What if the only thing that came out was Mermese? No time to wonder because the first one had reached her.

"Hi," he said. "We heard you singing."

"It was so beautiful," the second one said.

She liked their faces, especially the second one. He did not look at her directly, but hid his face slightly. Was this called embarrassment? The first one just stared, which was closer to what she was expecting.

"We've never seen you here before," the first one said.

"Your singing was so beautiful," repeated number two.

"You already said that, genius," said number one, while his friend turned red.

"Do you surf?" asked number two. What would she say? That she could ride the waves with more grace and strength than anything they could muster? That the ocean had been the only home she had known until this point?

"No, I don't," she said. "I was just taking a... walk... on the beach." The words flowed so beautifully and perfectly. She was doing it!

So excited, she let out a little giggle. Number one looked at her quizzically, but the second one, with the nice face that turned red, just smiled. So big that it took up his whole head. He finally held his head up long enough that she could look at it.

"My name is Peter," he said.

"I'm Aaron," said number one.

"My name is Claire." She heard the words come out of her mouth, but did not understand why. She never used her given name. Why hadn't she said Lalune?

This was a whole new life and required a whole new name. Clair de la Lune was too much, she guessed, for these land-walkers, but maybe Claire would work.

"That's a beautiful name," beamed number two, now known as Peter.

"Is that all you can say?" asked number one. Although his name was Aaron, all she could think of was arrogant. She wanted him to get out of the way so she could keep looking at Peter.

"We're going surfing now," Peter said. "I guess you don't want to join us."

"No, I can't right now. Do you mind if I just watch?" She did not know where these words were coming from, but she was pleased with them nonetheless.

"Wow, that would be great! Will you really wait here on the beach for us?"

It would give her time to recall all that Avanora had instructed her, to create this new life. There was a lot to review and plan.

"Yes. Yes, I will."

It was a beautiful day for a song.

Dearest Reader,

I hope you enjoyed Marco and Monique's remarkable love story. If you'd like to share your thoughts about the book with others, you can leave a review wherever you bought your copy. Reviews support independent authors!

For all the perks of being a cherished reader (which you are), and be the first to know about new releases, sign up to be part of the Smart & Sexy Reader Team. I regularly send out book bonuses, audio clips, playlists and other goodies to make the wild ride even more fun. Get on the list at www.pekavanagh.com/contact.

If you can't wait to find out what happens next, I've included an excerpt to SEX, MONEY, AND THE PRICE OF TRUTH, Book Two of The Price Series.

Thank you again, and I hope to see you soon between the pages of my steamy love stories.

Excerpt from SEX, MONEY, AND THE PRICE OF TRUTH
Book Two of The Price Series

The door to Galaxy Bar & Grill flung open and nearly smacked Aidan Connelly in the face. He stumbled back as a blur of honey hair rushed past him and continued down the sidewalk. The air around her shimmered as if she were on fire, magnified by a pace that screamed hot rage. He stared, transfixed, as a sea of blue suits parted to let her pass.

Everything about her stood out, like an exotic bird among pigeons. He hadn't seen her face but the view from the back - the flutter of a summer dress, sun-kissed skin, legs until tomorrow - left him gaping until she disappeared into the crowd. That was not the kind of woman he had ever expected to come out of that kind of place.

He reached for the discolored door handle, pausing in case some other pissed-off patron decided to burst out. The smell hit him as soon as he stepped inside, like getting slapped with a beer-soaked towel. When the door slammed shut behind him, the bright light of the afternoon and the golden veneer of Wall Street gave way to the dark gloom of neglect.

Galaxy wasn't just a seedy bar, it was an alternate universe, home to a couple of day-drinkers and a grime-covered collection of fake planets and black-light posters. This time of day, the other bars in the neighborhood would be booming with bankers and tourists, while this place echoed with a dusty emptiness. Maybe Mack had chosen it for that very reason.

Aidan could turn around and disappear into the bustling city streets, skipping the pointless conversation. Why had he come, anyway? He had no obligation to sit through another tirade about getting revenge on some woman. *What a waste of time.*

Before his good sense pulled him back out the door, he caught sight of Mack's blond hair, slicked back into an immovable mass that reminded him of the yellow ceramic bowls of his childhood. It wasn't even 5pm on a Tuesday and Mack was already drunk, as evidenced by the jerk and sway of his head.

Morbid curiosity overtook Aidan's pervasive apathy and growing disgust, and he took a seat at the bar. Everything about this place - the filthy glasses, the cloying darkness, the man sitting next to him - added to the revulsion. He closed his eyes, longing to replace the sights and sounds around him with the image of honey and heat.

Mack's slurred, nearly incomprehensible rants began without greeting or introduction. "You gotta do this for me, man."

As expected, that idiot's begging for help. "Listen, I know this woman messed with you. That's women, you know? But you can't get all twisted about it. Don't let it make you crazy."

Mack tossed back a shot of tequila, leaving three empty glasses on the bar. "That's not the point, man. She's evil. Came all the way down here to tell me to fuck off. Like she's so much better than me."

That must have been her.

Aidan swallowed and turned to the drunk man in disbelief. Mack had seemed cool enough when they met at work a few weeks prior. Aidan's bullshit bank, like so many others, had gotten caught with its pants down and Mack's fancy law firm had come in to clean up the mess. The two men were in their early thirties, living large in New York City, indistinguishable from every other hotshot in the cesspool of the young and powerful. All part of the unholy bond of lawyers and bankers that kept the madness alive.

"Either way, it's best to move on. You're young and rich in a city full of hot women. Just pick another one and get on with it. Why waste your time trying to get her back?" Besides, anyone who'd go out with that schmuck had to be either a saint or a lunatic, neither worth keeping around.

Mack lifted his finger to catch the attention of the bartender before bringing his hand back down onto the grimy bar with a thud. "I'm not trying to get her back, Connelly. I'm trying to get back *at* her."

Aidan had realized that something wasn't right with Mack within their first few encounters. It didn't matter if he was insane or on drugs or if it was something else; he'd taken the lunacy to a whole new level. But in comparison, Aidan's life didn't look so bad. Maybe that's why he stuck around.

"I get it. But shit like that never ends up how you want it to." *Trust me, I know.*

Mack slid his lips apart in a move that might have been a smile on another face. "All I'm asking is that you mess with her. Should be easy for someone like you."

Aidan clenched his fist, wanting desperately to hurl it against Mack's face. "You don't know anything about me. And I don't want to get involved."

Mack tilted forward, closing the space between them. Stale booze seeped through his pores. "I can pay you. You just left the bank, right? Maybe you could use a little cash."

Aidan's stomach lurched. Right there was the problem. Everything had a price in this world he had helped to create. It was all about taking and owning, possessing and controlling. Nothing was out of reach. Not someone's belongings, their time, their body, their soul. "I don't need any cash, thanks."

"Come on, Connelly. It's easy money."

All money was easy. Aidan could buy and sell that douche bag a few times over. "I don't need your money. And I'm not interested in messing with some woman I don't even know."

Mack lifted the newly arrived tequila shot to his lips, paused, then arced it into his mouth. He swallowed without a flinch, then slammed the glass on the bar loud enough to get the attention of two men across the room. "That bitch needs to learn a lesson. You wouldn't believe the shit she's pulling. Shoulda heard what she just said said to me."

"Sorry you got screwed. But I can't help you." Aidan pushed himself off the barstool, retrieved his wallet out of his back pocket, and dropped cash next to his glass. *Only in Manhattan could a few spoonfuls of warm gin set you back twenty bucks.* This city had made him jaded. Turned him into a different person. It was time to get out. This bar, this city, this life. He took two steps toward the door.

"Not even as a favor for a friend?"

We're not friends. "No can do."

Mack stood up, stumbled, and fell back onto his seat. "You're going to regret this, Connelly!"

Aidan snickered as he continued out of the bar. One more regret wasn't going to make a damn bit of difference in the mountain of remorse his life had become.

The sun accompanied Aidan nearly the whole walk to midtown, dipping behind the skyscrapers and into the Hudson River as he entered the lobby of his building. The elevator doors opened directly into his loft and to a spectacular view of the Empire State Building, a daily reminder why he had chosen to live far from the financial district.

Getting out from under all those soul-less financial towers helped him stand up straighter. Even the neighborhood was more peaceful. Not that he interacted with his neighbors much, but the occasional sighting of an artist or family made him feel less like an alien in a sea of clones.

He stood in front of the window, watching the buildings change from gold to grey in the fading daylight. This was a much better view than that repulsive bar. Going to Galaxy had been a mistake. There was no talking sense into Mack, hell-bent on revenge, as if he was the only guy to ever get dumped. Hopefully, he'd straighten out before doing something really stupid.

Aidan shook off the uneasy feeling around Mack's threats to him and that woman, and grabbed a beer before heading into the spare bedroom. The sight of the stack of boxes against the far wall, a reminder of his upcoming departure, brought relief. Two more weeks and all this hell would be in his rearview mirror. He could turn his back on the mess he'd made, as well as the one on the horizon when all his bad choices caught up to him. That same feeling of imminent disaster he'd gotten before each of the recent financial meltdowns buzzed through his veins. He couldn't be happier to be getting out.

He shoved the two small boxes labeled 'Jessica' further into the corner. His ex-fiancee would probably never get her stuff. Why was he even saving it? Maybe the same masochistic streak that kept him on Wall Street for so long kept him connected to her.

She was just like the rest of them, completely satisfied by a stallion on her arm, a huge diamond on her finger, and the good life in her future. Sure he thought all that crap was important too, until it fell apart. He shook his head at his own stupidity and gullibility. *I should have known better.*

It was book-packing day. The floor-to-ceiling bookshelves against the far wall contained some of his most treasured possessions. Most of them would have to go into storage with the rest of his stuff, but a select few would accompany him on his great escape. Whitman's *Leaves of Grass*, a book of Neruda's poems, and *Ulysses* by James Joyce were definites. Perhaps Jung's *Red Book* and something by Emerson, to get his mind right.

The promise of a dramatic escape had picked Aidan up off the floor, and given him hope that what had broken could be fixed. Southeast Asia was as far as he could get from Manhattan. He would start out in Thailand. Bali was a must, as was Vietnam. Other than that, he had at least a year, maybe two, to recover from the train wreck his life had become. Maybe he'd never come back. A permanent sabbatical. He called it his parole, even if nobody else got the joke.

Aidan frowned at the growing pile of books on the floor, already more than he could bring, and he'd only scanned the top two shelves. The whole point was to leave the city empty-handed. Only a total purge would begin to wash him clean, absolve him of his disgrace, wrest the life he never wanted from his clenched fists. If he could let go of all he was, maybe someone worth living would emerge.

———

Everything's different. Aidan stared out the taxi window at the city that used to feel as integral and familiar as one of his limbs. Exhausted from nearly three days of traveling across the planet, he welcomed in that familiar rush of energy that had sustained him for all those years. New York City was a miracle, even compared to the exotic sights of his recent travels.

As the taxi rounded the corner of his block, he perched forward. Other than different names on a few of the businesses, his neighborhood was unchanged. Maybe the world had stayed exactly the same, but he had very little in common with the man who had fled New York more than two years prior.

The doorman's eyes widened as Aidan stepped out of the taxi.

"Mr. Connelly! You're back!"

"I sure am, Edgar."

The uniformed man took the largest of Aidan's bags. "Welcome home, sir. You've been missed. I'm glad to see you looking so well."

Aidan ran a hand over his full beard. "That's kind of you to say. How's everything with you?"

"Can't complain, sir. Can't complain. Added two more grandkids to the stable. We nearly have a baseball team now."

Aidan patted the older man on the back as the elevator opened. "Congratulations, Edgar. That's wonderful news."

"Your place has been well taken care of. I hope you agree."

A sense of relief greeted Aidan as the elevator doors opened to his loft. During more than one dark moment, he'd imagined it had been looted and vandalized. Maybe the maintenance company he'd hired had stopped coming, and it would be a maze of cobwebs and dustballs. Or they had stolen every tangible piece of his life. Most of the time he didn't care.

But at that moment, seeing his familiar belongings made him swallow against the push of an emotion he couldn't quite name. Sadness had been his companion for so long. But this sensation was different, harkening back to a time so long before it might have only existed in his imagination. He was happy to be home.

The spacious emptiness felt like a glorious reprieve from the constant bombardment of people and activity that had accompanied him from place to place. Bangkok was crowded. Bali was chaotic. India was madness. But they were exactly what he needed, pummeling him into submission and breaking him of the fever that had taken over his mind. He breathed peacefully now, slept well, and lost the repulsion at being in his own skin.

Aidan walked through his home, checking each of the rooms. Edgar was right. It was pristine. Almost certainly cleaner than the day he left. Other than the boxes that filled the far corner of the living space, everything was exactly as he had left it.

He had taken a risk, shipping back all the art and decorative pieces he'd bought throughout Asia, but all the boxes appeared to be intact. Aidan ran his hand over the edge of the largest one, nearly as tall as him and three times as wide. Unpacking would have to wait. Maybe for a while. He wasn't sure he'd be staying.

This city held too much history, too much evidence of his mistakes, too many reminders of how far he'd strayed. He loved New York, but didn't know if he could be the man he wanted to be in this environment. Maybe he'd leave the city, head out west, re-create himself.

After a call to his parents, Aidan dialed his best friend. "Hey, Tommy. I'm back."

"Finally! How are you feeling?"

"Really good. Bleary, but happy. I'm sure I'm going to crash in a few hours, but for now, I'm loving all the buzz of New York. My place looks perfect, too. Like I never left."

"Well, we definitely felt your absence. I'm going to be in the city tomorrow morning. I'll drop by and we can hang. I want to hear everything."

"Sounds good, man. Can't wait to see you."

The line remained silent for long enough that Aidan checked to see if the call had dis-connected.

Tommy cleared his throat. "I'm so glad you're home, Aidan. I was scared you'd never want to come back. After everything."

"Can't say I didn't think about it. But I'm here."

"See you tomorrow."

Telling his best friend that he was thinking about leaving again, this time permanently, was going to be a hard conversation. At least he felt clear enough to make a decision. But there was no rush. First he'd have to re-acclimate to civilization.

Aidan cleared the steam from the mirror after a luxuriously long shower. He hadn't missed much of his previous lifestyle, but a shower hadn't felt that good in a long time. He picked up the tube of shaving gel, ready to eliminate the evidence of his transformation, and paused. Sure, he looked like someone who'd been living on a beach for a few years. But this was him, now. No pretense, no show, no being what he was supposed to be. He put the tube down and walked out of the bathroom. Civilization could wait another day.

His fatigue grew harder to ignore after getting dressed. He needed to stay awake for a few more hours to begin adjusting to the new time zone. A long walk was the perfect option, not only for his body, but for the thoughts tumbling around his head. Lots of decisions had to be made. Would he try to work? Going back into the financial industry was out of the question, but he was hardly qualified to do anything else. Thankfully, money wasn't going to be an issue for a very long time. Maybe never. But being idle for too long was asking for trouble.

He stopped in the lobby to slip a hundred dollar bill into Edgar's hand. That guy was a high quality human being - honest, caring, hard-working without being obsessed about money. Aidan needed more people like that in his life.

He walked out into the sunny day, grateful for the late summer breeze. There were times the stifling heat and humidity of the tropics had felt like a well-deserved punishment. He had run away to paradise, but a little bit of hell had followed alongside. Heading uptown to Central Park with a smile on his face, Aidan was certain of his redemption.

GRATITUDES

This book took a hold of me, like a highly skilled lover, and had its way. All my resistance to the process – so foreign for a spiritual essay writer – was no match for the intensity of desire and passion that filled me.

Like any fine ravaging, it took many hands.

Thank you Chela Davison for the vision that birthed the two primary characters and Graciela (Mamita) Masso for the cover inspiration. Profound appreciation and awe to the A-team (Bibi, Alex, Sarah, Kurt, Heather, Marianne, Renee, Lori, Allison, Carole, Cil), who read terrible drafts, over and over again. And still spoke to me in the morning.

Deepest thanks to the lovers who demonstrated how healing great sex can be, (you know who you are), the Muse whose light spankings I rather enjoyed, and the magical Universe that keeps feeding me blessings, lessons and fairy tales… in flesh and blood.

ALSO BY PE KAVANAGH

THE PRICE SERIES
  The Price of Desire (Book One)
  Sex, Money, and the Price of Truth (Book Two)

———

FRIENDS & LOVERS SERIES
  Collecting Secrets (Book One)
  Coming Home (Book Two)
  Claiming Power (Book Three)
  Consenting Adults (Book Four)

———

ZODIAC MAGIC SERIES
  Casting A Spell (Book One)

———

Available at your favorite online retailers.

ABOUT THE AUTHOR

I believe that everything we experience exists as a story within us.

My journey as a writer includes the award-winning poem I penned at the ripe old age of seven, decades of hiding and doubt, and then finally... finally!... realizing that art needs to be shared. Storytelling is part of my heritage, even though I denied it for so long. The stories I created - true and imaginary - have saved me numerous times.

My characters come to me, like old friends excited to tell me what's new.
They represent the world I see and the world I want to see.

More than anything, I care about recovery from life's setbacks... getting back on your feet after life has brought you to your knees... and my characters fight the hard fight for the lives they know are waiting for them.

I've drawn my inspiration from the many flavors of my life experience. Once a sad, shy girl, I've also been an MIT-educated engineer, biotech executive, professional dancer, yoga teacher and business owner, school founder, spiritual counselor, entrepreneur, and author.

And I own a magic wand that I'm certain will work one day.

When I'm not typing furiously trying to capture the stories that pour from me, you can find me loving my people to excess, globe-trotting to the next great adventure, and sporting bright red lips as a tango diva. And of course on my digital homes: pekavanagh.com and boldsoulcoaching.com.

For more information…
www.pekavanagh.com
me@pekavanagh.com